I0838533

The Cuban Girl

A Novel by Roger Neumaier

Published in Paperback and eBook, February, 2022.

Cover photo by Roger Neumaier

An uncopyrighted early draft of this book was printed in 2016 to share the rough manuscript with the author's family and friends.

Printed in the United States of America

Library of Congress Control Number: 2022902927

ISBNs: 978-1-956920-04-8 (paperback); 978-1-956920-05-5 (eBook)

1. A Flight from Havana

A black 1956 Cadillac Sedan Deville pulled in front of the portico of the Hotel Nacional de Cuba. The car was there to pick up Sam Erickson. Sam recognized the driver. It was the same soldier who had driven him to dinner with Fidel Castro the prior Saturday evening. Sam settled into the limousine's comfortable back seat as he rode silently to Havana's San Antonio de los Baños Military Airfield.

An hour later, routine airfield noise was drowned out by the massive diesel engines of a Soviet manufactured Ilyushin Il-12. As the two large propellers began to rotate, a young bearded Cuban diplomat sitting next to Sam said, "I've flown on this Soviet built rattle-trap to and from Mexico City a dozen times. It was built to carry military cargo. Then they threw a few seats into it and started calling it a passenger plane. While it's safe, you need to prepare yourself. This is going to be an uncomfortable and horribly noisy flight."

The young Cuban diplomat had not exaggerated. The plane's constant shaking and nonstop succession of hard bumps were accompanied by the unending thunder of its twenty-year-old engines. Sam tried to sleep with no success, finally stuffing a small wad of Kleenex into each ear to muffle the dreadful roar. The Kleenex reduced the roar a little, but nothing could be done to decrease the constant shaking of the bumpy flight.

In order to distract himself, Sam ran through all of the things that had happened to him over the past eight months—things that dramatically changed every part of his life and resulted in the trip to Cuba. The distraction turned the trick. In spite of the Ilyushin Il-12's thunderous noise, rattling and shaking, Sam fell into a deep sleep.

2. Growing up in Minneapolis

Growing up in Minneapolis in the early 1950s, Sam Erickson dreamed of becoming an adventurer—of finding lost treasures—of solving complex crimes. Sam entertained himself by reading detective novels. He would imagine he was a private investigator who everyone admired.

One winter day in 1954 during a junior high school lunch hour, Sam was describing his favorite movie, *The Maltese Falcon*. Another student smirked and said, "Your name may be Sam Erickson, but you think you're Sam Spade."

Sam wasn't offended. Being compared to Dashiell Hammett's fictional PI or to the actor Humphrey Bogart who played him in the movies seemed like a compliment— even if it wasn't intended as one.

*****

Sam's grandparents started a small downtown Minneapolis café named *Lucky's* in 1924. Somehow, they hung onto the café through the tough years of the depression. Sam's mother, Mary, waitressed at Lucky's and met Sam's father while serving him a hamburger, fries and a chocolate milkshake. It was love at first sight. It was also only a month after Pearl Harbor—and just a couple of days after Sam's father had signed army enlistment papers.

So, Sam's parents had to marry quickly because his father had to leave for basic training three weeks later. After basic training, Sam's father was assigned to a base in the Philippines. From there he went on to the Solomon Islands where he died in August of 1942 after stepping on a land mine at the battle of Guadalcanal.

*****

Sam was born on a snowy October morning in 1942. His crib was located in his mother's bedroom in the house she shared with her parents. Two weeks after his birth, Mary returned to work. Sam slept in a play pen that was placed in the café's break-room. For the rest of her life, Mary spent six days a week at Lucky's. She never went out on another date.

Sam spent much of his early years in that restaurant break-room. He wasn't ignored. In addition to his mother, grandmother and grandfather, the other kitchen staff played with Sam, read him books and told him stories. Sam grew into a quiet kid who often spent time by himself. He was well-behaved at school, though he did as little homework as was necessary to pass his classes and didn't socialize much. As a youngster, Sam played a little baseball near his home. He fantasized that one day he might become the third baseman for the Milwaukee Braves—just like his favorite baseball player, Eddie Mathews.

Sam stopped playing ball at age fourteen after his mom told him, "Sammy, it's time to join the family business. You need to wash dishes at Lucky's after school."

But late at night, after work and school, Sam listened to Milwaukee Braves baseball games on his clock radio. One of his happiest memories was the Braves winning the 1957 National League pennant. That year, Sam sported a smile for a full week after the Braves were crowned World Series champs.

*****

Sam was forced to take directions from his mother at home and at work. That turned out to be the source of many arguments. At the end of a long quarrel in early spring of his senior year, Sam said, "Mom, I have to do something more than just work at Lucky's. Life has to offer me something more than that."

Mary shook her head and laughed. "Sammy, your problem is you're just a spoiled little brat. You're lazy. You don't know what tough is. If you'd lived through the depression—well then Sammy—then you wouldn't be whining all the time."

Sam figured he couldn't win. His mom would never understand. The following day, Sam walked into his high school principal's office and announced he was quitting school. Then he marched down to a nearby armed services recruitment office. Sam would do what Elvis Presley had done. He would join the Army—just like his dad. When he entered the recruitment office, the first person he saw was an Air Force recruiter. The recruiter promised Sam that if he enlisted in the Air Force instead of the Army, he would be trained as a law enforcement professional. He could go abroad. That sounded good enough to convince Sam to sign on the dotted line then and there.

By the time Sam got home that evening, he regretted his actions. But there was no way he was going to tell his mother or his grandparents that he had made an error. So, within a few weeks, Sam became Airman Erickson.

*****

After completing basic training, Sam was assigned to Morón Air Force Base in Spain where he would be an Air Force Police Investigations Clerk. Sam had read about Spain in *The Sun Also Rises*. Now, he was going there. He looked up Morón in an Atlas. It was only thirty-five miles south of Seville. Wow! Sam was thrilled. This would be so neat.

A couple weeks later, Sam's military flight arrived at the Morón Air Force Base. The next day, Sam met with his new master sergeant.

The overweight master sergeant had a greying crew cut. He looked Sam in the eye and barked, "Airman, I'm going to make you work your butt off. But you need to know—this assignment is an opportunity. So, don't screw it up! Most of the investigators in my unit can't speak Spanish—they have to use a translator. You're replacing a colored guy from Puerto Rico--his tour of duty ended last week. The team depended on his ability to speak Spanish. Now, we got a big hole. You want to make a difference here? You want a quick promotion? Learn Spanish, airman. Fill that hole."

Sam recognized the opportunity. "Sir. I'd like to learn to speak Spanish, sir. When can I start, sir?"

"I am not your *sir*, airman. I am your *Master Sergeant*. Got that? You will address me as *Master Sergeant!* This base will give you free language classes—typical military crap—skip 'em. If you want to move ahead...if you intend to learn to speak the Spanish language, you're going to hire a local. Got it? There's a civilian tutor working in our office. Name's Alisa. Gives Spanish lessons on the side. She's good. You want my advice? Get lessons from her. Got that airman?"

Later that day, Sam approached Alisa, the investigation unit's civilian receptionist. Alisa was small in stature and high in energy. She had dark black hair, sharp eyes and an expressive face. When Sam asked her if he could hire her to tutor him, she quickly answered. "I will teach you to speak the beautiful language of my Spain. But you must be willing to work hard—very hard."

Then she flashed a large smile, looked him directly in the eye and added, "And after this conversation, senor, there will be no more English—we will only speak Spanish. *Estás de acuerdo?*"

An uncertain and confused Sam understood Alisa expected a response. He made a guess as to what that was. "Si." Alisa smiled and nodded. In their final English conversation, Sam and Alisa agreed to meet for two-hour lessons each Saturday afternoon.

In a letter to his mother a few weeks later, Sam wrote:

I am enjoying my work as an investigations clerk. It isn't very high-level. But it's interesting. And it's a start to a career in law enforcement. I am working hard on learning to speak Spanish. My teacher is demanding. She says I'm doing a really good job. Imagine that—me—a good student!

I've got something else to share! I wanted to explore the small villages and countryside of Andalusia—that's what they call this area. A week ago, I saw a for-sale ad on the base bulletin board. Another airman was selling a beat-up, ten-year-old BMW motorbike. It only cost a hundred and seventy bucks. For another forty-five bucks, a mechanic in a nearby town is putting it into good running shape. Hopefully, I'll be tooling around the hills of Andalusia within a few weeks.

Mom—It's all so exciting. I hope you, grandma and grandpa are doing well.

Once the cycle was running well and Sam had mastered riding it, he started exploring Andalusia. With only thirteen horsepower, the BMW R25 wasn't particularly powerful. But it offered as much acceleration as Sam wanted. During the months that followed, Sam spent most of his free time biking around the base, going to Seville, Jerez and Malaga, and enjoying Andalusia's rural mountainous hills and picturesque villages.

Spanish lessons seemed to be going well. Sam was motivated. It wasn't just that his new Spanish skills were making a huge difference at work and as a result his master sergeant kept assigning him more interesting assignments. But Sam admitted to himself that he had a crush on his tutor. He was working hard to impress her. One day after their lesson, Sam asked Alisa if he could take her out to dinner.

"Well, Sam," she responded in Spanish, "Ordinarily it would not be appropriate for me to date a student. But you have been making a lot of progress lately. So, as a reward, I will make a special exception this one time."

Sam tried to hide how pleased he was. Alisa laughed at his botched attempt to hide his feelings.

That Saturday, after the lesson and after telling Sam about her fear of motorcycles, Sam talked her into getting on the back of his cycle. Then he drove them to a gazpacho café in Seville. At dinner, Sam told Alisa about his life in Minneapolis. He concluded with, "Now you know all about me, but I don't know anything about you. What—uh—could you—uhm—tell me about your life?"

Sam watched her closely as she slowly savored a spoonful of cold seafood soup. Then, after swallowing the soup, she picked up her wineglass and took a sip of its dark red garnacha wine. It seemed like she was more interested in the food and wine than in responding to his question. Sam began to wonder if maybe it had been a mistake to ask Alisa about her life—even though he knew almost nothing about her—except that he had a crush on her.

But after one more sip of wine, Alisa responded. "Sam, since I started working at the base, I have been very careful to always keep my work life separate from my personal life. Today, because I am giving you a combination of a class and going out to dinner, it's a little different. So, I will give you a response. My daughter and I live in Utrera with my mother and father. I live in the same house in which I was born."

Sam was surprised Alisa had a daughter, but tried not to show it.

"I was a good student in secondary school. My father encouraged me to work hard on learning English. He told me that maybe, someday, I could get a job at the United States Air Force Base. That was attractive. The base pays more than any other job I could have gotten."

Sam waited. When more didn't come, he asked, "How old is your daughter?"

Alisa paused, took another sip of wine, closed her eyes for a moment, then said, "My daughter is three years old." She paused and added, "That is enough about my personal life. It is late. We should be going."

*****

Sam's investigation assignments were going well and he was enjoying his time in Spain more than any period in his life. He continued to push himself in learning Spanish and took Alisa out for dinner whenever she was willing. He looked forward to those dinners. One time, after a dinner of lobster paella and Tempranillo in Seville, Sam and Alisa went to a small bar hidden on a city back street. There, Sam was introduced to the elaborate footwork and brilliant music of flamenco. He was in awe of the emotion with which the performers sang, played their large guitars and danced their stories of love and betrayal.

After he told Alisa how much he enjoyed flamenco music, she said, "Sam, you should learn to play guitar." Inspired and wanting to impress, Sam bought an old handmade rosewood guitar and a couple of used guitar books. He started spending at least an hour a day learning to control the clear, soft and resonant tones from his instrument.

Sam also continued to exchange letters with his mother. About a year after he arrived in Spain, he wrote,

Life is good. My Spanish skills are improving. In my annual review, my master sergeant wrote, "Because you hustled and learned Spanish, we're going to assign you more complex cases that require interviewing locals. And I like that you are a good listener. You pay attention to details! Senior investigators have been asking for me to assign you to their cases. Keep it up!"

And mom, I'm having fun exploring Andalusia on my BMW and am loving playing the guitar. By the way, I've been dating a Spanish woman who works at the base. I like her a lot.

Mom, things are going really well. I hope things are good for you guys.

A couple of times a month, Sam and Alisa went cruising on his cycle along mountain roads, stopping at whitewashed tapas bars in thousand-year-old mountain villages to enjoy traditional local tapas and sherries. These outings made Sam feel happy. After returning home from one of their small adventures, Sam had trouble going to sleep—his heart felt so full. He realized he was falling in love with Alisa. But all that Sam knew about her life was what she had shared during their first dinner. He wondered if maybe he should tell her about his feelings. His fear was that she seemed so shy, that she would be intimidated by the power of his love for her.

One lovely April Sunday morning, they went riding East along a picturesque single lane mountain road. They stopped for a picnic in a large field next to the remains of an outdoor Roman theater. Alisa laid out a blanket on the ground. Upon it, she put the picnic she had packed of bread bastóns, Manchego cheese, Serrano ham, marinated olives and a small tomato, onion, and pepper salad.

Sam opened the bottle of Alberino he had purchased at a local bodega and poured a glass for each of them. He raised his glass, as if in a toast, and said, "Alisa, we have known each other for over a year now. You taught me Spanish. I appreciate that more than you can know. But the most wonderful part of it all has been spending time with you. You are a beautiful person."

He paused and took a deep breath. Then he took a large swallow of wine and finished what he had started. "I've given a lot of thought to what I am about to say. Alisa, I would like you to become my wife. I will love your daughter as if she was my own. And when my tour is up, we can all return to the States—together. Alisa—will you marry me?"

Alisa placed the pointer finger from her right hand on her lips. She said nothing for a minute. Then she sighed and said, "Sam. You are so sweet. But you are also so young. You don't know me at all—not at all. I appreciate the heartfelt nature of your proposal. But my life is away from the base. And Sam, I am sorry you did not realize—I am already engaged—to a man who I have known for many years. He is older than me and he is financially well off. He will be able to support my daughter and me."

She took another breath. Sam saw that she had more to say. He hoped that she would give him some encouragement. She exhaled and continued. "I had no idea you saw our relationship in that way. I wish you nothing but the best. But Sam, I am sorry. I must say no."

Sam was crushed. They sat there on that warm afternoon, quietly eating a small portion of the feast that was laid out on the blanket. Then they silently packed up their foodstuffs and climbed onto the cycle. As they rode back to the base, Sam didn't notice the scenic mountains or ancient villages that had seemed so beautiful just a short while before.

Their goodbye that evening was quiet and distant.

*****

A couple of days later, Alisa quit her job at the Base. By the time Sam learned that she had resigned, she was gone. He found a short note from her in his mailbox. It simply said, *Sam, I enjoyed getting to know you. I wish you nothing but the best.*

Sam didn't know whether he should be angry, sad, or somehow hope Alisa would change her mind. How could he have misunderstood her feelings so badly? His life was suddenly turned upside down. In one moment, the magic of Spain disappeared, the Air Force lost its luster. Being in the military began to feel confining.

Sam's two-year tour of duty was scheduled to end in a matter of months. His master sergeant was encouraging him to reenlist. But Sam was asking himself if the military was what he wanted out of life. Sam wasn't exactly sure of what that he wanted, but he decided whatever it was, well—it wasn't in Spain—and it wasn't wearing a uniform in the Air

Force. Sam decided to return to the States and swore to himself, he would never put on any sort of uniform again.

Then, Sam was surprised to realize something else. He was anxious to return home.

3. Trying to Start Over

In addition to his clothing, Sam transported three things from Spain: his motorcycle, his guitar and his painful disappointment in love.

It was the spring of 1962. Sam discovered that Minneapolis hadn't changed much. But Sam's family had—it had changed a lot. Both of Sam's grandparents had died in December of 1961. Sam's mother was now the sole-owner of Lucky's.

Sam moved back into his old bedroom in what was now his mother's house. Without another plan, Sam went back to work as a short order cook at Lucky's. He hated it. But when he complained to his mother, she said, "Remember, Sam. When I die, both the café will be yours."

Sam shot back, "Ma—I don't want the goddamned restaurant." He paused for a moment before adding, "or the house!"

Sam felt lost.

*****

In August of 1962, four months after Sam returned to Minneapolis, Sam's mother's statement seemed like a premonition. Mary suffered a fatal heart attack. And thus, before he was twenty years old, Sam owned the café—which he had no desire to run—and the only real home he had ever known.

Neither the home, a dark green two-story craftsman, nor its arts and crafts furnishings had changed much since the home had been built in 1910. Sam had always liked it with its large front porch, stone chimney, wide eaves and leaded and stained-glass windows. But it felt odd living by himself in a two-story house he had shared with his mother and grandparents.

And there was a financial surprise. Sam learned his mother had purchased a life insurance policy when he was born. He was the sole beneficiary. The policy's value had gone up over the years. Weeks later, Sam deposited its proceeds—$290,000.

Sam was ashamed of how he had treated his mother. She had had a hard life. He had often been disrespectful to her; deserted her during the last few years of her life. He told his mother's attorney, "Let's be honest. I wasn't that great a son. Mom always was thinking of me; wanting the best for me." Sam shook his head while looking down. "I didn't spend a lot of time thinking about her—or anyone but myself."

*****

The restaurant had enough regular diners to comfortably support a working owner. But Sam had no desire to be that working owner. He felt guilty admitting it, but he wanted to sell Lucky's. The attorney told Sam, "The business and the building aren't worth much. But the land underneath it—it is. Minneapolis's downtown district is hot. Your mom turned down multiple offers after your grandparents passed away. A couple of serious developers have contacted me since she passed. They want to purchase the property."

Running Lucky's had been a burden for Sam's grandparents and for his mother. Sam was not going to hang onto that burden. He took a deep breath, exhaled and told the attorney, "Sell the place."

So, Sam was the person who validated the café's name. Three months after his mother's death, Sam sold Lucky's for over a half a million dollars.

In the fall of '62, as Sam turned twenty years of age, he was financially secure. Not only did he own his home outright—he had almost three-quarters of a million dollars invested in the stock market.

*****

That winter was lonely. Sam didn't have a clue as to what he wanted to do with his life. He didn't have a single friend, not one living relative and there was no girlfriend. He just hunkered down at home, drank more beer than he should have and watched too much television. He was alone in the world—with one notable exception. Two decades before, the family's parish priest, Father Tom, had officiated over his mother and father's wedding.

Father Tom was a short, paunchy man with a round face and a jovial, calming demeanor. He was the only living person Sam had known throughout his life—the only person who stopped by to check in on Sam during that rough winter. During one such visit in the spring of 1963, while sitting on the couch in the living room, drinking coffee and discussing the weather and baseball, Father Tom turned to Sam and said, "You're set for life now—financially. But you're very young, Sam. What do you want to do with the rest of your life? What are your goals?"

Father Tom waited for a response. Sam was silent. He didn't know what to say—or how to respond. He was a little embarrassed. Finally, he just said, "I'm at a loss, Father. You're right. I haven't any goals." Sam looked down at the floor, silent for a moment, then added, "Do you have any advice?"

Father Tom sighed. "Well, Sam, most kids your age have to work if they're not in college. You don't have to work. Maybe you should consider enrolling in college. You might even find something you find interesting—and get a degree."

Silence again. Sam took a drink of coffee. "Hmph," was all he could get out.

Sam wasn't at all confident a high school dropout with only a military GED certificate could get into any college program. Probably more important, he wasn't sure he wanted to go to college. Why should he want to hang out with a bunch of spoiled kids studying God knows what?

Father Tom was still waiting for a response. Time passed. The silence in the room grew heavy. Sam knew he had to say something. Finally, not knowing how else to respond, he quietly said, "One thing I realize, Father, is that the status quo isn't working. Ok. I'll give it a try."

Over the next few weeks, with a lot of encouragement from Father Tom, Sam followed through on that commitment. He filled out applications for fall admission to two local colleges, Augsburg and the University of St. Thomas.

*****

In addition to leaving Sam her home and business, Mary had left him her pride and joy—a two-tone blue 1959 Rocket Oldsmobile Super 88. Mary purchased the Olds while Sam was in the Air Force. It was the biggest purchase of her life and the only new car she ever owned. In a letter to Sam written after she bought the car, she wrote:

> *Sammy, the car has low-slung fins shaped like jet engines. It looks like a spaceship. It has a 394 cubic-inch V8 engine. (Don't ask me what that is, because I don't know, but the salesman said it's really big and*

powerful.) The Rocket can seat eight adults! Four in the front and four in the back. But the most I've had in it is three—me driving, your grandpa in the passenger seat and your grandma in the back.

Mary had driven the car as one might expect an older widow to drive it—gently and not a lot. When Sam inherited the still shiny automobile, its odometer showed less than twelve thousand miles. And it didn't have a single dent or scratch—not one.

On hot summer evenings during that summer of '63, Sam cruised Hennepin Avenue, shutting off the air conditioning, rolling down the windows and turning up the radio. He listened to the likes of Roy Orbison, Bobby Vinton and Elvis Presley. Those rides were a distraction, but Sam knew he was just trying to escape the emptiness that was dominating his life.

*****

Sam was in Spain when the American League's Washington Senators moved to the Twin Cities, taking the name the *Minnesota Twins*. The Senators had been an awful baseball team and the Twins were no better. Still, in the spring of 1963, Sam purchased a Minnesota Twins season ticket. During that summer, he spent many afternoons and evenings at Metropolitan Stadium. And lo and behold, the Twins turned out to be competitive. Sam enjoyed watching Harmon Killebrew with his powerful compact swing. But it was the Cuban contingency that excited him the most. He enjoyed the likes of curve-balling pitcher Camilo Pascual, brilliant pinch hitter Julio Becquer, speedy shortstop Zoilo Versalles and the hitting machine Tony Oliva. Going to the games was the highlight of that empty summer. On game days, Sam would arrive at the stadium early—before batting practice. When the ballgame began, he would pull out a pencil and carefully scored the game in his program. The Twins won over ninety games that year. It was exciting...but there was no pennant.

One pleasant diversion during that summer was riding his BMW cycle through the rural hills of Southern Minnesota. Touring the Minnesota countryside brought back fond memories of satisfying rides on his bike across the countryside of southern Spain. But as the summer wore on, Sam worried that once the cold weather hit with its ice and snow, things would change. There would be no touring on the motorcycle and no cruising Hennepin Avenue with the windows down. And the baseball season would end. Life would be very empty.

In late July, Sam received notification that his application to Augsburg College was rejected. But a few weeks later, he breathed a huge sigh of relief when he opened a letter from the University St. Thomas. He had been accepted for the fall term as a freshman! St. Thomas was a Catholic liberal arts college. Father Tom had called St. Thomas's president to recommend they accept Sam's application. Sam wondered if he would have been admitted without the father's assistance. Probably not. And while that fact made Sam feel a little worthless, he was very relieved that he would have something to do during the upcoming winter.

*****

Sam made every effort to turn his experience at the University of St. Thomas into a success. He tried to make friends. But the students in his class seemed overly confident, awfully young and inexperienced in life. During the period in which Sam was enrolled at the University, there were only two courses he found satisfying or enjoyable. One was a Spanish language course. It brought back some good memories of Spain. The second was a modern poetry course. Sam was surprised how much he got into that class. He was fascinated by the poems of Ginsberg, Roethke, Plath and Snyder. Modern poems gave meaningful perspectives to the challenges that he faced in his own life.

He wrote a paper about one poem that reminded him of a couple of frustrating Air Force investigation cases. The poem also addressed the emptiness in his own life—something that hadn't stopped since his mother's death. The poem was written by Weldon Kees. The poem was called *The Crime Club.*

No butler, no second maid, no blood upon the stair.
No eccentric aunt, no gardener, no family friend
Smiling among the bric-a-brac and murder.
Only a suburban house with the front door open
And a dog barking at a squirrel, and the cars
Passing. The corpse quite dead. The wife in Florida.

Consider the clues, the potato masher in a vase,
The torn photograph of a Wesleyan basketball team,
Scattered with check stubs in the hall;
The unsent fan letter to Shirley Temple,
The Hoover button on the lapel of the deceased,
The note, "To be killed this way is quite all right with me."

Small wonder that the case remains unsolved,
Or that the sleuth, Le Roux, is now incurably insane,
And sits alone in a white room in a white gown,

Screaming that all the world is mad, that clues
Lead nowhere, or to walls so high their tops cannot be
seen;
Screaming all day of war, screaming that nothing
can be solved.

4. Life Decisions

Sam tried to make his college experience meaningful. But after two years of being around young people who seemed spoiled and immature; and after listening to countless lectures and reading too many books about things he in which he had no interest; Sam decided that college was not for him. He withdrew from the University of St. Thomas in May of 1965, three years after he left the military. He still had no idea what he wanted to do with his life.

During the summer of '65, Sam attended Twins ball games, read novels, played the guitar and drank an occasional bottle of beer. Life seemed empty. There had to be something more. Once again, he went to the only person he knew from whom he could ask for advice—Father Tom.

Tom was direct. "Young man—you need to make some decisions. The major one, Sam, is you need to find a vocation."

"But Father, I'm financially set up—I don't need to work—not as long as I don't blow my inheritance."

"If you don't need money, Sam, well good for you. But earning money is only one reason to have a job. You need to carve out a place for yourself in this world. Once you have a vocation, you will discover your place."

"Father, that's well and good. I'm open to exploring a vocation. But how do I figure out what that vocation should be?"

"You begin by identifying where you have skills. And within those areas, you identify what you enjoy. That's how you'll discover your vocation."

"I'll give it a try Father," said Sam with a lack of enthusiasm. Then, looked down and slowly shook his head from side to side.

After Tom left, Sam headed for the kitchen, opened the refrigerator and grabbed a bottle of Hamm's beer and opened it. What Tom was asking for was easier said than done. Sam had all the restaurant experience in the world; all the skills any commercial kitchen would want in a new hire. But he had sworn he would never again work in a restaurant—and nothing was going to change his mind. Sam took his bottle of Hamm's into the living room, sat down on the couch, put his feet up on the coffee table and began to sip the beer. He thought about the skills he had and the things he liked to do and ended up laughed quietly and thought to himself, *No hobbies—none worth focusing on. No one's going to hire me to play guitar—and, come to think of it, the Twins already have a third baseman.*

Sam went into the kitchen, shaking his head the whole way, and opened another bottle of beer. He went into the dining room and sat down at the table, continuing to try to figure some option. But Sam was totally discouraged. He sighed. His internal monologue continued. *My only work experience other than Lucky's was in the Air Force as an investigator. Sure, that was cool. And, yah, I did a good job...but...but.... Hmmm.*

Sam sat up straight, took a big swig from his bottle of Hamm's and finished his thought with a question. *Maybe...just maybe, maybe I could become some sort of investigator?*

*****

That night, Sam could not stop tossing and turning in his bed as he wrestled with the idea of trying to become some sort of investigator. The next morning, Sam woke up inspired. After a couple of cups of coffee and some strategic planning, he made a telephone call to the Federal Bureau of Investigation's Minnesota administration office. His experience in the Air Force had to make him an attractive candidate for the FBI.

However, Sam quickly learned the FBI required a college degree. And while the personnel officer he spoke seemed to be trying to let him down gently, she added that the FBI put little value in military police experience.

Back to the drawing board. When he left the military, Sam had sworn he would never put on a uniform again. However, police detectives don't wear uniforms. And maybe, Sam just needed to become a little more flexible? Maybe he should explore a career in a state or municipal police force?

That afternoon, Sam went into St. Paul's office of administration for the Minnesota Highway Patrol. Good news—they were hiring. More good news—no college degree was necessary. But in speaking with the jabbering woman in the personnel office, Sam learned that most Highway Patrol troopers spend their entire careers driving around in Ford Fairlanes chasing speeding cars and arresting drunk drivers. No. That wasn't going to work. Being a State Patrol Officer wouldn't be any more pleasant than washing dishes.

But Sam wasn't done. He jumped into the Rocket Oldsmobile and headed for the Minneapolis Police Department's personnel office. He received good news on two fronts. They were hiring and they valued military police experience. The receptionist sent him back to speak with a personnel officer.

What he learned next was not so inspiring. If he was hired by the police, it would take more than ten years of boring beat patrols before he could even hope to move into a detective position—and the sort of work he wanted to do. In the interim, the job would be similar to the Highway Patrol. He would wear a uniform and enforce rules. Sam crossed off the Minneapolis Police Force—and after asking the personnel officer if things would be different in the St. Paul Police Department, he decided to eliminate them as well.

Sam asked himself, *What job could I could I get that would let me use my investigation skills right away?* After a while, Sam decided there just wasn't such a job. He put his vocation search aside and tried to enjoy the rest of the summer—as much as he could. Instead of focusing on trying to find a vocation, Sam turned his attention to baseball.

1965 turned out to be a fantastic year to follow the Twins. Six of their players were on the American League All Star team. Shortstop Zoilo Versalles, who hit .321, became the American League's most valuable player. The Twins ended up winning 102 games and the American League pennant. What a year to follow the Twins!

The Twins played the Los Angeles Dodgers in the 1965 World Series. Sam attended all four games played at Metropolitan Stadium. He had never seen anything quite as festive or as full of pageantry as the World Series. But the Dodgers were too good. Their team featured the two best pitchers in baseball, Sandy Koufax and Don Drysdale. The Twins lost the series in seven games. Still, it had been baseball at its best and Sam had thoroughly enjoyed it.

But the season ended and the weather cooled. It was mid-October. There was nothing to do. Once again, Sam sat on his living room couch asking himself, *What can I do with my life?* He took a long drink of Hamm's and chuckled as he admitted to himself, *Father Tom was right. I have to find some sort of work.*

But what could that be? One evening a few days later, Sam was sitting on the couch, sipping a beer and rereading his favorite Sherlock Holmes book, *The Hound of the Baskervilles*. He had just read where Holmes turns to Watson and says, "The world is full of obvious things which nobody by any chance ever observes."

Sam closed the book and put it down on the couch. His solution was in front of him! Sam began to laugh—then spoke out loud—as if there was someone else in the living room listening to him. "I've been missing the obvious. Solving cases as an independent investigator, no matter how simple those cases turn out to be—that will be so much more satisfying than joining any bureaucratic investigative force—anywhere. Holmes was right. The solution is obvious. I need to start a detective agency."

*****

The next morning, Sam went to the Hennepin County Library to research how to start a detective agency. He asked a reference librarian for help. She led Sam to the periodicals section. They found a relevant article in *True Detective Magazine*. The article by an ex-cop was entitled *Establishing a Successful PI Agency*. In the article, the author stated:

> *Trying to start a commercial detective agency*
> *without a bunch of connections would be tough*
> *because it takes time to develop enough clients to pay*
> *your fixed costs. And after fixed costs, you need to*
> *have something left over to pay yourself. I benefitted*

*from the connections I built up over fifteen years in
the Sacramento Police Department.*

Sam was just looking for a part-time job. He didn't need
cashflow and shouldn't have many fixed costs. If it took a
while to get clients, well, that'd be just fine.

Sam became animated. He told the librarian, "This is
exactly what I was looking for. Now, I have to figure out how
to set up a detective agency."

As Sam said this, he spotted a full-page ad across the
article. Its banner headline read: "Are you ready to take on
an adventurous career in sleuthing?" The advertisement for
The Private Investigation Institute promised that after
completing their three-month correspondence course,
students would be prepared to get a Private Investigator
License and set up their own agency.

Sam didn't need to learn how to investigate—he had
those skills. But, in addition to investigation skills, the
course promised to teach the business fundamentals of
establishing a detective agency. That evening, Sam filled out
and mailed in the *Private Investigation Institute*
registration form that he'd torn out of the library's copy of
True Detective. He enclosed a check for two-hundred-
dollars, the cost of tuition.

Then Sam called Father Tom and told him, with a great
deal of pride, "Father—I did it. I've made my vocational
decision! I'm going to be a private detective."

*****

When the course materials arrived in the mail a week
later, Sam tore open the package and looked through the
materials. There were several course sections covering basic
investigation techniques. But, as promised in the ad, there
was also information addressing legal, financial, and

licensing requirements for a PI agency—exactly what Sam needed. There was even a section on marketing. Sam was ready to dig into the course.

Each week, over the next two months, Sam read one section of the class's materials. Then he completed that section's examination and submitted it to *The Institute* by mail. Nine weeks after starting the course, Sam received a graduation certificate. His new agency, *Sam Erickson Private Investigations,* was ready to go.

Sam decided to operate the agency out of his home. Most of his clients would contact him by phone and Sam would generally meet with them in their offices, their homes or over lunch at restaurants. But Sam could also meet with them at home. His back bedroom could easily be converted into an office.

That bedroom already had a large fifty-year-old carved mahogany desk and matching chair. Sam donated the room's maple bed and dresser to the Salvation Army, replacing them with a leather couch, an easy chair and a coffee table purchased at Dayton's Department Store. He brought a Tiffany stained-glass lamp and Persian oriental carpet down from his attic. Then, after framing his freshly acquired private detective and business licenses, he hung them next to his Air Force honorable discharge paper. His office looked pretty official.

As far as weapons went, Sam had learned in the military that the easiest way to get shot—by himself or by an adversary—was by pulling out a handgun. And with the types of investigations he planned on conducting, a weapon wasn't going to be necessary. Still, just to be cautious, Sam acquired a permit to carry the compact Beretta pistol he'd inherited from his mother—in case there ever was a need. But the pistol would stay in his desk drawer unless needed.

Next, Sam put together a marketing plan. In a nutshell, his plan was that each week, he would visit at least three Minneapolis or St. Paul legal firms or insurance agencies; introduce himself; and offer his investigation services. Sam also placed an ad in the yellow pages, ordered five-hundred business cards, had the phone company add a separate business phone line to his home and signed up with a local answering service.

The Sam Erickson Detective Agency was open for business on February 1, 1966.

*****

Each weekday morning for the first couple of weeks of February, Sam dressed in his new tweed sport coat, a clean shirt and tie and made cold calls on law firms and insurance agencies. Those visits didn't result in a single customer inquiry. At the end of the second week, Sam was discouraged.

5. Meeting new People

The Triangle Bar on Minneapolis's West Bank was built at the turn of the century. Its name reflected its shape as well as the pie wedge shaped lot upon which it had been constructed. The Triangle offered cheap beer, live music and cool, young clientele. Sam often went there to listen to live musical performances. A beer, burger and some music from the Triangle never failed to lift his spirits.

On Monday, February 14, 1966, Sam needed that lift. He had already been feeling blue. But now, his business appeared to be dead in the water—and, to top it off, it was Valentine's Day and Sam didn't have a girlfriend to be his valentine. Sam decided to escape the misery and go to the Triangle for dinner. He was disappointed to learn that the Triangle's entertainment for the evening was a local performer who sang folksongs and played the accordion. He had heard the guy perform before and hadn't been impressed.

Sam took a seat at the bar, ordered a beer, burger and fries. The performer's act was worse than Sam remembered. Sam ate quickly and was getting ready to leave the bar when the accordion player left the stage and a young Cuban woman—a student at the University of Minnesota—came onto the stage to sing a few songs between the accordion player's sets.

*****

The Cuban woman, accompanying herself on guitar, started singing in Spanish. She sang with a rich, throaty voice while playing her guitar with a skill and intensity that reminded Sam of the flamenco music of Seville. The songs' lyrics were stories of love and pain. The crowd at the

Triangle paid almost no attention to her. Most probably didn't understand the Spanish lyrics. But Sam was gripped by the emotion she brought to the stories she sang. He moved to a small table in front of the stage.

She was tall—as tall as Sam—with square-shoulders and an almost muscular build. She had long curly jet-black hair, a dark complexion, ruby red lipstick and big brown eyes. Her bright red cowboy shirt was embroidered with yellow and blue flowers. Well-worn blue jeans and fancy inlaid turquoise and brown cowboy boots completed her unusual look.

She introduced each song in English that was textured with a thick accent. She informed the audience—anyone who was listening, anyway—of the story behind each ballad she was about to sing and shared a little about the person who had taught her that song. Her set lasted about half an hour. Then the accordion playing folk singer returned to the stage.

*****

As the Cuban performer knelt, carefully putting her guitar into its case, Sam surprised himself by walking up to her and saying in Spanish, "I enjoyed listening to you so much. Your songs are so rich, so full of happiness, sadness and beauty. Would you join me for a drink?"

The woman looked up from her guitar case, gave him a sly smile and said in her thick rich voice, "Si Señor. If you're buying, I'm drinking. I will have a daiquiri."

Sam ordered two daiquiris from a waitress. As they waited for the drinks, Sam wasn't confident as he tried to start a conversation. "Uhm—my name is—uhm—well, it's Sam Erickson. I—uh—enjoyed your performance—er—so much."

Sam was thankful when the ice-cold daiquiris in stemmed glasses were set on the table in front of them. He tasted his drink and said, "I've never had a daiquiri. I always thought it was a woman's drink. But this is good stuff."

The woman replied, "I bet you didn't know that daiquiris were Ernest Hemingway's favorite drink."

"No. I guess I didn't know that."

"They were. In fact, my father often fixed a daiquiri—several daiquiris—for Señor Hemingway. He would visit our home—or, more often, we visited his—just outside Havana. Papa and Hemingway would go out onto the veranda and drink daiquiris until the sun set—or until they no longer could see straight—whichever came last."

She laughed after saying that. Her name was Isabelle. Sam may have been tongue tied, but Isabelle certainly wasn't. She told Sam about herself. Her mother had died shortly after her birth. She had been raised by her father in that small home near Havana.

"My father was a good friend of Fidel Castro—going back to the 1940s. In 1956, when I was thirteen years old, Papa joined Fidel, his brother Raul, Che Guevara and a few other patriots in the Sierra Maestra Mountains. They waged the battle to free Cuba from Batista and his like. That was when Papa sent me to live with my mother's brother in Miami. The plan was that I would stay in Miami until the revolution was complete. Then I would return home. My temporary visit became a permanent move when, in early 1958, Papa was killed in an ambush by Batista's army."

After saying this, Isabelle paused, took a deep breath and looked down at her painted finger nails. After a moment of silence, she shook her head as if she was casting aside some unwanted thoughts and continued to speak. "Uncle did not like my father. He was not sympathetic to Castro or to the Cuban revolution. Uncle hated Castro. He had been a person of privilege in Cuba and wanted to forget all about Cuba—to become a middle-class American. In Uncle's home, I was not allowed to bring up memories of my father—or of Cuba."

She was fascinating. Sam was enjoying himself more than he had in a long time. And it helped that Isabelle was doing most of the talking.

"So," she continued, "after graduating from high school and spending a year attending Miami Dade College, I escaped Uncle. I moved to the Twin Cities—far away from Miami. I picked the Twin Cities somewhat by chance. I had never seen snow. And I had heard people in Minnesota are nice. At first, I supported myself working as a sales clerk at Donaldson's. I saved enough money to enroll at the University. Now, I support myself and my studies as a teaching assistant in the University's Spanish Language Department.

*****

The waitress returned to the table. "Another round of daiquiris, guys?"

Sam was about to nod yes. But Isabelle spoke to the waitress, "Ask the bartender if he would fix the daiquiris using lime juice, grapefruit juice and a touch of maraschino liqueur."

Minutes later the waitress returned with the drinks. "I repeated your request to the bartender. He just smiled at me and said he knew exactly what you're asking for. He said, 'The Cuban gal wants a Hemingway Daiquiri.'"

The second round tasted better than the first. The potent rum drinks began to loosen Sam up. He started speaking! The two of them laughed and shared personal stories with one another as they moved on to a third round of drinks.

Sam appreciated Isabelle's intensity in the stories she told about joy and sadness. Her Spanish was different from what he had heard in Spain. Her pronunciation was much less precise. Sam asked her about that accent.

Isabelle laughed. "Cubans, my dear friend, do not come from Spain. They come from Cuba. They speak Spanish like Cubans. When I listen to someone who comes from Mexico or Spain, their accents sound strange to me—yours included."

With the daiquiri's help, Sam had begun to feel totally at ease. He talked about himself, though he felt his life was woefully boring as compared to all Isabelle had experienced. But she listened intently and asked questions about things he had never even wondered about. *Did his mother regret she'd married his father? How had his grandparents met?*

Her questions took Sam aback. He had to pause before responding to many of them. More than once, he had to respond by saying, "I'm sorry, Isabelle. I just don't know."

Sam liked that Isabelle was able to talk about herself so freely and still be interested in him. They ignored the accordion playing folksinger—and every other person in the bar as they drank daiquiris and exchanged life stories. Their conversations jumped back and forth between Spanish and English.

*****

Sam suddenly realized that not only had the accordion player left the stage, but he and Isabelle were the only customers left in the bar. The bar staff were watching them.

It was time to leave. Sam offered Isabelle a ride to her home. She quickly accepted.

Outside, the snow was falling. As they approached Sam's Oldsmobile, Isabelle said in her thick accent full of rolling r's, "How magnificent! You will drive me to my home in your own rocket ship. How romantic!"

Sam felt proud—Isabelle was impressed with his car! After he unlocked and opened her door, she slid across the seat ending up close to him. Sam was aware that the alcohol in the daquiris had done its work on him. He drove carefully, avoided major thoroughfares and stayed on back streets as much as possible.

When the Rocket Oldsmobile pulled in front of the house in which Isabelle rented a room, Sam surprised himself one more time. "Would you—would you like to go out with me—for dinner—this weekend?"

Isabelle gave a pensive look which caused Sam to have a panicky moment in which he thought, *Oh god, was that a mistake?*

Then Isabelle laughed and said, *"Por supuesto"*. She wrote down her phone number on a piece of paper and gave it to Sam. He proudly offered her his business card and added, "I'll pick you up at six on Saturday."

As Sam drove home, he realized he was grinning. What a wonderful Valentine's Day! He had a date coming up— with a girl he liked!

*****

The daiquiris may have gone down smoothly on Monday evening, but when Sam woke up early Tuesday morning with a terrible headache, he realized that they had taken their toll. He decided to stay in bed and try to get over his hangover.

Finally, he fell asleep. Then the phone rang. It was Sam's first call on his business line. A representative of Midwest Insurance—a Twin City based insurer—was responding to the marketing information Sam had delivered to their office. "Could you meet with me," the caller asked, "to discuss a possible contract? We need someone to investigate a few insurance claims. It will involve travel."

Sam agreed to meet with the Midwest Insurance Company representative on Friday morning. Before the conversation ended, the caller said, "By the way, I've tried to call you a couple of other times. There was no answer."

Sam tried to finesse it. "Sorry. My answering service must have screwed up again and didn't pick up the calls. I'll call them and let them know what's what. My clients deserve better service than that."

After the call, Sam did call his answering service to complain. He learned that if he wanted the answering service to pick up his phone calls, he had to flip the switch on the side of his office phone. Once the switch was flipped, calls would go to the answering service and when he flipped the switch back, he could receive the calls at his home. Sam had wondered about the purpose of that switch.

Sam went back to bed and slept most of the day. When he finally got out of bed, he felt like a million dollars. He realized things were beginning to turn his way.

6. Progress

Friday morning Sam went into Midwest Insurance's headquarters. The insurer wanted a freelance contractor for routine investigations of property and car insurance claims. The contracts manager was an Army veteran. He told Sam, "Your Air Force experience makes you highly qualified for the job." Then he offered Sam the contract.

Sam had to hold back a grin when he signed the contract. Now, when someone asked him what he did for a living—well, he had an answer. He rewarded himself for getting his first client by deciding he would stop making cold marketing calls. He had hated them. Instead, Sam could now focus on investigations—something he would enjoy.

****

Sam couldn't stop thinking about his upcoming date with Isabelle. He decided to go all out to impress her. His grandparents had celebrated Sam's tenth birthday by taking him and his mother to dinner at the Nicollet Hotel's Waikiki Room. That wonderful dinner was one of his happiest childhood memories. He hadn't been to the Waikiki Room since. But on Saturday, that's where Sam was going to take Isabelle.

Saturday evening, as Sam drove Isabelle to the Nicollet, the easy flow of their conversation mixed with constant laughter confirmed to him that none of their Valentine's Day chemistry had disappeared. As they walked through the Nicollet Hotel lobby, Isabelle commented with delight on the hanging chandeliers, ornate wooden paneling, marble floors, luxurious oriental carpets and, sophisticated overstuffed furniture.

When they entered the Waikiki Room, her jaw dropped. "Sam, this reminds me of a Havana restaurant my father once took me to—I was about eight. Entering that dining room was magical, just like this. And the music—Sam—the music. I love the gentle sound of the ukulele and the soft voices singing Hawaiian songs."

A Hawaiian headwaiter—Sam recalled from years before that all of the waiting staff had been Hawaiian—led them to a candlelit mahogany table under a lifelike palm tree. Isabelle and Sam sat down on bamboo and wicker chairs. Isabelle continued to look around, in a sort of awe. She inspected the carved statues of frowning gods, the bamboo tiki awnings and all of the other Polynesian decorations. Then she took a deep breath, leaned back in her oversized bamboo wicker chair and drew a long sip from the straw in the mai tai Sam had ordered while she studied the room. Then she took the pink paper umbrella out of her mai tai and twirled it between her thumb and forefinger and winked at Sam who simply blushed.

After an appetizer of Polynesian barbecue spareribs, their waiter brought each of them a small white plate that held a hot, wet linen napkin. Isabelle and Sam wiped the sticky sweet sauce off of their fingers as their main course arrived. They dove into the mandarin duck with plum sauce accompanied by snow peas and Polynesian fried rice. That evening they only spoke Spanish. Isabelle recounted happy memories of her dinner with her father at the Havana restaurant that had reminded her of the Waikiki Room.

Then, Isabelle asked Sam about his house.

"Well, Isabelle. Let me see—uhm—it's a really nice house. It has—well there is the main floor. It has a living room that's attached to a dining room—and of course there's a kitchen. And—uh—on the second floor, well on the second floor, there are three bedrooms—and there's a bathroom there too."

Sam stopped speaking for a moment, then nodded; confident he had covered everything. "I guess the house is about fifty or sixty years old. And it's in a nice neighborhood, you know, near Lake Harriet. There are a lot of expensive homes nearby. Though my house, well, it isn't big and it's not fancy—but it's nice."

"Sam, I know that part of Minneapolis—the lakes—the homes—it's simply wonderful. But your description, Sam, it tells me nothing—nothing at all. You're going to have to show me your house."

The waiter briefly interrupted their conversation as he placed a piece of moist pineapple upside-down cake in front of each of them.

Then Sam said, "Gee Isabelle, I—uh—would you like to come over—I mean come over to my house and see it—I mean after we polish off our desserts?"

Fifteen minutes later, Isabelle and Sam left the restaurant. As he drove the Rocket Oldsmobile toward his home, Sam was feeling on top of the world—almost like the powerful Oldsmobile really was a rocket ship and that he, Sam, was the pilot, guiding it and his precious cargo to his home port.

*****

During Sam's tour of the home, Isabelle did not stop asking questions. "Who owned the house before your grandparents? Was all of the arts and crafts furniture in the house when they bought it? Didn't your grandmother and mother just love the furniture's style? Who is that in that framed photograph? Is that sculpted statue of the Indian an original? Where did they get that amazing art deco vase?"

Sam tried, but failed, to respond to each question. Isabelle asked so many questions that Sam couldn't answer that he finally told her, "I'm embarrassed. Isabelle. I just never paid a whole lot of attention to my own home. I ignored all of the details. But seeing the house through your eyes, Isabelle; looking at all of these arts and crafts pieces of furniture, the pottery, and the art; well, I feel like I just discovered that my home is a classic—you know—it's sort of like the Rocket Olds."

Isabelle pointed at the family photo album on a bottom shelf in the living room. "Could we look at that?"

Sam said "sure' and while Isabelle sat down on the living room couch, he went into the kitchen and returned a minute later with two small, delicate crystal glasses filled with Crème de Cacao and a touch of cream.

Sam sat down next to Isabelle on the couch and started to page through the photo album, one photograph, one page at a time. He realized he was doing a much better job explaining the photographs than he had done with the furnishing of his house. More than a decade before, Sam had sat on that same couch—more than once—with his grandmother—looking through the album—hearing her describe each of those photos—her memories of the past.

Isabelle and Sam took time examining and discussing each page of the album. There were time-tinged photos of Sam's great-grandparents, wedding photographs of Sam's parents and grandparents, worn snapshots of Sam's father in uniform taken in the South Pacific and a series of Lucky's Cafe pictures spread across time.

When the album was closed, Isabelle sighed and looked thoughtful. Then she said, "Sam, one thing jumps out to me. There are not many pictures of you."

Sam thought about that for a moment. Then he just shrugged his shoulders and said, "I guess the restaurant always was the family's real baby."

They finished the photo album and put it away. Isabelle took a deep breath. She gave an emphatic exhale and said, "A good friend recently invited me to her wedding. It will be in two weeks at a church in St. Paul. The reason I am telling you is because the reception will be in the ball room at the Nicollet. Having seen how grand the hotel is, I am certain the reception will be fabulous. I want to go to that party. But Sam, I don't have a date. Would you be my date, Sam? It will be such a wonderful celebration with fantastic Cuban food and music. It will give you the chance to see the beauty of my culture and you will meet some of my beautiful Cuban friends. Would you like to be my date for this?"

Sam grinned from ear to ear—almost laughing. "Yes, absolutely. I'd love to be your date."

Isabelle matched his grin and said, "And we will have so much fun dancing, Sam. There is going to be such a wonderful Latin band at the reception."

Panic set in. Sam cleared his throat—a couple of times. Then he said, "I'm really pleased to be going to the party with you, Isabelle. But I gotta be honest. I don't know how to dance. The only dances I know are—well, the twist and the two-step—and I don't do them very well."

Isabelle's big smile got even bigger as she said, "That won't be a problem. I will give you lessons before the party. I'm such a good teacher, Sam. I guarantee that at the party, you will dance well."

Wow. This was working out better than Sam could have planned. Isabelle was offering another chance to get together. They agreed that Sam would pick up Isabelle the following Saturday for his first dance lesson.

Isabelle looked at her watch. It was late. Sam drove her to her home.

*****

Monday morning, Sam met with the Midwest Insurance's Risk Manager, Dennis Davis. Sam would investigate all questionable claims in small towns across Minnesota, Wisconsin and Iowa. He would meet with claimants and local insurance agencies; confirm reported facts with local police and fire departments; check out local pawn shops and junk yards looking for items reported lost or stolen; and snoop around with other local sources like bankers to learn if a claimant had financial problems that might have precipitated a claim. When Sam identified a potential fraud, he would report it to Midwest Insurance and they would take it from there.

The assignment seemed straightforward. Sam would be on the road about a week a month. The work wasn't dangerous. Sam would be reimbursed for all his travel expenses and his detective agency now had a regular revenue stream. Davis gave Sam a background file for each of his first set of investigations—all in Iowa. Sam would spend the next week on the road, carrying out investigations.

*****

Saturday morning, Sam picked up Isabelle for his first dance lesson. As he drove his home, she began to tell him about Cuban dance. "The *rumba* was created in Cuba by former slaves almost a century ago. In its music, you hear the primitive drumbeat of Africa. The *cha cha*, *mambo*, and *Cuban son*—they all emerged from the *rumba*. For our lesson today, we'll focus on my favorite dance, the cha cha. If the only Latin dance you know when you get to the wedding party is cha cha, we'll still have lots of fun dancing."

When they got home, Sam poured two mugs of strong coffee and they sat down at the dining room table having the small talk conversation of two people who are just beginning to know one another.

Then Isabelle announced, "OK, Mr. Fred Astaire. No more stalling. We dance."

They went into the living room. Sam pushed back the couch, moved the coffee table aside, rolled up the rug and the lesson began.

"We begin our work without music," she said in a businesslike manner. "In addition to taking small steps during the dance, cha cha requires hip movements. You do this by shifting your weight from one foot to the other. See—like this."

A completely intimidated Sam watched as Isabelle demonstrated.

She continued. "As one knee bends, that hip drops. When your knee straightens, your hip will rise. Then you take three steps and—well—that's *cha cha-cha*." She demonstrated the steps and movements several times while counting out aloud.

Then it was Sam's turn to try. He felt awfully awkward. "I know I am doing a half-ass job of mimicking your dance steps, Isabelle. The problem is I have two left feet—I was born that way."

Isabelle gave a chesty laugh as he struggled to move his feet and body in time with her beat. "I agree Sam. You are clumsy—but nice clumsy. I can work with this."

By the time they broke for lunch, Sam had learned the basic movements and was beginning to feel the rhythm. All this while, as he mimicked her moves, he had been dancing next to Isabelle rather than holding her in his arms.

"Isabelle—I think the movements are beginning to come."

Isabelle laughed and said, "Si, quizas. But after lunch, you will have to try it with some music."

*****

For lunch, Sam served grilled cheese sandwiches, dill pickles and canned tomato soup. Afterwards, Isabelle put a cha cha LP on Sam's hi-fi and they began to dance together—accompanied by music. Sam was surprised. He was beginning to feel some confidence. In addition, he was enjoying holding Isabelle in his arms. They worked throughout the afternoon. For dinner, Sam fixed spaghetti with meat sauce and a green salad. They drank a bottle of chianti and then went back to dancing. By the time they quit for the evening, Sam was beginning to feel like maybe he might not make a total fool of himself at the wedding.

During the day, Sam and Isabelle had spoken mostly in Spanish. But as he drove her home, they spoke in English. He enjoyed hearing her rich, exotic Cuban accent. Her emotive voice was complimented by animated hand gestures and expressive eyes.

Sam was thinking about the party and began to panic. "Isabelle, what am I supposed to wear—I mean to the wedding?

"A suit will do for both the wedding and the reception. However, you will find many of the attendees will be specially dressed for the party. It will be quite an occasion."

"What do you mean by *specially dressed*?"

"This will probably be the most festive Twin Cities Cuban occasion of the year. The bride is from Miami. The groom is local—the brother of a Minnesota Twins baseball player. The women will wear bold colored gowns that have lots of lace, sequins and ruffles."

They were at a stop sign and Isabelle stopped speaking. Sam looked at her. Isabelle gave him a quick smile followed by a wink he hadn't seen from her before. "Some men will wear suits to both the wedding and the party. But all of the stylish men will wear tuxedos or dinner jackets to the evening party—some will be quite formal. And in case you are wondering, Sam—and I can see on your face that you are—my gown will be magenta and black."

Sam was relieved he'd asked. His old suit would probably still fit. But now, he knew he needed to rent something special for the party. And he had no clue what color magenta was. He suspected it was either red or blue—but maybe it could be yellow? Sam decided that if he was a smart man, he would figure out what color magenta was before he ordered his dinner jacket. Sam really wanted to please Isabelle—to have her believe he was a stylish man.

*****

Sunday, Sam went through the claim files that Davis had given him. He learned that on the trip, he would investigate four thefts—two in Des Moines, one in Iowa City, one in Mason City—and two fires, both on farms near Cedar Rapids. Sam would be on the road Tuesday through

Thursday. He was looking forward to driving on Iowa's two-lane highways past snowy post-harvest cornfields.

Monday morning, he phoned the claimants, local insurance agents, police and fire station officials to set up meetings. He also went into a tux rental store to reserve a dinner jacket for the party. He described the wedding party to the salesman.

The salesman responded enthusiastically. "Seems like a really big deal. Baseball player's family, eh? Could be fun. What d'you wanna wear, bud?"

"I want my tux—or dinner jacket—or whatever I should be wearing—to go with my date's dress. Her dress is magenta and black."

"Sounds like she's got quite the fashionable gal. What shade of magenta is her dress?"

"Huh?" Sam paused and his face turned a littler red. "Uh—I don't know. I don't even have a clue what color magenta is. I thought maybe you could help me."

The salesman chuckled. "You're not asking an easy question, fella. I could rent you a really sharp looking magenta dinner jacket. But then, there are so many different shades of magenta, you're be pretty certain to have the wrong shade and then, you'd be totally screwed. I recommend a white dinner jacket. I'll throw in three sets of cummerbunds and matching pre-tied bow-ties—a black set and two in varying shades of magenta. That'll cover your bases—to borrow a baseball term."

Sam wasn't done asking questions. "One other thing—should I buy her a corsage? I've never taken a date to a wedding and I don't know if I should—I mean—give her a corsage."

"Buy a corsage for the prom, pal. But this ain't your prom. No corsage."

Sam left the shop feeling relieved and informed. The salesman had shown him an assortment of magenta cummerbunds. He now knew that magenta could be any one of a million shades of purplish-red.

Live and learn.

*****

The Iowa trip went well. There was only one claimant he didn't meet—a farmer. Sam saw the other claimants, their insurance agents and various police and fire department officials.

Sam was suspicious about two of the claims. One was the Iowa City claim for a vehicle reported as stolen. It had been demolished in an accident and Sam was not able to confirm the damage to the car because it had been sold to a junk yard which had immediately destroyed it. When he spoke with the Iowa City policeman who had filed the original accident report, he learned that the University of Iowa student who had filed the claim had a drinking problem. The cop told Sam he had seen no evidence that the car had been broken into. Sam met with the student and told him the car's value was about a thousand dollars.

"You know," Sam told the student, "If it somehow turned out that the report of the car theft was a lie, well, the impact on your life would be a whole lot greater than a thousand bucks. At least, that's what I think."

Later that day, without admitting any guilt, the student called the local insurance agent and said, "The hassle of the claim isn't worth it." The student retracted his claim.

The other problematic claim was the Cedar Rapids fire claim from the farmer who was out of town when Sam came to interview him. Sam learned the farmer was actually visiting relatives in nearby Davenport. The county's fire commissioner comment was: "Farmer Skalrud's barn is a total loss. But it's common knowledge he was on the verge of bankruptcy. Where the fire started—well—I have no real evidence...but the claim might be a tad bit suspicious."

Sam decided to recommend Midwest Insurance initiate a formal arson investigation into that claim. The other four claims raised no questions. Friday morning, Sam called Dennis Davis at Midwest Insurance to report on his progress. Davis was pleased with the what he heard. Sam promised to send him written reports and a bill by the end of the following week.

Sam was satisfied that his detective agency was now a reality instead of just a dream.

*****

Sam hadn't worn his suit since he was in high school. When he tried it on, he found that the seat of its pants was full of moth holes. Friday afternoon Sam went to Donaldson's Department Store to buy a new charcoal grey pin striped suit. Donaldson's tailor raced to complete putting cuffs on the suit while Sam purchased a pair of black Allan Edmonds wingtips, a white shirt (that he could wear with his grandfather's gold cufflinks) and a red satin tie.

On the way home, Sam picked up his dinner jacket complete with the three sets of cummerbunds and ties. After having the Rocket washed and waxed, he got home and called Isabelle to confirm when he would pick her up the following day.

Sam was ready for the weekend.

*****

Just after noon on Saturday, the gleaming two-tone blue Rocket Eighty-Eight glided to a stop in front of Isabelle's home. Isabelle came out of the house with a big smile on her face. Sam carefully placed the garment bag that held her dress onto the back seat of the Oldsmobile. After the wedding ceremony, Isabelle would change into her evening gown at his house.

Sam had often driven past the site of the wedding, the Cathedral of the Apostle Paul. He had always admired its two-hundred-feet-high exterior dome. But he had never been inside the church. As the couple entered the cathedral, Sam was stunned with the beauty of the sanctuary. Its granite interior was set off with soft blue painted paneling and delicate gold leaf trim. But what was especially breathtaking was the sunlight that streamed through the dome's stained-glass windows. Sam stared up at the windows, then surveyed the magnificent church's delicate architectural details as an usher in a black suit led him and Isabelle to their seats.

Once seated in a carved wooden pew in the middle of the cathedral, Sam looked down from the dome to view other wedding guests. His jaw dropped. There, in the rows of guests (most of whom were speaking Spanish), were several Minnesota Twin ballplayers alongside their stunning wives or dates. They included Camilo Pascual, Zoilo Versalles and Tony Oliva. Even Harmon Killebrew was there! Sam looked at Isabelle. He blushed when he realized that Isabelle had been watching him and was laughing at him.

"I was wondering what your reaction would be when you saw the ballplayers. I thought you might be impressed. You did not disappoint."

Several of the ballplayers' wives and dates turned around, smiled at and waved to Isabelle. Two or three also lifted their thumbs up—messages an embarrassed Sam took to mean he had just received their approval. While he realized that that was good, his face turned an even deeper shade of red. Sam tried to avoid their watchful stares by looking down at his printed program. Sam understood he was not just a guest. He was on display.

*****

After a long wedding mass conducted entirely in Latin, the bride and groom left in a chauffeured shiny black Cadillac Fleetwood limousine. Sam and Isabelle went back to the Rocket and drove to Sam's home to change clothes for the evening celebration. On the drive, Isabelle was animated—obviously pleased with everything that had just transpired. She spoke quickly in Spanish giving Sam background on a series of individuals he had met that morning. As Sam listened, he realized Isabelle had a lot more friends than he had ever had. And he hadn't missed how much affection those people had for her.

"And Julia, you know, the woman in the red dress, she is like a sister. Her date, the big guy in the black tux, he is brother of the groom—well you know him from watching baseball. And Luciana, the woman in the yellow dress—oh, my God, she is so beautiful. But she is more than just a little bit of a gossip...."

"I'm sorry, Isabelle. The only people whose names I can remember are the baseball players."

"That's ok Sam. You will have many opportunities to be with my friends, to get to know them, to learn their names."

That sounded good to Sam.

*****

After dressing in his rented outfit—but not yet putting on a bow-tie or cummerbund—Sam sat down on the living room couch and waited for Isabelle. She was preparing for the evening in the middle bedroom. A half an hour later, when she descended on the staircase, Sam learned which shade of magenta his date was wearing. But more important, he recognized her unusual beauty and style. Her jet-black hair picked up on the black lace jacket she wore over a strapless magenta knee-length gown. And, for once, Sam noticed a detail. Isabelle's lipstick matched the color of her dress.

Sam swallowed. All he could manage to utter was, "Wow."

Sam showed her his cummerbund and bowtie alternatives. Isabelle frowned at the two magenta sets and quickly selected the black. Sam put them on and they were off to the ball.

*****

After walking through the Nicollet Hotel's impressive lobby and then riding up to the second floor in what Isabelle described as "the most perfect art deco elevator she'd ever seen", Sam and Isabelle entered the hotel's grand ballroom. The room was lit by immense sparkling crystal chandeliers. Toward the back of the ballroom, three long buffet tables were packed with dishes and platters of food. A hosted bar was on each side of the buffet tables. A couple of dozen dining tables bearing white linen, dinnerware and crystal were set up between the buffets and a large wooden dance floor.

Formally outfitted men and vibrantly dressed women conversed as they drank from glasses that held an array of alcoholic drinks. Isabelle was immediately greeted by a series of friends—some of whom Sam had met at the wedding—others who he was meeting for the first time. It was a good thing that Sam was fluent in Spanish. Few guests were speaking English. While Isabelle spoke with an acquaintance, Sam walked over to the bar and asked for a mojito for himself and a daiquiri for Isabelle. He noticed that the bartenders did not skimp on the rum.

When Sam rejoined Isabelle, she introduced him to her friend, Rosaline Martinez. "I knew Rosaline when I lived in Miami. Rosaline is like family. No, actually, she's closer than family. Rosaline and her husband Luis came here from Chicago for the wedding."

Rosaline was the sort of woman that causes people to look twice and to wonder if perhaps she might be a movie star. She had auburn hair, dark brown eyes and was wearing a strapless black sequined cocktail dress with a red silk scarf draped back over her shoulders. As Sam watched Isabelle and Rosaline talk, it occurred to him that a major part of Rosaline's beauty was the confidence with which she carried herself.

Rosaline grabbed her husband Luis by the arm, led him to Sam and introduced the two men. Luis Martinez was a retired major league pitcher. (Sam remembered seeing him pitch against the Braves on *The Major League Game of the Week* a few years back. Now, he was bowled over to meet Martinez in person.) Luis was dressed in a black double-breasted tuxedo with an elaborately ruffled white shirt and black bow tie. His black hair had streaks of silver in it, but he looked fit enough to be ready to go to spring training tomorrow.

Sam asked Luis if he missed playing baseball.

Luis responded, "I enjoyed my baseball career. I pitched for several major league teams—the last being the Cubs. But after I met Rosaline, I decided to make the Windy City my permanent home. When the Cubs traded me to the Mets, it was time to retire. I wasn't going to move away from her. Rosaline and I married. I bought a Cadillac dealership in the suburbs and the rest; well, the rest is history. By the way Sam, if you ever are looking to buy a Cadillac, come to Chicago. I'll sell you a beautiful car at a great price."

As he said this, Luis reached into his lapel pocket and took out two cigars. He offered one to Sam. "It's the real deal, Sam. The quality of the tobacco is better than any cigar you can buy in the States. Real Cuban cigars are made perfectly in every way—they do not contain a single flaw."

Sam had only smoked a couple of cigars in his life. After Luis cut off an end of the cigar, Sam took it and Luis held out a lit wooden match. Sam sucked in the smoke. He immediately had to fight off a cough. The cigar was much stronger than any other cigar Sam had smoked.

Sam was enjoying himself as he stood next to Luis, Isabelle and Rosaline, sipping his mojito and puffing on his cigar. He tried to look like he was used to this sort of social festivity. When Luis asked Sam what he did for a living, Sam felt so good being able to give an answer other than—*well— uhm—nothing*. After Luis heard Sam ran a detective agency, he appeared more than casually interested. He asked a series of questions about Sam's experience as an investigator in the Air Force. Luis and Sam were interrupted when Rosaline came over, took Luis' arm and told both of them it was time for dinner.

As they headed to the buffet table, Luis told Sam, "I want to speak more about your detective agency later."

*****

At the buffet, Isabelle and Sam filled their plates from an expansive assortment of traditional Cuban dishes. Sam had never seen a spread like this. The visually beautiful dishes were labeled with exotic names. There was Mojo Chicken with Mango Salsa, Cucina Cubana Baby-back Ribs, Coconut Chicken in Banana Leaves, and Fried Sweet Plantain, Avocado, Watercress, and Pineapple Salad.

The four of them filled their plates and then sat down together at one of the elaborately set tables. After eating, he tasted and enjoyed nearly every exotic dish from the buffet, Sam watched Luis and Rosaline walk off into the crowd, hand in hand. Sam and Isabelle, also hand in hand, began to tour the ballroom. Sam met more and more of her friends. She continued to down daiquiris and he kept pace with the minty, citrusy and slightly sweet mojitos.

This party was fun! A highlight of the evening was chatting for several minutes with his favorite major league pitcher, Camilo Pascual. Pascual offered Sam a second cigar. Sam, now an old hand, quickly accepted. Pascual held out a wooden match and Sam lit his cigar. As he inhaled, he felt like he was getting comfortable with these earthy, woody and aromatic Cuban cigars.

Pascual liked to talk about cars. "I have a friend who owns a sweet Cadillac two-door convertible. I love the its style and size. But my friend lives in Miami. And you know, having a convertible in Miami is much more practical than having one here in freezing Minneapolis. I have been talking to Luis about getting a white two-door Calais."

Sam felt comfortable discussing cars. "You know, Camilo, the Caddie and the Olds are built on the same chassis. They both have those crazy large engines. It's true that the Cadillac has retained the fins and has a different front grill. But other than that, the two cars are similar. Of course, my Rocket doesn't have an adjustable electric leather seat or the deluxe speaker options. But overall, there are more similarities between Cadillac and Oldsmobile than differences."

Pascual listened politely. A moment later, when he saw a friend across the room whom he hadn't seen in years, Camilo Pascual excused himself.

*****

The festivity was changed by the syncopated rhythm of a five-piece Latin band from Miami. Fortunately for Sam, the first song was a cha cha. Isabelle grabbed his hand and they were quickly doing their steps on the wooden dancefloor. Sam had enjoyed his mojitos enough to avoid any sense of self-consciousness. He was into the music and enjoying dancing. But the real treat for him was being able to watch Isabelle. She had saved her best moves for the ballroom.

As he danced, Sam looked around. There were a few others who, like him, were having fun without depending upon too much skill. But there were quite a few accomplished dancers. When the music changed from cha cha to rumba and then to the Cuban son, Sam saw Isabelle had been correct—the cha cha steps worked perfectly with each of the other Cuban musical genres.

*****

The wedding couple danced a slow dance followed by applause. Then the crowd began to murmur. Something special was about to happen. Most of the couples, including Sam and Isabelle, left the dance floor. Isabelle said, "Now you will see, Sam. Some of the best dancers will demonstrate how fabulous Cuban dance can be. They will dance the tango."

Sam responded, "I thought the tango was an Argentinean dance."

Isabelle laughed. "Common misconception. We Cubans lay claim to tango. It grew out of a traditional Cuban dance called the *habanera*. And we dance the tango extremely well, Sam. The Argentinians just copied us."

Among the six couples waiting for the music to start were Luis and Rosaline who had not yet been on the dance floor. Sam had figured they were just not into dancing. A moment later he recognized how wrong he had been.

When the tango music began, Luis took Rosaline in his arms in a formal manner. As they moved across the floor, Luis and Rosaline's stared into one another's eyes. As the pace of the music picked up, they moved more quickly—totally in sync with one another. Other couples were doing similar steps. But Luis' formal presence—his forceful and deliberate movements juxtaposed to Rosaline's strong but graceful response—made them the stars of the dance. As Luis guided Rosaline through twisting turns, her scarf whirled out—accentuating the speed of her pirouettes. When the music stopped, the ballroom erupted into applause. Sam realized he was not the only person there who had been enthralled watching Luis and Rosaline.

Isabelle whispered, "Luis and Rosaline's dancing skills are well known across the United States. They once won an important international tango competition held in Miami."

*****

Sometime after midnight, the combination of rich food, tasty mojitos and deeply flavored Cuban cigars caught up with Sam. He began to feel a little ill. He slurred some of his words as he spoke in a spontaneous fusion of Spanish and English, "Perhaps, should I be driving you on the way home?"

Isabelle agreed that the evening had been great, but it was time to say *hasta luego* to her many friends. As Sam waited for her to deliver her goodbyes, he looked around. He could see that he was not the only person in the ball room who had consumed their limit of rum.

*****

When they reached the Oldsmobile, there was no doubt Sam's mojitos had hit their mark and Isabelle suggested she drive. Sam was relieved. While Isabelle drove the Rocket Eighty-Eight out of the hotel parking garage, Sam focused all of his cerebral energies on not throwing up inside his beautiful Rocket. In spite of the freezing weather, he lowered his window. The fresh cool air helped—but not enough. Fortunately, the lowered window gave Sam a path for quick release when he needed it most. While waiting for a red light a couple blocks from the hotel, Sam sent the last of his mojitos and the remnants of his exquisite dinner out, through the open window of the Oldsmobile, onto Hennepin Avenue's pavement.

7. A Missing Person

When Sam woke up the next morning feeling awful. He couldn't remember getting home—or changing into his pajamas—or getting into bed. He just hoped he hadn't made too much of a fool of himself at the wedding party. He rolled over and opened his eyes. Isabelle was in bed next to him—wearing his pajama tops. She slowly opened one eye, then the other, and said, "Good morning, Sam. Did you have sweet dreams?"

Sam was embarrassed—confused—he stuttered—then threw out a jumbled set of questions. "Uhm—uh—did you dress me? I mean, how did we get into the house last night?" He was quiet for a moment and then added, "Did you spend the night here?"

Sam realized he was making a fool of himself. But he wasn't done. He had one more uncomfortable question, "Did we—uhm—did we—uh—do anything...," he paused, trying to figure out the best word to complete his thought, "uhm—intimate?"

Isabelle responded with a smile, "If you don't remember last night, Samuel Erickson, you don't deserve to know."

What could he say? He got out of bed. As he stood up, his head felt even worse. What a hangover! Sam threw on his robe and staggered down to the kitchen to make a pot of coffee. A half an hour later, Isabelle, wearing one of Sam's old cardigan sweaters as a robe, joined him. They sat quietly at the kitchen table, sipping from mugs of hot strong coffee.

After a while, Sam asked, "Did I make a fool of myself— I mean at the party.

"I can assure you that you did not do anything at the Nicollet that you need to be too ashamed of. I totally enjoyed everything at the party—especially my date."

Sam decided it might be a good call not to ask any other questions about what might have happened after the party.

*****

Isabelle looked up at the kitchen clock. It was eleven o'clock. "Sam, we should start getting ready if we are going to meet Rosaline and Luis for lunch at one."

Sam's face flushed. While he remembered Rosaline and Luis very clearly, he had no recall of any plan to get together with them for lunch.

Isabelle read Sam's face. "Luis was impressed with you, Sam. He is interested in your detective agency. He wants to talk to you about a missing person. Since Luis and Rosaline are going to drive back to Chicago this afternoon, we agreed to meet them today for lunch. Luis will tell you about the case. You said last night *it sounded interesting*."

Sam couldn't remember the conversation. "What sort of case were they talking about?"

"It is terribly upsetting. Rosaline has not seen her teenage daughter Fidelia for more than a month. She has no idea where Fidelia is—or even if she is—still alive. Rosaline and Luis want to see if you would be willing to help them find her. Luis asked you if there was a place where we could meet for lunch that had good food. You suggested Cecil's Delicatessen in St. Paul. I was pleased. You've told me more than once about Cecil's excellent food. But I have never been there. We need to leave soon so I can change. If I come to lunch in my evening dress or your pajamas...."

A short while later, Sam drove Isabelle by her home where she changed into blue jeans and a white cotton

59

blouse. They arrived at Cecil's a few minutes after one. Luis and Rosaline hadn't yet arrived. They walked around the deli's black and white tiled grocery area. Isabelle inspected its traditional delicatessen fresh baked goods, kosher meats, cheeses, breads, deserts and condiments. Then they were seated at a table in the restaurant part of the deli.

*****

A few minutes later, Luis and Rosaline arrived. Rosaline seemed even more stunning than she had the previous evening. Greetings were exchanged and all attention turned to the serious job of examining the menu while the waiter poured each of them a cup of coffee. Sam and Luis each ordered hot corned beef on rye with a cup of matzo ball soup. Isabelle and Rosaline agreed to split an order of cheese blintzes served with strawberry jam and sour cream. They chose that entree after receiving promises from their men that they would receive bites of corned beef sandwich and tastes of matzo ball soup.

There was no talk about Rosaline's daughter during the meal. Wedding party reviews and gossip about old friends were the focus of a conversation dominated by Isabelle and Rosaline.

Sam and Luis had a side bar conversation about the 1965 World Series. Luis concluded, "Koufax and Drysdale should be outlawed—they're just too damned good. It doesn't seem fair."

Sam nodded his agreement.

*****

After the waiter cleared the dishes, the foursome sat quietly for a few minutes. Luis took a deep breath, looked at Rosaline. She nodded. Then Luis turned to Sam and said, "Rosaline's daughter Fidelia is a wonderful girl—perhaps a bit impetuous—oftentimes passionate. But those qualities are the reason I love her—and her mother. Anyway, at about ten in the morning on the second Saturday in January, Rosaline went to Fidelia's room to wake her. Fidelia wasn't there. We've not seen her since—nor have we been able to learn anything about where she is—or what may have happened to her. We're sure she didn't just run away. Fidelia loves her mother too much. She would have done anything possible to avoid causing her mother the pain that Rosaline has endured as a result of her vanishing."

Sam pursed his lips, looked up at the ceiling for a moment, took a deep breath, let it out and then said, "Have the police had any success—I mean have they found any clues—at all?"

"The police did not do anything about her disappearance other than to write down what we reported into their missing person's log. They gave us the same pat answer the school gave—*she probably ran away*. The cops told us that when she returned—which of course according to them she would have already done—we ought to sit down with her and figure out what's troubling her. Thanks a lot."

Sam had his notebook and pen in front of him and started to write. He looked up and said, "Ok. Let's go over everything from the beginning. You need to give me background information about Fidelia, yourselves and anything else that could turn out to be a factor. If I take the case, I need to understand Fidelia—have some insight into what she might have run away from—or to. I need to know about her friends, about any possible enemies she has—or you have—and any theories you have about anyone or anything else that could be involved in this. We need to find a clue—any clue. Then, we will build on it."

Sam's turned toward Rosaline. "Rosaline—I need to know about your background—about your family, your friends and if there was anyone who might want to hurt you. I need to know about Fidelia's father." He paused, looking intently at Rosaline, "I need to know about anyone who might have any interest in her—at all. And Luis," Sam turned to him, "I need to know—might you have friends or enemies who could be a part of this?"

Sam paused and took a deep breath, then blew it out. He was quiet for a moment while the others at the table watched him closely. "If I am to help you, you need to be completely honest with me. I must consider every variable that could be a factor in your daughter's disappearance. And you need to tell me if there are any reasons that could have caused the police to choose not to investigate this case more thoroughly."

Sam waited for Rosaline or Luis to respond. He had a laser focus, ready to take notes, document each statement, each assumption and every nuance.

Luis began. "Rosaline and I understand what you need. Rosie—you ought to start."

Rosaline tightened her lips, looked at each of the others at the table, then looked down at her hands that were folded together in front of her. She began to speak. "Sharing my history, as you are about to learn, will bring back personal sadness. But I understand why you need to know everything. When I am done, you will understand why we have not pushed the police to investigate Fidelia's disappearance."

She looked at Luis who signaled her with a nod of the head to continue.

"My mother was a dancer in Havana before she met Papa. After they married, she joined him in Santiago where he ran a bank. Mama died when I was ten. I inherited some of her—well—some of her beauty. When I turned twenty, I entered a beauty pageant. I became *Miss Cuba, 1946.* The world opened up to me. I left home, moved to Havana, enjoyed myself—and benefitted from how attractive men found me. Papa did not approve."

Rosaline looked at Luis. With another brief nod of his head, he encouraged her to continue. "Some of these men were wealthy and powerful. Others were exciting and handsome. I met men who were involved in dangerous politics. I even dated Fidel Castro. Fidel married shortly after that. But he introduced me to one of his closest friends, Miguel Garcia. Miguel was attractive and financially secure. He was also very considerate. He treated me with tenderness—was demonstrative with his affection—brought me many beautiful bouquets of colorful flowers. Miguel and I fell deeply in love. I moved into Miguel's apartment only a couple of months after I met him. But Miguel was an intellectual radical. He told me that while he wanted to spend his life with me, he did not believe in marriage."

Rosaline stopped speaking briefly while the waiter filled their coffee cups. "In 1949, I became pregnant. In 1950, Fidelia was born. Miguel was a proud father. But he soon responded to what for him was a higher calling. He joined Fidel—to begin the revolution. I was left in Havana with our beautiful young daughter. Miguel saw to it that I received a monthly check that covered our living expenses."

Isabelle interrupted Rosaline to say she needed to go to the ladies' room. Rosaline joined her. Sam and Luis sat waiting for the two women, saying nothing, each lost in their own thoughts.

After the two women returned to the table, Rosaline continued. "Castro's first attempt to overthrow Batista was in 1953. He planned to storm a military garrison in southeastern Cuba. Castro calculated that once the dictator Batista had been challenged in a military confrontation, the people of Cuba would rise to overthrow him. The attack on the garrison was botched. Miguel was captured, tortured and killed. He was one of the first to die in Castro's revolution."

Rosaline took out a cigarette. Luis lit it. She took a sip of her coffee, then continued. "Papa was strongly against the overthrow of Batista's government. He had prospered in Cuba while most other Cubans suffered. But he was smart enough to see that a big political change was about to occur, that there was no long-term future for him in Cuba. In 1954, he moved to the United States, to Miami. Before he left Cuba, he told me in no uncertain terms how deeply ashamed he was of the way I was living my life."

Rosaline turned to Luis and asked, "Is this what I should be sharing?"

Luis responded, "Yes, Rosie. Go ahead. Sam needs to hear all of this background."

"After Miguel was killed, his estate sent me monthly support checks for two years. When those payments ended, there was no source of income. Fidelia and I had no alternative but to ask Papa if we could live with him in Miami. We came to Miami in early 1956. Papa allowed us to live with him because he was happy to have his granddaughter there. But he treated me like the fallen and unredeemed prodigal daughter—often making clear his disgust with the life's path I had taken."

"Have you had had any contact from Miguel's family or friends since you left Cuba?"

Rosaline nodded. "Yes. Yes, I have. I received two letters from Miguel's father—one from Miguel's sister. In each of these letters, they inquired about Fidelia and invited my daughter and me to visit them in Cuba. I sent them pictures of her, but told them that we were unable to visit Cuba."

Rosaline stared ahead, took a deep draw from her cigarette, looked up and exhaled. Turning back to Sam, she continued. "I also received two handwritten letters from Fidel Castro himself—one in 1960; the other in 1963. Castro wrote that he had promised Miguel if anything happened to Miguel, that Fidelia and I would be safe and secure. I did not respond to either of these letters. I have heard nothing from Fidel—or from anyone else in Cuba since 1964."

Rosaline stopped for a moment while the waiter refilled their coffee cups. Sam asked for the bill. The waiter told him Luis had already paid for their lunches.

"So, my daughter and I moved to Miami. While I did not have many marketable job skills, I could speak English well. I found employment as a bank teller. In the fall of 1959, a wealthy client of the bank, Tony Giarri asked me to go out on a date with him. I refused. I hadn't gotten over losing Miguel. Tony Giarri visited my bank teller's station often. We would exchange pleasantries and he often asked me to have dinner with him. Each time, I told him *no*. Somehow, Tony found Papa's home address. Without any invitation or encouragement from me, he called on me one Sunday afternoon. I refused to meet with him. I was furious that he would not accept my *no* as an answer. But Papa invited him into the house."

Luis reached out and took Rosaline's hand, squeezing it and giving her a smile. She returned a half-hearted smile. "Giarri and Papa hit it off. Papa was impressed with Tony's description of himself as *an investor*. Papa came to my bedroom while Giarri was there. He said that this man had been so gracious—he had brought me a dozen roses! The least I could do would be to come out and visit with him for a few minutes."

Rosaline took another deep breath and looked down, shaking her head from side to side. "Under intense pressure from Papa, I did leave my room to say *hi* and *thank you* to Tony. Then I returned to my room. But Tony stayed and chatted with Papa for over an hour. During the next month, Tony made similar unwelcome Sunday visits. I did not encourage him. Finally, after a lot of pressure from Papa, I agreed to let Tony take Papa, Fidelia and me out to dinner. After that, I accepted dates from Tony. He would take Fidelia and me to the cinema or he and I would dine at posh restaurants. He even escorted me to parties at his friends' mansions. I actually began to enjoy his company—he was always the gentleman. Papa was so pleased with this that, for a while, he stopped calling me *the Marxist, the whore* or any of the other cruel names he liked to use."

Rosaline looked down at the table. She said nothing for a couple of minutes. Sam recognized she was collecting her thoughts and that sharing these memories was obviously causing her quite a bit of anguish.

Then Rosaline looked up, sighed and said, "Tony and I dated for about ten months. Then he started pressuring me to marry him. I have to admit I was tempted to say *yes* even though I knew I wasn't in love with him. Maybe I would never fall in love again, so why wait? The idea of financial security for Fidelia combined with the opportunity to get out of Papa's home was so tempting. One Sunday morning, I was reading the Miami Herald on Papa's porch when I came across an article about the gangster Meyer Lansky whose organization-controlled heroin distribution and prostitution houses were prospering throughout Southern Florida. The article touched upon a key lieutenant in his organization who happened to be a nephew of Lucky Luciano. The man's name was Tony Giarri. There were pictures of Tony and several pictures of his deceased ex-wife—who, according to the Herald, had died under *unusual circumstances.*"

Isabelle interrupted and said to Rosaline, "Rosa, I had no idea. This is so horrible. I am sorry. You must have felt awful."

Rosaline turned to Isabelle. "I was dumbstruck, Issa. Tony had lied when he said he was an investor. He had lied when he said he had never been married. And God knows what else he lied about. I showed the article to Papa. He told me, 'Relax—there is probably a reasonable explanation.' *Relax*—that was the word he used! I realized that I not only needed to end the relationship with Tony, I had to move out of Papa's home. Fidelia and I had lived with him for four years. I needed to get out."

Rosaline looked up with a bit of fire in her eyes. "When I inquired at the bank about a job transfer, I was offered a position in Chicago at the bank's headquarters. I had friends from Miami who had moved to Chicago. They had said it was cold and windy. But they liked it. I jumped at the chance. I wrote Tony telling him I had read the article in the Herald, that I now realized he had lied to me—in so many ways and I told him we were done."

Rosaline looked at Sam directly while saying, "I refused to see him again or to take any of his phone calls. Finally, he came to Papa's home. He would not leave until I spoke with him. So, I came out briefly and repeated several of the most horrid things from the Herald article. I told him I never wanted to see him again. He became angry—said many things that were mean—things that were not true."

Rosaline stopped speaking. There were tears in her eyes. She shook her head. Her hands were shaking as she lit another cigarette, then looked out across the deli. She did not continue speaking until she had finished smoking her cigarette. Sam, Isabelle and Luis waited, watching her, saying nothing.

"Papa became horribly angry and abusive, criticizing me for breaking it off with Tony. He told me he was glad I was moving out of his house; that I was a poor excuse for a daughter. And he told me I should leave Fidelia with him—I was not fit to be her mother! Imagine that! I asked him, 'what part of me is not fit?'"

Rosaline smiled sadly and she sighed. "Papa told me I had lived in sin with a communist revolutionary and had had a child out of wedlock! He said I was a sinner, a communist and a terrible mother! I could not believe how many cruel things were being said by my own father! I packed my things, took my ten-year-old daughter by the hand and we marched out of Papa's house—out of his life."

Rosaline took a long drag from her cigarette, blew the smoke to her side and said, "I have not spoken with that man since."

Isabelle interjected, "Good for you, Rosa. Your papa sounds like such a monster!"

Rosaline smiled at Isabelle. "Thank you, Issa. You are a special friend."

Then Rosaline turned back to Sam. "Tony Giarri has tried to contact me only once since then. Two years ago, I received a letter from him. He told me he knew where I lived and that he accepted I would not love him. But he told me he wanted to be able to visit Fidelia who he had come to love as a daughter. The letter had a New York City return address. I thought about not responding to his letter, but decided it would be better to be direct with him. I wrote that Fidelia now had a father and that I would never allow Tony to see Fidelia again. I have not heard from that horrible bastard since."

Sam uttered the punch line from a bad joke, "Other than that, how was the play?"

No one even smiled. Rosaline seemed to have no idea what Sam's wise crack meant. She paused, ignoring his comment, and continued. "Fidelia and I made the long drive to Chicago. For the first few months, I stayed with my Cuban friends. Then Fidelia and I got our own place. About a year later, my friends introduced me to Luis. He has been kind to both Fidelia and me ever since."

Rosaline shook her head from side to side as she looked down at her empty cup of coffee. She put her hand in Luis' and looked at him before saying, "I moved in with Luis in 1961—about a year after arriving in Chicago. We married a year later. Since then, Fidelia has come to love Luis. She calls him *Father*. Everything was quite wonderful until a couple of months ago—when I walked into her bedroom to wake her on a Saturday morning—and I saw—I saw she was gone—no warning—nothing. Of course, Fidelia and I had the usual teen age daughter-caring mother disagreements. But you expect those. No. There was just no warning."

And at that point, Rosaline paused, looking straight forward with a sad look on her face, covered her face with her hands and quietly cried.

There was silence at the table. Finally, Luis spoke. "The reason we did not push the police to initiate a more thorough investigation is that the cops in Chicago have a reputation for having a more than cordial relationship with the mob. And Rosaline was afraid what could have happened if she had contacted Tony. And the FBI? Fidel Castro is *Mr. Hated-by-the-American-Government*—so we couldn't go there. Rosaline was afraid she would end up being investigated by them if we asked for their help."

Luis reached over and took one of Rosaline's cigarettes out of her pack and lit it. He took a deep drag, blew the smoke up toward the ceiling and said, "Sam, I don't know if you know this but many immigrants are afraid of being deported—even after they have their United States citizenship. We also feared that if either Tony Giarri or Rosaline's father found an opportunity to hurt Rosaline by making statements to public officials, they would do so. Anything that would link Rosaline and Castro would be seen by the government as an opportunity to hurt Castro rather than help Rosaline."

Luis looked intently at Sam and said, "For those reasons, we could not ask the police for more of an effort. We waited, hoping Fidelia would return home. But that hasn't happened. When I heard about your agency, I realized—you could help us. And Sam, you speak Spanish well. That is absolutely critical. Last night, Isabelle assured us you are trustworthy."

Luis looked at Rosaline who signaled with a facial gesture that he should continue. "So, if you are willing to take the case, Sam, I'm prepared to pay your per diem charges as well as all of your incidental expenses plus an additional five thousand dollars when you find Fidelia—dead or alive."

When Luis finished his statement with *dead or alive*, Rosaline bent over and wept. Luis consoled her and said to her, "We will find her Rosie—she will be alive. She will be home. Everything will be ok."

Rosaline continued to weep. Luis clearly did not know what to do or say. Isabelle took Rosaline by the hand. They left the table going to the ladies' room. Luis quietly shook his head, then buried his face in both hands. When he looked up, Sam told him he would take the case. Luis proceeded to write an advance check to Sam for two thousand dollars.

"When you need more, you let me know."

Sam told Luis, "I'll come to Chicago soon. I want copies of letters, photographs of Fidelia and some other documents. I'll also interview staff at Fidelia's school and speak with the police."

Moments later, Sam and Luis agreed Sam would come to Chicago that coming Thursday.

*****

After Rosaline and Isabelle returned to the table, Rosaline was once again a model of composure. There was no sign that, minutes before, she had been full of sorrow. The sharing of background on Fidelia's disappearance was over. The two couples made small talk for a few minutes before leaving the Deli and saying their goodbyes. Sam and

Isabelle watched Rosaline and Luis depart in a shiny red Cadillac Coupe de Ville convertible headed back to Chicago.

As Sam drove Isabelle home, he tried to review in his mind's eye the different pieces of information Rosaline had shared. There was the father, the ex-boyfriend, her first husband's family and the officials in Cuba—including Castro. The other explanation, of course, was that Fidelia was a victim of a random act of violence. But the fact that she disappeared from her room—that sort of ruled that out. And—could there be a boyfriend? Well, Sam was glad he had taken a lot of notes during the conversation. He needed to review and digest them carefully. He had to be certain that before he began to investigate the case, he had separated the facts from Rosaline and Luis' assumptions.

As Sam pulled up to a red light. He glanced over at Isabelle having realized he had been ignoring her.

"Welcome back from outer space," she said in Spanish. "I was concerned you might be lost for the rest of the ride home."

She smiled and added, "But I do appreciate your being so kind to two of my closest friends. Luis and Rosaline are— they are good people who have been a little lost—unsure of how to proceed. Rosaline told me she likes you. She said you and I make a good couple."

Sam found himself blushing—he was now part of *a couple*. But he was relieved Isabelle was not frustrated with his absent-minded voyage into his right brain.

For a while, they drove in silence. Then, Isabelle spoke again. "Sam, I like you. I don't want to intimidate you. But I am enjoying getting to know you. I think we are a good couple."

This was good. Sam listened attentively, wondering where Isabelle was headed in this conversation.

She continued. "We are good for one another. It is nice every time we are together. But Sam, it is just too complicated for you to drive to pick me up and take me home each time we get together."

Sam thought to himself, *Shit. She is going to tell me goodbye. How could I have screwed this up so badly when it all looked so promising?*

Isabelle was not finished speaking. "I would like to change that, Sam. I would like to move into your home—to live with you. What do you think?"

At that point, Sam totally forgot about Luis and Rosaline. He stared ahead at the road, uncertain of how to respond. He silently processed what was going on. In his mind, he went back and forth—processing pros and cons. *The big question is what do I want? Sure, Isabelle is right. We have fun together. But I like being by myself as well. I'm attracted to her—that's true. But I don't really know her very well. However, it would be fun being part of a couple— I enjoyed that with Alisa in Spain—but then I ended up getting hurt so badly. And I have never lived with anyone except my mom and my grandparents—and that's nothing like a girlfriend.*

Sam continued to drive while considering his options. *I don't want to hurt Isabelle's feelings by saying "no". That would end everything between us. On the other hand, if we spend too much time together too quickly, I might get on her nerves. She might get on mine. Isabelle was open and direct. Now the ball is in my court. I'm not sure what to do.*

Finally, as Sam stopped at a red light, he took a deep breath, turned to Isabelle and asked, "Will you give up your rented room?"

"No, Sam. I don't think that would be wise. My fear of being hurt is as great as yours—I mean my fear of getting stuck in an uncomfortable relationship. I think it might make more sense for me to continue renting my room—you know, until you and I decide whether we like living together."

Sam didn't say anything, but his shoulders relaxed. Nothing more was said until they arrived at her house.

As he pulled up to the curb, he said, "Well, I guess what you said makes a lot of sense. I like you too, Isabelle." He paused and added, "—a lot. Why don't I wait out here—I can review my notes from the meeting with Rosaline and Luis. You go up to your room and pack whatever you want to bring over to my house."

It was Sam's turn to wait for a response. He was wondering if he might have seemed a little cold. Maybe he had been too aggressive?

After a minute looking ahead in silence, Isabelle turned to him. "OK," she said, taking a deep breath. "I guess the quickest way to get into the water is to jump into the pool. Give me fifteen minutes, Sam. After I tell my housemates about our plan and have organized my things, I will come out and get you. You can help me carry my stuff out to the car."

Then she added, "There will be a lot of stuff."

Fifteen minutes turned into an hour. Sam did not focus on his notes or on Rosaline's missing daughter. He just sat in the car wondering if he had just committed to something that he was going to regret later—a lot.

Finally, Isabelle returned to the Rocket Eighty-Eight. "Sam—come in. Meet my housemates. Then, you can carry my things to the car." In saying that, Isabelle hadn't hidden any enthusiasm and concluded her statement by flashing a big smile.

Sam's smile became as big as Isabelle's. Meeting the roommates was a blur. He just wanted to pack the Oldsmobile and head home. But it took a while to load the Rocket. In addition to clothing and books, there were pots, pans, boxes of food, two guitars and a cardboard file box full of personal papers. Sam was relieved that the Oldsmobile's trunk was so large and that the back seat had been so empty.

When they got back to his place, he carried her stuff into the house. They would sleep in the front bedroom. Sam suggested that Isabelle use the middle bedroom as her study since he had the use of the back bedroom as his office.

Isabelle communicated her agreement with a kiss.

*****

While Isabelle put her things away, Sam sat down at the dining room going over his notes. Then he began to put together a plan for finding Fidelia. He identified and wrote down all of his thoughts, organizing them into the following categories:

- Copies of documents and photographs he would request from Rosaline and Luis;
- Things he knew—facts that were solid;
- Assumptions that needed to be explored;
- Contacts that he should meet with in Chicago, Miami, New York and maybe Havana; and
- Uncertainties that might affect his investigation.

Isabelle came downstairs while he was finishing his lists. She told him she wanted to fix dinner that evening. He told her that sounded great, then returned to his review of the information he would request from Luis and Rosaline.

*****

Isabelle fixed omelets on an old cast iron skillet. Sam heard her singing as she went about her business in the kitchen. After half an hour, she brought out plates with omelets bathed in salsa and dollops of sour cream. Sam put his papers in a pile on the couch and sat down at the table. Sam poured wine from a bottle of Rioja, lifted his wine glass holding it out towards Isabelle, and said, *"Salud, amor y pesetas y tiempo para gustar los"*, a toast he had learned in Seville. It meant *health, love, money and time to enjoy them.*

They ate without speaking.

Finally, Sam interrupted the silence. "This is the best omelet I've had ever had. What's the trick?"

Isabelle smiled softly and said, "One day, Sam, I will show you how to create an omelet."

"What's in the salsa?"

"Tomatoes, jalapenos, garlic, limes, red onions, cilantro, honey and olive oil. I transported them from the kitchen in the house I shared. From now on, Sam, we always keep fresh vegetables in our kitchen."

They went back to their omelets—each lost in their own thoughts. It had been an intense weekend. That evening, before they turned in, Sam completed going over his notes. He felt like he did not know enough to begin an investigation. It seemed more like he was about to throw a net randomly into a river hoping a catch a specific fish.

But he understood he had to start somewhere.

*****

The next morning, as Isabelle and Sam sat drinking coffee in the dining room, each reading a section of the morning Minneapolis Tribune, Sam realized he was smiling. He had no difficulties remembering the prior night.

Sam looked up. He saw that Isabelle was smiling as well. Things were good.

8. Beginning the Investigation

Monday morning, Sam called Luis to confirm his plan to visit Chicago. He told Luis the type of documents he hoped to receive during the visit. When Sam asked for a hotel recommendation, Luis told him he should stay at their apartment. That sounded great to Sam. He would arrive in Chicago on Wednesday and return home on Friday.

Sam faced a transportation conundrum. If he drove, Isabelle would have to take the city bus to her classes at the university—an hour's bus ride away. He decided to leave the Rocket with Isabelle and go by rail to Chicago. The train ride would be the perfect opportunity to think through his investigation plan, read through his notes from lunch at Cecil's and finalize the list of questions for Luis and Rosaline.

But Sam was aware that taking the train on this trip was a onetime solution to an ongoing problem. Sam would have to use the Rocket on his insurance claim investigation trips. Isabelle's commuting problem hadn't been addressed.

*****

Wednesday morning, Isabelle drove Sam to the Minneapolis Great Northern Depot. Sam had always liked that train station. What its facade lacked in modern design, it made up for in grandeur. As he walked into the cavernous terminal, he looked up at a large WPA mural of a Native American warrior wrapped in a blanket looking out across a lake. He recalled that the first time he had seen the mural, he had been with his grandmother. She had told him the story behind the mural which he had long since forgotten it.

Sam walked past across terminal's heavy wooden benches to the ticket counter. He purchased a roundtrip ticket on the Great Northern Empire Builder—the same passenger train route he had taken almost twenty years before when his grandmother brought him with her to visit a friend in central Wisconsin.

The last few weeks had been intense and Sam was drained. As the Empire Builder pulled out of the Twin Cities, he gazed out the window, losing himself in the scenery along the Mississippi. The clickety-clack sound of the coach as it rattled down the tracks was relaxing. After about an hour of that meditation, he opened his brief case and began to go over his plan of action.

*****

In addition to getting documents and other information from Luis and Rosaline, Sam planned to interview Fidelia's school contacts. He also wanted to meet with the police officer to whom Luis and Rosaline had originally reported Fidelia's disappearance.

Sam's tentative plan for after the trip to Chicago was to set up a meeting in New York City with Tony Giarri. There was an obvious reason for not putting off that meeting. A connected guy like Tony might have *helped* someone disappear—using one tactic or another. And even if Tony wasn't involved in Fidelia's disappearance, his mob connections might prove useful in finding her. On top of that, New York was a whole lot closer to Minneapolis than Miami or Havana.

If the trip to New York didn't solve the case, the next visit would be to Miami to meet with Rosaline's father. Visiting a bitter old man like her dad would not be pleasant. But it could turn out to be productive. Sam believed Rosaline's father might be the culprit. He seemed like a self-centered person capable of a vile action like taking his granddaughter from his daughter. Hopefully Rosaline could give him the names of some of her father's contacts in Miami. They might be able to offer Sam information that would be useful.

Finally, if those two visits weren't fruitful, Sam realized he would have to go to Havana. He wasn't looking forward to organizing that trip. Traveling into a Communist country that was an enemy of the United States would be a bureaucratic nightmare. Sam would deal with that challenge if and when he had to. Hopefully, he wouldn't need to make the trip.

*****

The Empire Builder pulled into Chicago's massive Union Station at 4:30 that afternoon. He carefully followed Luis's instructions, identifying the appropriate station exit, finding the correct bus stop, then boarding the right bus, the Lakeview, which he rode to West Belmont Avenue. There, Sam exited the bus and after a five-minute walk, arrived at Luis and Rosaline's vintage 1920s apartment. Sam was warmly welcomed into their flat. As Rosaline greeted him, Sam once again was struck with her stunning beauty. He could tell she enjoyed being noticed.

A moment later, Sam sat with Luis in the living room drinking a dark rum with a slice of lime on the rocks. Sam, as he sipped on the rum, looked around him. He was appreciative one more time of Rosaline's excellent taste. The flat had been restored beautifully.

Rosaline called to Luis and Sam. She had finished preparing *Chuletas de Puerco,* grilled pork chops in mojo sauce. It was time to come to the table. During the meal that followed, there were no discussions of Rosaline's missing daughter. Conversation turned to the wedding celebration and then on to Rosaline's excellent cooking.

But toward the end of the meal, Rosaline steered the conversation toward Sam's relationship with Isabelle. Sam was amused by her protective—almost big sister—attitude toward Isabelle. He decided that what was occurring was essentially an interview regarding his background and intentions. Sam responded openly to each question about himself and his family.

But he wasn't quite sure what to say when Rosaline said, "Isabelle has told me how happy she is to be living with you. You know she has never lived with a man before, Sam. You need to understand that Issa is a sweet and innocent person who could easily be hurt—if a man was thoughtless."

Luis bailed Sam out. "Sam, you have been warned. And Rosie—you have outdone yourself once again with a brilliant dinner. You are going to make me fat. Now Sam, while Rosie clears the table, let's go have a cigar and a glass of a very special dark Añejo rum before we begin to review your investigation plan. Everybody happy with that?"

*****

A half an hour later, Rosaline joined them in the living room. Luis began the discussion by asking Sam for his initial analysis of Fidelia's disappearance as well as his high-level strategy for finding her.

"Well Luis, there hasn't been much to analyze yet. What I know is what the two of you shared with me at Cecil's. My strategy is to contact each of the people you spoke about and learn as much as I can from them."

Then Sam reviewed the questions he had put together for each party. He shared the plan to visit New York after

Chicago; then, if necessary, go to Miami; and only if he hadn't found Fidelia, would he need to visit Havana.

After Sam finished speaking, Luis puffed on the cigar he had been nursing throughout the conversation. Luis exhaled a stream of smoke and watched it curl toward the ceiling. "Sam. Your approach and questions makes sense."

Rosaline nodded assent. She asked, "How confident are you that you will find Fidelia? And how long do you think it will take?"

"Unfortunately, Rosaline, I don't truly know more than when we spoke on Sunday. What I've laid out is a conceptual approach for finding her. I hope it'll be successful—and I hope sooner rather than later. But I would be lying to you if I promised anything definite. If it turns out I have to visit all three cities—well, the investigation could easily take six months. I just can't be certain how long it's going to take—or what turns in the road I—or I should say—we might encounter."

Sam asked for a photograph of Fidelia. Rosaline brought out a framed color portrait of her daughter. Sam did a double take. Fidelia was a younger version of Rosaline—a second extraordinary beauty.

After looking at the picture for a couple of minutes, he looked up and said, "Does Fidelia have a driver's license?"

Luis looked at Rosaline, then responded, "She passed the driving test in October. She kept all of her identification in her wallet. It must have been in her purse. Her purse is the only thing we know for certain is missing from her room."

Sam gave a thoughtful look, jotted something in his notepad, then said, "I have a few questions about Fidelia. I'll just throw them all out there. Then you go ahead and tell me about your daughter. Try to hit on as many things I asked as you can. Afterwards, there will be more questions."

Rosaline said, "Go ahead—ask."

"Did Fidelia's behavior change over the few months before she—uh—disappeared? How was school going? Did Fidelia seem happy or sad? Who did she hang out with? Did she have a boyfriend? Were there any changes in anyone she was seeing? Did either of you ever have a strong disagreement with her—a confrontation? And, Luis, anytime you have anything to add to Rosaline's responses, please speak up."

As Sam spoke, Rosaline had taken notes in a spiral bound notebook. Now, she stopped writing, looked up and spoke in a slow measured tone. Luis's eyes were glued on her. Sam could see how painful this was for her. But she was focused and collected.

"Fidelia is a good student—not exceptional—mostly Bs. The amount of time she took to study and the quality of her grades did not diminish prior to her disappearance. She didn't share a lot with me about her social life at school. But I know she didn't have a lot of close friends; did not have a boyfriend—although she had gone on a few dates. She also did not participate in any regular afterschool activities. Fidelia hated winter. She used to curse the wind, snow and cold of Chicago complaining that I should have stayed in a warm climate. Once she asked me what had been so bad about Miami."

Rosaline looked at her notes, then continued. "Fidelia spoke Spanish well. She once told me she wanted to be in a place where other people could also speak Spanish. She told us she sometimes was teased at school because she was from Cuba. A few times she was called *a communist*. Some of that was just kids being kids. But it used to sting. Some girls teased her for not being from North America. Young people can be so awfully insensitive."

Rosaline held a cloth hankie in her hand and stopped for a moment and wiped away a few tears. Luis watched with a serious, intent look on his face. Sam waited.

"Fidelia and Luis get along well. Fidelia sometimes picks fights with me on small stupid issues—never anything important. You know—I'm not cool enough; I cook too many Cuban dishes; I don't dress casually as often as I should—stuff like that. When I have had enough of that sort of talk, I snap at her. She weeps and falls into my arms. Fidelia and I are really close." Rosaline sighed. "My daughter and I have been through a lot together."

Sam listened closely. These responses seemed open, honest. But as Rosaline spoke, it seemed like she didn't know much or wasn't sharing anything she did know about Fidelia's personal life. Maybe Fidelia had run away like the school officials had said? Maybe she had a boyfriend?

Finally, Sam did interrupt her. "Have you looked through her things—I mean to see if she packed any clothing before she disappeared?"

Here Luis took over and anticipated Sam's next questions. "Fidelia liked being independent. We respected that. Her monthly allowance was sufficient to purchase lunches at school, buy most of her clothing and allow her to go to a concert or movie whenever she wanted. For the past couple of years, when Fidelia purchased a new outfit, she often didn't tell us. We looked through her room after she disappeared. But because she had purchased her own clothes, we couldn't tell what may have been missing from her closet. She did not have a credit card or bank account.

But we don't know how much cash she might have had when she left. It's entirely possible she had several hundred dollars."

Sam nodded, looked down and uttered a *Hmmm*. Then he asked, "Can you tell me a little about her school?"

Luis answered. "Fidelia's School—St. Benedict Preparatory School—has been cooperative. They were quick to respond to us when Fidelia disappeared. But the school officials believe she probably ran away—although they have no explanation as to why. They simply said *teenage runaways are not unusual*. They were absolutely confident Fidelia would return home within a few days—as soon as she was cold and hungry. Obviously, they were wrong."

Luis looked seriously at Sam and leaned forward. "The reason we are in such a fix and so relieved to have your assistance is that we cannot share Rosaline's background with the school officials or with the police. School officials would flip out if we told them about Rosaline's connections with Giarri—and his with the mob. And even if the cops are not—how can I say it—biased in favor of the mob, Giarri would certainly not be open with them. Then, there is Rosaline's father. If he knew anything that could help us, he would hide it from law enforcement. People who live in Miami's closed Cuban-American community shun outsiders. They're not going to share anything with the police."

Sam was taken aback with the Luis' openness. He felt a lot of Chalets sympathy for the fix they were in. It wasn't just that their daughter had disappeared. They had no one else to turn to.

Luis finished up. "And finally, if we need any sort of assistance or information from Havana—well, any American official who tried to get information from anyone in Cuba would be unsuccessful—and would actually end up hurting the chances we would learn anything from Cuban officials."

Luis shook his head and gave a sad chuckle. "And, given the current state of affairs between our countries, Rosaline and I would certainly end up on some American government watch list."

There was silence in the room. For several minutes, Sam reviewed his notes, trying to figure out what he should ask next. He was baffled. There was so much he didn't know.

Luis broke the silence, "Fidelia was a good student, but she also had her challenges at school. There is one issue I should tell you about. In November, a counselor from school notified us that Fidelia had skipped several classes. She had never done that before. When Rosaline and I asked Fidelia where she had been and why, she got defensive. She told us we were out of touch—she was sixteen years old—a junior in high school—missing a few classes was not a big deal. She said old people never understand anything. So why should she try to explain it to us?"

Luis leaned forward. "I wasn't going to let her get away with that. We insisted on an answer. Fidelia finally said that she and a girlfriend had taken a few afternoons off to just talk. And she wasn't going to tell us more than that because it was none of our business. Then, she broke down crying and left the room. After that discussion, Fidelia didn't miss any more classes. We thought the issue was resolved."

Sam was writing intensely. He looked up and said, "That could be very important." He stopped and looked at each of them. "Is there anything else like that—anything similar?"

Luis responded. "You need to speak with Mr. Webb, Fidelia's counselor at the school. Webb met with her each time she skipped a class. Maybe he can give you some insight that we can't."

Sam jotted down a couple more notes and said, "Tell me more about this Mr. Webb."

Rosaline was glaring at Luis. Sam surmised that she was not pleased that Luis had shared anything about Fidelia skipping classes or that now, he had put Mr. Webb into the equation.

Rosaline took over the response. And having been warned by Rosaline with that look, Luis sat back. "When a student skips a class, they have to speak with a counselor. Fidelia met with Mr. Webb a few times. Luis and I spoke with him after Fidelia disappeared. He said she hadn't shared anything of consequence. That's it."

Sam looked up. "You're probably right. Webb will probably not have anything to add. But I need to check in with him—just to confirm that—and to see if there is anything else the school has to offer. I also will check in with the Chicago Police—see if they can offer me anything I can use."

Sam spent the next couple of minutes writing in his notepad. He tore out the last page on which he written and gave it to Rosaline. "Here is a list of the items I need. Can you get them together for me?"

The list included:
- Pictures of Fidelia;
- Her birth certificate, passport and social security number;
- Addresses and phone numbers for all of the parties discussed in New York City, Miami and Havana;

- Names and phone numbers for health care providers as well as Fidelia's closest friends; and
- Copies of all of the letters Rosaline had spoken about that expressed interest in seeing Fidelia.

"I'll spend tomorrow morning at the school and try to set up a time with the police for later in the day. Before the trip, I drafted a request to Fidelia's school for Rosaline's signature. It authorizes their cooperation on the investigation and asks that I be allowed to speak with school officials as well as Fidelia's school friends. I will tell the school officials that one person I want to meet with is this Mr. Webb."

Sam handed the letter to Rosaline who looked weary. She signed the letter without reading it; then handed it back to Sam.

*****

They had covered the territory Sam wanted to review. He told Luis and Rosaline he was exhausted. Within half an hour, Sam was in bed. But he didn't go to sleep. He lay in bed going back and forth over a swirling list of facts and questions. It became obvious that there were many more questions than facts. That evening, no one had mentioned the possibility that Fidelia might be dead. If that turned out to be the case, he would have to determine who had been responsible. And Sam wondered, how would Rosaline deal with that?

Before he fell asleep, Sam remembered, with some irony, the final verse of Weldon Kees' poem *The Crime Club*.

Small wonder that the case remains unsolved,
Or that the sleuth, Le Roux, is now incurably insane,
And sits alone in a white room in a white gown,
Screaming that all the world is mad, that clues

*Lead nowhere, or to walls so high their tops cannot be
seen;
Screaming all day of war, screaming that nothing
can be solved.*

*****

The following morning, a reenergized Sam entered Rosaline's classic 1920s-style kitchen. Its warm cherry wood cabinets stood out nicely against white counters with black trim. In the center of the kitchen's green and white checkerboard flooring was a chrome and red Formica kitchen table with four red vinyl and chrome chairs.

"Your kitchen is lovely, Rosaline."

"Thank you, Sam. Isabelle, said you wouldn't notice. She was obviously wrong."

"Well, maybe. The only reason I noticed is because Isabelle is teaching me to pay attention to details. She expects a thorough report on your home when I get back to Minneapolis. So, I sorta got to pay attention."

Rosaline smiled and said, "I will report to her that her student has been diligent."

Rosaline handed Sam a cup of hot cafe con leche and small plate that held a fresh cinnamon roll dripping melted butter. Sam sat down, inhaled the cinnamon roll's sweet woody fragrance, then lost himself in its taste. Sam looked up. He was embarrassed when he noticed that Rosaline was quietly laughing at him.

Rosaline said, "Isabelle also told me you like your food. I wasn't exactly sure what she meant. Now, after seeing you almost faint as you inhaled the aroma of that hot cinnamon roll, I know."

Luis joined them at the breakfast table. Rosaline brought him a cup of café con leche and a cinnamon roll.

Luis handed a section from the Chicago Tribune to Sam. They ate their breakfasts in satisfied silence.

*****

Sam studied a map he'd picked up on the bus. He was looking for a direct connection from the Martinez home to St. Benedict's School—with no luck. Getting there would require a forty-minute walk in the cold. Luis saw Sam looking at the map. "Sam—there is no quick way to get to the school. Here." And Luis tossed Sam a set of keys on a keychain with a Cadillac coat of arms. "Today, you will discover why Cadillac is the best car in the world. Have a good day and enjoy the Caddie!"

Sam was pleased to drive a Cadillac. But he didn't let that on. He just thanked Luis and took the building's old-fashioned birdcage elevator down to the basement garage.

Even if he had tried, Sam couldn't have stopped the big smile that emerged on his face when he saw the '66 convertible Coupe de Ville. Its long luxurious lines and streamlined fins were gorgeous. The shiny red convertible's top was cream colored; its leather interior white with red detailing. Sam slid into the driver's seat and manipulated the electronic controls guiding the soft leather driver seat down and back until he was more comfortable than he had ever been in a car seat. As he drove the Coup de Ville out of the garage, Sam felt like he was piloting a classic Chris-craft powerboat through a marina on a quiet day. The engine created no sound, no vibration and the car's acceleration gave a sense of unlimited torque. With some embarrassment, he recalled that at the wedding party, he had told Camilo Pascual that there was not a lot of difference between a Cadillac and an Oldsmobile. Man, was that ever a load of crap. Every detail on this car said luxury, style and class!

*****

Ten minutes later, the Coupe de Ville coasted into St. Benedict's visitor parking area. After entering the main building, Sam spotted the school's administrative office. As he waited to speak with the principal, he remembered his own high school experience. He had been in the principal's office a few times—but it had never been a very positive experience.

A small plump nun led Sam into a sparsely decorated office where Sam was greeted by a balding priest who introduced himself as Father Robert. They shook hands and Father Robert glanced at Rosaline's letter of introduction.

He looked up and said, "Luis just called. He asked me to be as helpful as possible. I am aware Fidelia is missing. But unfortunately, I don't have much to share that would be useful. Your best contact will be Frank Webb, the counselor who met with her. Webb will give you the best information the school has. And he might also be able to suggest other contacts at St. Benedict. Frank's office is a couple doors down from here. You walked past it on your way into the building."

Sam thanked Father Robert and headed down the hall to meet Frank Webb. A moment later, Sam was greeted by a stout, medium height man whose thinning grey hair sported a crewcut. Webb's suit pants were wrinkled and his white dress shirt had large yellow sweat stains under each armpit. There were team pictures of boys' basketball teams on the small office's walls. Obviously, Webb also happened to be St. Benedict's basketball coach.

Webb stuck out his hand and gave Sam a firm handshake. "Hi. Name's Frank Webb. You can call me Frank. Ok if I call you Sam?"

Sam simply responded, "Sure".

"Father Robert says you're the dick who's trying to figure out what happened to the cute little Martinez girl. What a fox, eh? I met with her three or four times late last year—you know when she was skipping classes. We didn't hit it off a whole lot. She'd walk into my office, slouch down on the chair and look at her fingernails. Occasionally, she'd roll her eyes, tell me she'd been taking long walks. Come on. You and I both know that was a bunch of hooey! You don't do that in Chicago—not in November and December. It's just too damn cold!"

"Did any of her school mates join her when she skipped the classes?"

"Nope. No other absences at those times. And to be frank—and Sam, I am Frank," Webb chortled for a moment before continuing, "I figured she probably had some boyfriend on the outside—maybe was smoking dope or doing something else her parents wouldn't have approved of. After our third meeting, the girl stopped missing classes. So, it wasn't a problem anymore. In January, when her parents called the school and said she'd disappeared, it was a surprise to me. I don't know what more I can add. I spoke with a local cop assigned to her missing persons case—to be frank—and there I go again—I'm always Frank—the cop figured she'd probably run off with a boyfriend. He found no clues—didn't know any more than I did. So that's all I can think of, Sam. If you have any questions, let me know. I hate to see any of these kids get into any trouble —the white ones or the colored."

Sam realized Frank Webb was a poor excuse for a counselor—and probably a lousy basketball coach. He thought to himself that Frank should change his first name to *Useless*. He could start out his sentences with, *to be useless—wait—I guess I am Useless*. But Sam chose not to share that witty insight. Instead, he asked if Frank knew who Fidelia's close friends were.

"A girl by the name of Lois often hung out with Fidelia. Lois is in a study hall right now in room 114—down the hall. I told her teacher you might stop by to ask a few questions. I told her to tell Lois to be helpful. Maybe you'll get lucky and the girl ends up knowing something."

Sam asked for the name of the cop who had investigated Fidelia's disappearance. Frank pulled out a card with the name *Detective Pat Miller*, a phone number and an address for Precinct Number 19 on Halsted Street.

After they shook hands and he had left the office, Sam thought to himself, "Thanks Useless."

Before going to the classroom to speak with Fidelia's friend Lois, Sam walked back to the school office and called Detective Miller. When Miller answered the phone, Sam introduced himself and asked if Miller could get together with Sam to share information about the disappearance of Fidelia Garcia.

Detective Miller paused for a moment before responding. "Sure, uhm yeah. I can meet with you here—at the precinct station—this afternoon—say 1:30."

As Sam walked down the hall to meet with Fidelia's friend Lois, he focused on the one important thing he had learned so far that morning, Fidelia had lied to her parents. She had not skipped classes with another student. That told

Sam that Fidelia was hiding something. Sam wondered what it was that she was hiding.

*****

Sam knocked on the study hall room's heavy oak door. A nun in a black knee length habit with short salt and pepper hair opened the door. She exuded all of the warmth and energy that had been missing in Frank.

"Good morning. I'm Sister Eileen. I guess you're here to speak with Lois. You can meet with her in the room across the hall. I was thinking maybe it would be worth your while to chat with me after you speak with Lois. I knew Fidelia fairly well. She took a couple classes from me. I'd be glad to answer any questions you have."

Sam liked Sister Eileen and was more than pleased to receive an offer of help. He spoke with Lois first. That exercise turned out to be one of no value. Lois was cute, blond and a teen-ager. She made clear she thought all adults were a total waste of time. While Sam explained that he was working for Fidelia's parents to discover any information he could about Fidelia's disappearance, Lois looked out the window with a smug look.

When he stopped talking, Lois looked him directly in the eyes and said defiantly, "I'll tell you the same thing I told Webb, that I told the cop and that I told Father Robert. I don't have a clue what Fidelia is up to or where she is. She's a nice enough girl. But she isn't my sister. I mean, how am I supposed to know what's up with her?"

Lois used the back of her hand to brush her blonde bangs from her eyes. Then she straightened her back, turned her head at an angle and gave Sam a *so-there* look.

Sam asked several more questions, "Did Fidelia have a boyfriend? Was she fighting with her parents? Was she afraid of anything? Did she like school? Did she ever talk about wanting to visit old friends or family?"

As Sam asked the questions, Lois' body language continued to announce that she was totally bored. She shrugged her shoulders or gave an eye roll in response to each question. But she said nothing.

Finally, Sam asked, "Is there anything that you know that would be of help to her parents in discovering her whereabouts?"

Here, the spoiled teenager responded with a word that should have had only one syllable, but she managed to stretch into two, "No-oh."

Sam stood up. His words to Lois were, "Thank you." His thoughts were *This kid's poor parents. What a little creep!*

*****

Sam walked Lois back to her study hall. He waited patiently while Sister Eileen told her students, all wearing dark pants or skirts, white shirts with green and blue plaid sweaters, to be quiet while she was out of the room. Then Sister Eileen went with Sam into the empty classroom where he'd met with Lois a moment before.

"Thanks for offering to help, Sister. Unfortunately, neither my time with Frank nor with Lois has been useful. Any assistance you could give me would be appreciated."

Sister Eileen looked at him thoughtfully. Then she spoke in soft voice. "I was worried about Fidelia. It was clear something was on her mind. I asked her what the problem was. She just looked a little lost and told me I couldn't help. I asked her if the problem was with her parents. She gave a wistful smile—and—I remember her exact words. *No, Sister. My mom and step-dad are innocents.* She skipped a few afternoon classes. I think she must have been meeting someone. After the last time she skipped class, she returned to school looking upset. She was obviously worried about something."

The Sister paused and sighed. Her words were spoken with sadness. "She didn't hang out with any of the girls during her last couple of months here. I think part of Lois' tough attitude is that she was hurt when Fidelia stopped sharing personal things with her. Lois isn't a bad girl—though I recognize she is a tad bit spoiled. As far as Frank goes, he coaches the basketball and track teams and—well—he offers little more than that." Sister Eileen chuckled as she finished her thought, "to be frank."

Sam also chuckled. He decided that Sister Eileen was ok and he ought to be more open with her. "Can I share some information on a strictly confidential basis?"

She smiled gently. "You've asked the right person."

Sam told her about Rosaline's history in Cuba, with her father in Miami and with Tony Giarri in New York. Sister Eileen listened intently. She did not comment or give any reaction while Sam spoke.

Sam finished up by saying, "Do you think there is any chance that Fidelia was meeting with one of these men from her mother's past? Could there be a boyfriend? Was there any chance she'd gotten into drugs?"

Sister Eileen looked down, pursed her lips, then responded. "With teenage girls, there is always a chance of a boyfriend. God knows Fidelia was attractive enough to have a lot of boys interested in her. But I didn't see the typical signs that she was involved with a boy. While she seemed distracted when she returned to school after skipping classes, she didn't show any signs of doing drugs. And as far as whether she had been contacted by someone from Cuba, Miami or New York, I just don't know. But what I do know, Sam, is that she shared no information about what she was doing. I believe she was meeting someone from outside of the school—partly because there is no other explanation that makes sense. If that was the case, she obviously wanted to keep whoever it was a secret. I just hope she's not been hurt—that you find her quickly—and that she's ok."

Sam was quiet for a few moments, processing what he'd just heard. He had learned very little during the morning's earlier meetings. Sister Eileen was the only sympathetic person he'd met at St. Benedict. But she hadn't given him any leads. "Do you have any suggestions for how I should proceed? Any other relevant information that might be useful?"

Sister Eileen couldn't think of anything. Sam gave her one of his cards and watched as she walked back into her classroom. Walking down the hall and out of St. Benedict, Sam wondered if Sister Eileen had been correct about Fidelia meeting with someone—and who that might have been.

9. Finishing up in Chicago

As the Cadillac eased out of the parking lot, Sam relaxed into its plush leather seat. He glanced at the Cadillac's chrome rimmed clock and was surprised to see it was almost noon. The morning had been intense. Now he was hungry. Sam spotted a diner that reminded him of Lucky's. Ten minutes later, a waitress brought him his order of a kielbasa with sauerkraut on a fresh baked bun. Sam started on the lunch, continuing to ponder the facts of the case. There wasn't much to go on. He must be overlooking something. But he couldn't figure out what that might be.

After what seemed like only a moment, Sam looked down at his plate. The kielbasa was gone. He had been so absorbed in his thoughts that he'd finished his lunch—and had forgotten to taste it.

*****

Sam returned to the Coupe de Ville and opened a street map. He quickly located Miller's 3120 Halsted Street precinct station. Fifteen minutes later, he was walking up to an old two-story red brick police station building. Engraved in granite above the entrance was *Police Station; 1888.*

Sam entered the building. He approached the duty sergeant's counter which was at the front of a large room filled with old wooden desks. Minutes later, Sam was shown into a small interview room. Detective Patrick Miller was standing next to a table. Miller was of average height, had a stocky build, combed back greasy hair and a bristly moustache. He was wearing a dingy white shirt with a worn necktie opened loosely at the neck.

Miller shook Sam's hand and said, "Sorry pal. You shouldn't expect a whole hell of a lot from what we've done.

Each year, Chicagoans commit over a hundred thousand crimes. Our force has to investigate them with thirteen hundred detectives. Each year, twenty thousand people get reported missing. Eight thousand are juvenile females. Suffice it to say, when we run into a situation where there are no facts saying that a crime was committed, we spend less time than we do if, say, an old man gets knifed by a couple of punks."

Miller gave a heavy sigh. "Luis Martinez calls in to report his step-daughter missing. And even though there's nothing to indicate a crime's been committed, well— ordinarily—I'd just let the guy just fill out a form. Then I'd file it. But since Martinez is a big shot ex-ballplayer, I was told by my superiors I had to investigate it—which I did."

Miller sat down and pointed to the other chair for Sam to take a seat as well. Then he took out a Camel cigarette, tapped its end against the table and lit the cigarette with a silver inscribed lighter. Miller inhaled the smoke, savored it, then blew it up toward the ceiling. "So, I headed over to the girl's private Catholic school; asked to speak to the principal. He was polite, religious and knew nothing from nowhere. He couldn't have told me the time of day if I lent him my watch. Anyway, he sends me to speak to some asshole counselor."

Miller laughed and shook his head. "The counselor was dumber than the principal. He didn't know anything except that the girl was no longer in school and had skipped four or five classes. Four or five classes? That makes this girl one of the best students in this whole damn town!"

Miller took another long deep drag from his cigarette, held the smoke in for a moment while he gave Sam a serious look, then exhaled and said, "The department shares its missing person lists, descriptions and photographs with the morgue, with all the city hospitals and with the federal government. I can tell you pretty reliably this Cuban girl didn't end up in the morgue or in an area hospital. We notified the national missing person's network. So, what else am I supposed to do? You tell me, Mr. Detective. Should I drop the murder investigation of the bank vice-president's wife? Stop working on the armed robbery at the diamond store? Or maybe, just maybe, I should just start working weekends full time—sort of like a new hobby? The wife would love that. One more opportunity for her to tell me I ignore the kids. I really hope you have something new for me because otherwise, pal, you are just wasting my goddamned time."

Miller seemed like a real loser. Sam would have liked to ask him if he would work the case if Sam gave him a dozen glazed doughnuts. But Sam knew that saying or doing anything other than kissing his ass would be the end of the meeting.

So, Sam puckered up. "I know you're right, Detective. You have the toughest job in America. Do you get credit for your efforts? No way. I was a police detective in the Air Force. I know how tough it is when everyone wants an answer right away—and they give you nothing to go on."

Miller's body language relaxed.

Sam continued. "The girl's mother is worried. But I understand you can't take time on this. Maybe I could just look at your file on the case and you can get on with your more pressing investigations. After I look at the file for a few minutes, I'll tell the family I tried."

Miller smiled as he squished his cigarette into an ash tray that was already full of butts and ashes. "I'm not supposed to share an official missing person's file, but hey, for a former cop—yeah—go for it. Here's the file."

Miller handed Sam a thin legal-sized dark green file folder. Then Miller, stood up, shook hands with Sam and took off to go save the city.

Sam sat down at the conference room's table and opened the file. It was quickly evident that Miller's summary had been accurate—he had done almost nothing on the case. The file included the original missing person form signed by Luis dated Monday, January 17th. There was a typed summary of Miller's meeting with Rosaline and Luis that took place on January 20th. The typed notes were brief and referred to the original missing person's form. Sam found some of the report's misspellings innovative. Miller was not only a lousy detective—he couldn't spell as well as an average eighth grader.

> *I reviewed the report submitted by the girl's step-father, Luis Martinz, a retired base ballplayer. As told to by Captain O'Malley, I met with Martinz and his wife, listened to their story and told them I would investigate. They have no clue where the girl is and no reason to assume she was a victim of a crime. But I was polit to them both.*

The notes summarized Miller's meeting with Frank Webb dated Thursday, February 3. Miller briefly described the uneventful meeting and concluded with:

> *Webb's statment that the girl had been skiping classes leads me to believe that the kid probably ran away from home—probly with some Cuban boyfriend.*

That was the extent of the official paperwork. It confirmed that no investigation had taken place. But there were three handwritten phone messages stapled to the inside of the file folder. Two of the messages were from Luis asking for a status report on the investigation. There was no indication Miller had returned Luis' calls. The third message dated January 24th was from an area code Sam did not recognize. But Sam did recognize the name of the caller—Tony Giarri. A hand written note on the message reported that Miller had returned the call, spoke to Giarri and relayed to him the facts of the case. The final sentence in the note stood out.

Giarri has asked to be informed if there are any developmnts. I agrreed. Giarri is clearly connected.

Sam was taken aback by that statement. It was mildly amusing that Miller had left the phone message and his personal comments in the file. Sam thought to himself, "I guess Miller's sloppiness has its rewards."

The Giarri call might turn out to be an important clue. Sam jotted down Giarri's phone number, returned the file to a precinct clerical worker and left the police station. He did not mention Giarri to anyone at the station. Hopefully the cop had forgotten his commitment to Giarri. Anything Sam said about Giarri might remind Miller to report Sam's visit.

****

When Sam returned to the Martinez apartment, he thanked Luis for the use of the Coupe de Ville and praised the car. Luis responded warmly, "I had good reasons to want to become a Cadillac dealer."

Sam described his experience at St. Benedict. Luis and Rosaline laughed at Sam's description of Frank Webb, agreeing that Frank should change his first name to *Useless*. Rosaline commented that Fidelia's friend Lois hadn't impressed her either and she had liked Sister Eileen from the moment she met her. Sam recapped his meeting with

Miller leaving out the information about Giarri's phone message. He would follow up on that when the time was right. But at this point, he was concerned that if Rosaline knew about the message, she might contact Giarri herself. That would definitely not help.

After the report of the day's activities was complete, Luis told Sam they were taking him out for dinner. Sam asked if he could have some time to go through Fidelia's room before they left. "I want to see if there is anything that might give me more insight into Fidelia's disappearance."

Luis simply responded, "Have at it".

*****

Fidelia's bedroom had shiny oak floors and light blue and pink wallpapered walls. There was a mahogany chest of drawers, a full-size bed, a bed-side table, a desk and a chair. The bedspread's pink color matched the flowers on the wallpaper. Sam was struck with how everything was neat and tidy—waiting for Fidelia's return. He wondered if Fidelia was that organized—or if the room had been cleaned and put in order by Rosaline after Fidelia's disappearance.

He checked out the usual hiding spots—between the mattress and the box springs; in the shelf above the closet; in the desk drawers; and underneath her clothing in the dresser drawers. He found nothing of interest.

There was a book shelf above Fidelia's desk. Sam removed the high school yearbook and paged through it. There was nothing unusual. He chuckled when he came across a hand written inscription next to a picture of Lois, Fidelia's friend who Sam had interviewed earlier in the day. It read, *To a real sweetie pie. Pals forever—Lois.*

The shelf held two John Steinbeck books, *Cannery Row* and *The Grapes of Wrath*. There was a diary with nothing written in it and an almost new spiral bound notebook. When Sam paged through the notebook, he found a nicely handwritten address, *612 Hibiscus Drive, Hallandale Beach*. Next to the address in the same script was written *just north of Miami*. There was no name or other descriptive information included with that address. Sam jotted down the address in his notebook.

*****

When Sam returned to the living room, Luis handed him a manila file folder and said, "Rosaline and I put together the information you requested."

Sam removed a small stack of papers from the folder. On top was a two-page hand written listing of names, addresses and phone numbers. Below that were four photographs of Fidelia: a high school portrait, a picture of her in tennis garb, a snapshot with several other girls and a photo of Fidelia standing in between Luis and a Chicago Cub ballplayer. Sam was taken aback. He recognized the other athlete. It was Ernie Banks—*Mr. Chicago Cub*—one of the finest power hitters in the history of baseball. He stared for a moment at the photograph. Then his face flushed. He had become totally distracted—focusing on a famous baseball player instead of the missing girl.

Sam returned to leafing through the papers. The rest documents were Xerox copies: Fidelia's birth certificate, her social security card, a series of letters and a newspaper article. Among the letters were:

- Two typewritten letters from Fidel Castro dated 1960 and 1963— inquiring about Rosaline and Fidelia.

- Two letters from Miguel Garcia's father Carlos dated 1962 and 1964. They inquired about Fidelia and invited her to visit Cuba.
- A letter from Miguel's sister Maria dated 1963 asking Rosaline how Fidelia was doing. Maria requested that Rosaline allow Fidelia to write to her.
- Letters dated 1963 and 1965 from Rosaline's father Hector Diaz. The 1965 letter began with the statement, *I'm an old man, Rosa. Have a heart. Let my sweet granddaughter visit me before I pass away.*
- Finally, there was a 1965 letter from Tony Giarri asking Rosaline if Fidelia could visit him in New York.

Except for the letters from Rosaline's father and Giarri, all of them were in Spanish. After Sam finished reading the letters. Rosaline said, "I did not write responses to any of the letters from Cuba. As we told you, writing to Cuba would have attracted unwelcome attention from American authorities. And, while my father's letters deserved no response, I did send him a picture of Fidelia at some point and told him about Luis."

The last item in the file was a brief Chicago Tribune newspaper article. It included a picture of Fidelia and was dated January 25th. The article stated *Fidelia Garcia has been missing for over a week. Any information about her whereabouts should be reported to Detective Pat Miller of the Chicago Police Force.* The article gave Miller's phone number.

After leafing through the file, Sam scanned the list of names, addresses and phone numbers. He noted that the phone number for Tony Giarri was the same one he had seen on the phone message in Miller's file.

Sam was brought back from his thoughts as Rosaline made another comment. "The only item on your list that we were not able to find was Fidelia's passport. We hadn't looked for that until today. We searched for it. We thought Fidelia had it in her desk. But it was not there—and we looked in every other place we could think of. It is nowhere to be found. She must have taken it with her. I can't imagine her losing her passport."

Sam was silent. He just gazed down at the stack of papers in his lap. That could be a big deal.

*****

Before coming to Chicago, Sam had mentioned to Isabelle the possible trip to Cuba. She had responded, "The United States will not allow you to go there. If you decide to travel to Cuba, you must pass through Mexico. In addition, you'll need a Cuban visa and that might be difficult to get. I have friends who have waited many months to find out if they would be granted a visitation visa by Cuba. For some of them, the answer ended up being *no*."

As Sam sat in front of Luis and Rosaline, he recalled that conversation. "You know Rosaline, Isabelle told me how tough it is to get a Cuban visa—and the amount of time it takes. I know this is asking a lot, but it would make a huge difference if you were willing to write Fidel Castro and ask his assistance. If you told him about Fidelia's disappearance and asked for help in getting a visa for me and Isabelle, it might make a big difference in my investigation."

Rosaline didn't hesitate. "How soon will you need the visa?"

"If I go, I may want to go there as early as June—so the sooner the better."

"I will write to Fidel immediately. I'll put the letter inside a correspondence to a friend of mine who lives in Mexico City. She'll post it to Fidel. A letter sent directly to Fidel Castro from the United States—well, you can imagine. It will never get to him. It would end up on the desk of some inquisitive American official. The review that would then occur could cause problems, not the least of which would be the fact that you did not request United States authorization for your trip to a communist country."

"That makes sense, Rosaline. And thank you. It could make a huge difference."

Sam paused, glanced at the pack of papers for another moment, then said, "I think that wraps up the business side of my visit. I'm going to need to spend time looking over these letters and going over my notes from my visits to Fidelia's school and the police precinct before I have more questions for the two of you."

Luis changed the subject. "How about a drink before we leave for dinner? I make an excellent dry martini."

Sam said he'd like that.

A few minutes later, the three of them quietly sipped ice-cold gin out of tall stemmed martini glasses. Each martini had two large stuffed olives pierced with a clear miniature glass sword. Rosaline brought out a small silver bowl filled with smoked almonds to accompany the martinis. Luis put an album on the stereo and the three of them kicked back and enjoyed their cocktail hour while listening to the easy swing of Astrud Gilberto and Stan Getz singing *The Girl from Ipanema*.

As he sipped on his martini, Sam got lost in the song's lyrics.

When she walks, she's like a samba that swings so cool and sways so gentle that when she passes, each one she passes goes A-a-a-h.

*****

A little while later, as they drove to dinner, Luis described their destination to Sam. "The Pump Room at the Ambassador, is a swanky American dinner club. Keep your eyes open, Sam. It attracts famous people who want to be seen. You might see some big stars."

After giving the keys to the Cadillac to a hotel valet, they entered the hotel restaurant through a classic 1920's style entrance. When the maître d' saw Luis, he smiled and said, "Good evening, Mr. Martinez. Your favorite table waits for you."

As they followed the maître d' to the table, heads turned. Luis in his camel cashmere sport coat and button-down collar white shirt walked with an easy stride that attracted attention from others. Meanwhile Rosaline, wearing a nicely fitted red silk suit topped off by a mink stole, was easily the most attractive woman in the restaurant. As they passed, Diners looked up from their dinners and whispered to one another, probably speculating on whether or not they were seeing a famous couple.

Once at their table, Luis ordered a round of martinis, individual Caesar salads and an appetizer of fried calamari. After looking through the menu, Sam ordered southern fried chicken and greens bathed in savory hot sauce. Luis' choice was a New York steak, medium rare, and Rosaline selected shrimp scampi.

After sipping on his drink, Sam surveyed the Pump Room. There were other diners who had a confident celebrity air, but Sam didn't recognize any of them. However, as their entrees were being served, Frank Sinatra, Sammy Davis, Jr., and Dean Martin casually sauntered into the restaurant. They were seated at a table on the far side of the room. Sam would have liked to go up to their table and get their autographs. But he realized that wouldn't have been cool.

Not a lot was said during dinner. The conversation about Fidelia earlier in the evening had been draining; the food was excellent; and watching the Rat Pack entertain two buxom platinum blondes who had joined their party proved to be a satisfying diversion.

At one point, a young man approached their table. "Mr. Martinez—would you give me your autograph? I always enjoyed watching you pitch. I would really appreciate adding your signature to my collection."

Luis artfully signed his name on the sheet of paper the young man handed him. Rosaline smiled. Her pride in her husband showed.

It had been a delicious meal. There was no room for dessert. After a final glass of chardonnay, Sam—stuffed, exhausted and suffering from heartburn—was happy to leave the Pump Room and head back to his warm bed at Luis and Rosaline's apartment.

*****

The next morning, Luis gave Sam a ride to the train station. On the way, he asked, "Did you achieve everything you hoped to get done on the visit?"

Sam thought for a moment before responding. "This is an investigation. You never know for certain what you'll need or what you'll find until you need it or find it. I got enough information to confirm everything you told me at Cecil's. My next step is to spend some time going over what we know and try to piece together where it might lead us. But it's all going to hang on whatever comes out of the trips to New York, Miami and Havana. Of course, I'll keep you and Rosaline informed as the investigation moves forward."

Sam looked out the window for just a moment, hesitating. Then he looked at Luis and asked, "But one question—I noticed that Fidelia's room was in perfect order. Was it straightened up after she left? Did Rosaline clean up the room or is Fidelia really that neat?"

Luis chuckled. "At times Fidelia can be totally irresponsible. But at other times she is rigorously organized—excruciatingly thorough. The extreme order you saw in her room—well, that's an example of her orderly side. Rosaline left the room as we found it."

Luis paused, a somber look on his face, then added, "Rosaline knows it is possible she will never see her daughter again. But we must never regret that we didn't try. We accept that your search for Fidelia has no certain outcome and know we haven't given you any large clues. But, Sam—what other approach can we take? We can't do nothing. The Chicago Police—they're not going to help us. And Rosaline is, with very good reasons, totally distrustful of how the United States government would manipulate any request for help with the objective of blaming it all on Castro or accusing Cuban expatriates of being in league with Castro."

As Luis pulled the Coupe de Ville over in front of the train station, he added. "We know we are fortunate that you have taken our case. Thank you, my friend. And be certain to send me the bill for all the costs incurred to date."

They shook hands and said their goodbyes. Sam got out of the luxurious Cadillac and walked into Chicago's Union Station.

After boarding the Empire Builder, Sam went to the dining car and ordered a small pot of coffee. As the train pulled out of the station, moving through the tunnels and industrial areas of Chicago, Sam gazed out the window. Questions without answers ran through his mind. Did Fidelia run away? If so, what was she running from—or running towards? Would he find her in New York—in Miami—in Havana? Or would he find clues in one of those cities that would lead him elsewhere? And what guarantee was there that he would even come across a meaningful clue?

Luis' observation about Fidelia's thoroughness and the missing passport troubled him. Maybe Fidelia had put together and carried out such a complex plan that Sam would never find her.

*****

While investigating for the Air Force, Sam had learned to structure important facts and assumptions into a single case summary. Such a document had been his primary technique for focusing a case's analysis. As the train rumbled through western Illinois, Sam began to lay out what he knew—and what he didn't know—on a sheet of paper. He organized those elements by city—New York, Miami and Havana.

Beneath each city section he wrote *Who* to identify the key player; *Evidence* for key information that would cause him to focus on the players from that City; and *Questions* to note major unresolved issues related to those players. As he sat sipping his coffee and thought about the case, Sam realized that his supposition that Fidelia's disappearance was linked to one of those three cities was still only a hypothesis. He added a fourth piece—*Other Possible Explanations.*

New York
- *Who: Tony Giarri*
- *Evidence: Phone Call Message to Detective Miller; 1964 letter to Rosaline.*
- *Questions: Why did Giarri call Miller? What was Giarri after? Is Giarri still connected with the Miami mob?*

Miami
- *Who: Rosaline's Father, Hector Diaz,*
- *Evidence: 1963 and 1965 letters to Rosaline, Handwritten Florida address found in Fidelia's book.*
- *Questions: What was the address handwritten in Fidelia's book? Is Giarri working with Diaz? Are there neighbors of Hector who can give me some information?*

Havana
- *Who: a) Fidel Castro, b) Miguel Garcia's father Carlos and c) Miguel's sister Maria*
- *Evidence: Letters dated 1960 to 1964*
- *Questions: Why was Castro so interested in Fidelia? What is the connection between the Garcias and Castro? Is there more to Rosaline's relationship with Castro?*

- *Questions: Could Cuba be the reason for the missing passport? Might the Cuba travel ban become a major headache?*

Other Possible Explanations
- *Runaway—a real possibility for age bracket.*
- *Could there have been an unknown boyfriend?*
- *Victim of random violence?*
- *Kidnapping? Keep watching for any evidence that could suggest kidnapping or violent crime. Luis has money, but there has been no ransom request.*

After assembling these pieces into a document, Sam felt he had a case summary that was meaningful. He looked it over—did anything stand out? Were there any elements he had ignored? He put those items into a fifth category.

Other Items
- *Why did Rosaline pause before responding when I asked her if she had had any communication with the letter writers regarding Fidelia's disappearance?*
- *Missed classes or disappearance from home with passport are not indicative of either kidnapping or violence.*
- *Have Luis and Rosaline been totally forthcoming?*
- *Did Luis and Rosaline overlook (or exclude) any enemies in Chicago?*
- *Are all the addresses and phone numbers current?*

Sam looked over his summary, took a deep breath and exhaled. This was a start. His pot of coffee now empty, Sam walked a crooked path down the aisle to find a seat in a passenger car as the speeding train bumped, zagged and rolled down the track.

Once seated in a nearly empty coach car, Sam laid out the letters Rosaline had given him on the empty seat facing him. There was a lot to learn from these letters. He began with the two from Fidel Castro—one from 1960, the other from 1963. They were the only letters that were typewritten. Both appeared to be typed by someone who was not a good typist. Hand written corrections and edits in the letters appeared to be in the same hand as the signature—about as sophisticated as Sam would have expected from an eighth grader. Sam guessed that the letters probably had been typed by Castro. It seemed unusual that the leader of a nation would take the time to type a letter himself. And the simplicity and personal nature of the letters made Sam feel Castro's request for information and his desire to help Rosaline and Fidelia were sincere—not just a goodwill gesture from a politician.

In the first letter, Castro explained that he had promised a dying Miguel Garcia to watch over Garcia's wife and daughter. That was touching. But of course, Sam didn't know anything about Castro. It could just be manipulative. Still, Sam read into the letter an honest expression of caring. The second letter just reiterated Castro's continuing desire to be in contact with Rosaline and Fidelia.

After reading those two letters, Sam spent about a half an hour looking out the window as the Empire Builder passed snowy forests and farm fields on its way to Minneapolis. *This is one weird-ass case,* he thought to himself. *The person I am trying to find has the attention of a modern-day revolutionary, a highly ranked Mafia boss and an angry Cuban expatriate. Wow!*

Next, Sam read the two letters from Miguel Garcia's father Carlos; then the single letter from Miguel's sister Maria. All three were brief and focused on Fidelia. Carlos Garcia's letters were printed in square handwritten capitals. Maria's letter was written in a beautiful cursive. But all three letters started out the same—by greeting Rosaline and hoping she was doing well. After that, each letter passed on warm thoughts about Fidelia. Finally, each letter concluded by encouraging Rosaline to have Fidelia respond with a letter. While Sam understood the interest that Miguel's father and sister would have in Miguel's only child, their parallel structure caused him to wonder if they had been following an outline as they wrote the letters.

Tony Giarri's note left no doubt that there was no love lost by Tony for Rosaline.

March 15, 1964

Dear Rosaline,

Your dad gave me your address. He encouraged me to write to you.

This letter is about Fidelia—not about you. You made it clear you don't want to see me. I am more than happy to grant that wish. I offered you a lot. You responded by kicking me in the teeth. That being said, I am a big man. I can take it.

Now, I am happily settled with a wife and kids here in New York.

The only thing that you did that really hurt me was taking Fidelia away without letting me say goodbye to her. She is a really good kid. In fact, I always enjoyed her company more than yours. I think she liked me too.

I would like to visit Fidelia. I come to Chicago from time to time on business trips. I could be like an uncle for Fidelia. She and I even could go visit your dad in Miami. He misses her a lot. He told me that not seeing her anymore is the saddest thing in his life.

Let me know if I can visit Fidelia when I am in Chicago. It would be a good thing you would not regret.

Tony Giarri

The letter had been written on stationary that displayed the Brooklyn Ocean Parkway address Rosaline and Luis had included in their list of addresses. There was no subtlety in Giarri's message. When someone is in the business of brute force, subtlety is probably not a primary tool. What did stand out was that someone high up in the mob who has his own kids said he cared enough to want to visit a child he had only known for several months—years before!

Why?

*****

It was 1:15. The conductor walked down the aisle calling out *Last call for lunch. Last call for lunch.* Sam put the letters back into his briefcase and headed to the dining car. He knew from prior experience that the food on the train was quite good. Once seated in the dining car, Sam ordered a bowl of cream of broccoli soup, a bacon lettuce and tomato sandwich and a Budweiser. His grandmother had introduced him to broccoli soup on a train trip years ago.

Sam was finishing his soup when he was joined at his table by a grey-haired lady from Milwaukee. She was traveling to visit her daughter and grandkids in Winona. She looked at Sam's plate, then ordered a BLT. For the next couple of hours, she told Sam about her life on a family farm, about her kids and her grandkids. Sam decided she was a pretty nice old lady. Between enjoying the meal, watching the snow falling outside and hearing about her life on the farm, the next two hours passed quickly.

*****

The conductor walked through the dining car announcing, *Train will arrive in Winona in five minutes.* As the sweet old lady got up to return to her seat in coach, she apologized for chattering so much about herself. But Sam had enjoyed riding with her and told her as much.

Sam stayed in the dining car. After ordering a small pot of tea, he pulled out the last couple of letters. They were the 1963 and 1965 letters from Hector Diaz. Sam wondered, *why did Diaz wait until 1963 to write to his daughter. Maybe he didn't have her address? Maybe he was too angry? I'll need to ask him that—when we meet—if Diaz is willing to speak with me.*

The first letter started out by giving Rosaline general news about distant relatives and Miami neighbors. It was chatty, maybe trying to normalize their relationship. Diaz asked how Rosaline was doing. He hoped things were good. Then he turned to what was obviously the purpose of his letter.

"I hope Fidelia is doing well. I miss her a lot. Could she write a letter to me and include a picture of herself? In fact, would she like to visit me? I would gladly pay her airfare. I am an old man. This would make my life complete."

The letter closed with a thank you to Rosaline for assisting "this loving grandfather and his only granddaughter in getting together." Sam thought it was interesting that there was no polite request for Rosaline to visit. Evidently Hector's hard feelings toward Rosaline had not diminished and he saw no reason to pretend they had.

Sam turned to his second letter. It was brief. The script was definitely from the same hand. But it was shakier. Rosaline's father was aging.

September 12, 1965

Dear Rosaline,

I'm an old man, Rosa. Have a heart. Let my sweet granddaughter visit me before I pass away. I got your response to my letter two years ago. I appreciated the picture of you and Fidelia. But it would have been kind if you had allowed her to write to me herself. I am getting older. I would like to see my granddaughter again before I die.

I am happy for you that you have a boyfriend. Wouldn't it be nice if you and your 'boyfriend' could make things legal? Is it healthy for an innocent girl like Fidelia to see her mother living in sin? But then, I guess I was always old-fashioned.

I am asking one more time for you to allow Fidelia to visit me. The anger—no, the hate you have for me is something I will never understand. But it is something I have come to accept.

At least you can allow my granddaughter to write to me. She deserves to be able to choose whether she gets to know me better, or not.

Still your father,

Papa

Sam shook his head as he finished reading this letter. He thought to himself, *each of us has our own world of pain. There is a lot of anger in this old man's sadness.*

*****

Sam looked at his watch. The train would arrive in Minneapolis in about an hour. He went back to the passenger car, found an empty seat and stared out the window. Sam was quietly considering all the things he had learned in the past few days about this young Cuban American girl named Fidelia.

10. Moving Forward

It seemed like it was only minutes later that the train jerked and jolted to a stop at the Minneapolis Great Northern Depot. Sam was one of the first off of the train. He trotted across the lobby and exited the station; quickly spotting Isabelle waving both arms at him as she stood next to the Rocket. She had a big smile on her face.

Sam was happy to come home to someone who wanted to see him—someone he was happy to see. As Isabelle drove home, she told Sam how her time had been spent while he was in Chicago. Classes had gone well. She had enjoyed the house and had had a lot of fun reorganizing the kitchen. Sam was amused to hear that Isabelle had been rearranging stuff in the kitchen. During her lifetime, his mother would have flipped out if anyone had dared to try to change where anything was placed in those drawers and cabinets.

*****

Once they got home, Isabelle proudly showed Sam the changes she made in the kitchen. "Why have the mixer out? We never use it. And we use the press pot instead of the percolator. So, we can get rid of the percolator—right? And the silverware—why would anyone have the silverware in that drawer when it is so much more convenient in this drawer?"

Everything had a new spot. But it all sounded fine to Sam. He told Isabelle how much he liked the changes, then sat down at the dining room table. Isabelle checked the pot in which their dinner was heating, then sat down across from him.

"How did the trip go," she asked. "Did you discover where Rosaline's daughter is?"

Sam gave a fifteen-minute summary of the trip including what he had learned about Fidelia, a description of Rosaline and Luis' apartment and a detailed menu of everything Rosaline had cooked.

Isabelle inquired, "Does Rosaline cook better than me? You know, I make really good cinnamon rolls. I think you will like my *rollo de canela* more."

Sam assured Isabelle that she was the vastly superior cook. Then he gave a complete description of Thursday evening's dinner at the Pump Room climaxing with the sighting of the Rat Pack.

Isabelle smiled and said, "Sam, I am so jealous of that dinner. Tell me more about Rosaline's outfit. *A red suit with a mink stole* tells me nothing—at all. That could describe Santa Claus! It amazes me how you men are so incapable of noticing anything important."

Isabelle went into the kitchen and returned with two plates of *arroz con pollo*—chicken and yellow rice served with a tomato sauce complete with black beans, corn, olives and green peppers. Sam opened a bottle of Rioja, poured them each a glass.

Isabelle watched Sam as he tasted the *arroz con pollo*. "Now isn't that better than Rosaline's cooking?"

"Isabelle—it is so much better than anything I ate on the entire trip."

After dinner, they each took a glass of wine into the living room. Sam asked, "Would you be willing to sing some of the Cuban ballads you sang the night we met?"

After a couple of soft protests, Isabelle retrieved her guitar from the middle bedroom. Then, while Sam slowly drank a third glass of Rioja, Isabelle sang songs she had learned as a child.

The last song Isabelle sang was *Guantanamera.* Before singing it, Isabelle said, "This is a song about a woman from Guantánamo. It tells the story of a doomed love affair. But more importantly, Sam, this is the song of the Cuban people. Different people have written lyrics for *Guantanamera* over the years. But the original lyrics by our country's hero José Martí are the best. Its most important line is, *With the poor of the earth I want to share my fate.*"

Isabelle turned her attention to her guitar, tuning it for a moment, then singing with intense emotion. When she finished singing, tears were running down her cheeks. Isabelle flushed and quickly wiped the tears away.

After regaining her composure, she turned the table on Sam. "I see you have a guitar in your office, Sam. But I have never heard you play. Do you play this guitar, Sam? If you do, why have you not offered to play it for me?"

"I've fooled around with playing guitar since I was a teenager, Issa. And I began to play it more when I was in the service. But I'm just an amateur—you're the artist!"

"Bring down that guitar now, Samuel, and start playing. I have played for you. It is only just that you do the same for me."

"You're awfully good, Issa. It'd be intimidating to play in front of you."

"You aren't being fair, Sam. I played my guitar for you. Now it is your turn. I want to hear you make music. I promise not to be a cruel critic."

"OK. Sometime soon—but not this evening. I need a chance to practice a little before playing in front of someone as skilled as you."

Isabelle caught herself, paused, looked up at the ceiling, then looked at Sam and said, "That is acceptable—but it is only a deal if you play for me soon—that means in the next week."

Sam was relieved and quickly agreed to her terms.

*****

March days in Minnesota are generally cold. But for a day or two during the month, the weather sometimes warms up into the high thirties or low forties. Minnesotans know it won't last. But after a cold winter, they treat it like an early taste of spring. When Sam woke up that Saturday morning, it was sunny. The Tribune said the high temperature would be in the mid-forties. He was inspired to take Isabelle for her first ride on his cycle. The *Old Mill Restaurant* would be an excellent destination. It was small eating place on the banks of the Straight River in Owatonna—about seventy miles south of Minneapolis. Its food was good and the winding country road that led to Owatonna was picturesque. And Sam figured Isabelle would be intrigued by the restaurant's history. In the 19th century, the structure had been a flour mill powered by the Straight River.

When Isabelle came into the kitchen, Sam announced enthusiastically, "Let's ride down to Owatonna on my cycle. We will take a really a wonderful route and then, have a fantastic lunch!"

Isabelle roared with laughter. "You expect me to sit behind you on a motorcycle? And you add insult to injury—you ask me to take this crazy ride in the middle of winter? What you drinking, boy? You loco! I would not ride on the back of a motorcycle—even in the summer—for all of the rum in Cuba!"

She continued to laugh as Sam licked his wounds. After a few minutes, he amended his request. "Would you take the trip in the Rocket?"

Isabelle gave Sam a hug and a kiss and said, "When do we leave?" Obviously, the problem had been the vehicle—not the driver—nor the destination.

*****

The drive down to Owatonna was scenic. The sunlight streaming in through the car windows made Sam feel uncomfortably warm. But when he complained about how hot it was in the car, Isabelle said it was just right. Sam shrugged his shoulders and turned on the car radio. They listened to the music and sang along with The Beatles on *Yesterday*, with Bob Dylan on *A Hard Rain's A-Gonna Fall* and with Patsy Cline on *Crazy*.

I'm crazy for trying and crazy for crying
And I'm crazy for loving you.

*****

At the Old Mill Restaurant, Isabelle immediately spotted the chicken salad sandwich on the menu. "It says the chicken salad is made with apples, walnuts, raisins and seasoned with curry. That sounds good."

Sam and Isabelle each ordered one with a glass of locally pressed apple cider. They were not disappointed in either.

On the ride home, Sam told Isabelle how he had learned about the *Old Mill Restaurant*. "My grandparents belonged to a restaurant association. Three times a year, restaurant owners and professional staff came together and celebrated their industry for an evening. My grandparents used to take me to those meetings. I learned about quality—whether that meant preparing good foods or presenting them in an appetizing manner. These culinary folks never spoke about the hardships they faced. Anytime I go to a fancy restaurant like the *Waikiki Room* or to a down-home diner like the *Old*

Mill Restaurant, I appreciate not only the quality of what I eat, but the hard work that made it possible."

Sam was pensive for a while. "You know, Issa. I hated working at Lucky's. But I learned what quality and hard work are from my grandparents—and from their friends in the industry. When we walked through the lobby of the Nicollet, I saw a beautiful and expensive investment. I knew—it was aging. I didn't miss that the decor needed repair and updating. But I appreciated someone's vision and hard work that created that hotel."

They rode in silence as Sam navigated the rolling hills of southern Minnesota. After a few minutes, Sam went back to complete his thought. "I have no desire to ever work in a restaurant again. But whenever I walk into one—or into a hotel, I am humbled by the amount of commitment—the hard work that created it."

Sam suddenly felt a little embarrassed, a little surprised at his compassion for all of those who operate a restaurant or a hotel.

****

On Sunday morning it snowed. Large snowflakes blanketed and insulated everything in sight. Sam and Isabelle sat in their living room; Isabelle doing homework in preparation for her winter quarter finals; Sam putting together his to-do list for the coming week.

Later that morning, Sam went out by himself for a walk into the snowy day. He had always found peace and clarity in fresh snow. Now, with a new awareness gained from Isabelle, he also studied the architectural detail of his neighbors' craftsman homes. They were particularly beautiful now, covered by a new coat of snow. As he walked, he thought about all that had changed for him in the past few months. Two months ago, he was living alone and getting ready to start a detective agency. There had been an emptiness in life. Now he was living with a fascinating woman, had a detective agency with a corporate client and was investigating a complex missing person's case.

When he returned from his walk, life got even better. He was greeted with a cup of hot buttered rum.

*****

Monday morning, Sam was all business. He knocked off the first few items from his to-do list and was ready to take on the most uncomfortable task on the list—calling Tony Giarri. It was early afternoon in New York—a good time to call. This would be Sam's first communication with one of the suspects from Rosaline's past.

Sam dialed Giarri's number. The phone rang four or five times with no answer. Sam was about to hang up when he heard, "Hallo—Giarri here. What can I do you for?"

Sam suddenly didn't feel so organized, "Mr. Giarri. Uhm—my name is Sam Erickson. I have a small investigation agency in Minneapolis. I—uh—am assisting a friend—to find her daughter. Rosaline Martinez needs to locate her daughter Fidelia. The reason..."

Giarri interrupted. "So, what's your point. The Chicago copper—Miller's his name. He already called; told me you were checking around for the kid. But the bitch, Rosaline—she never made one damn effort to communicate with me. Now I get this call from you. So why should I help her? And why are you calling me? You figure I kidnapped the girl?"

Sam gulped—he had learned in the military that if someone who thinks they're a big shot gets testy, your best strategy is to ask them for advice. In that way, you appeal to their oversized ego.

"I'm going to be in New York City next week—on Thursday and Friday. Miller told me you had called him and were concerned about Fidelia's welfare. So, I thought since I was going to be in town, I'd get together with you and share what I know and the approach I am taking on the case. I thought maybe you might have some suggestions for how I could approach the search."

The deferential tone worked. Giarri responded as Sam had hoped. "Sure—yeah. I can sit down with you and listen to your story—what you're doing and if you're finding anything—and I can tell you if I'd do anything different."

Giarri paused for a moment, probably checking his calendar, then continued, "Looks like I'm free on Thursday evening—that's March 24th. Why don't we meet for dinner at Angelo's restaurant—146 Mulberry—at 7:30? It's just off Canal and Bowery in lower Manhattan. You'll get to taste some real *Cucina Italiana*. See you on Thursday. Ciao— gotta run."

And Tony Giarri hung up the phone.

Sam was left sitting in his living room, thinking about the unusually abrupt manner in which Giarri had ended the conversation. But his plan was in motion. He could go ahead and make flight and hotel reservations.

As Sam got off the phone with Giarri, Isabelle drove up in front of the house. She had just finished a class. Sam went out to meet her. He told her he would be going to New York City to meet with Tony Giarri on Wednesday of the following week.

Isabelle's face brightened. She gave Sam a big smile and said, "Oh Sam, that's wonderful. I love New York. My cousin Christina lives there and I haven't seen her for more than two years."

Sam explained, "The trip to New York will only be for a couple of days. It doesn't make much sense for you to have to come along."

It was at that moment that Sam was introduced to a new opportunity for growth. Isabelle teared up. She was silent; made no accusations; and appeared to be embarrassed by her tears. But she was clearly crying. Sam realized he had moved into new territory. What he had said seemed simple and obvious. Apparently, he had been wrong. It was neither simple nor obvious—at least not to her.

So, Sam clarified his position. He accomplished this by making the following deft statement, "It will just be for two days. I felt that you would be as happy here as you would be in New York—and we can save some money."

Saying this made Sam feel relieved. Isabelle went into the kitchen and started fixing dinner. About five minutes later, she returned to the living room. Sam was rereading Tony Giarri's letters to Rosaline.

Isabelle stood silently in front of Sam. When he looked up, she said, "And I suppose you will have to go to Miami and Havana without me as well. I mean, why should I visit those cities? I am not a detective. So, what if I have many more connections there then you do. You're the man. I should stay at home. Even though I will be done with my finals on Wednesday, I can stay here and clean the toilets—something that you, no doubt, feel I, as a woman, am highly qualified for and certainly a task that will be much more useful than traveling to New York City."

This was new territory—their first argument. Sam put down the letters, stretched his arms back over his head and looked at the ceiling. Meanwhile, he had a silent dialogue with himself. It went something like this: *What do I do here?*

Isabelle and I have lived together for only a few weeks. I shouldn't have to feel everything I do is going to be done in tandem. On the other hand, it's pretty nice that she cares enough to want to go somewhere with me. Still, am I ready to give up my independence? But how happy was I when nobody wanted to challenge that independence...when I was always by myself? However, it could be dangerous in New York. No—that's just bullshit. It will not be dangerous in New York.

The silent conversation with himself went on for a while. Throughout it, Sam looked up at the ceiling and Isabelle stood in front of him with her arms crossed in front of her—waiting for a response.

Sam considered the cost; *it would only be the airplane ticket. That shouldn't be such a big deal. I can afford it. And what the hell. I have the time. There'll probably only be the Giarri meeting. We could enjoy ourselves the rest of the time.*

He looked at Isabelle and said, "We leave on Wednesday of next week and come back Friday. Does that work for you?"

Clearly it worked. Because Isabelle gave a big grin—and then starting crying again. This time, Sam figured that the tears were probably happy.

After dinner, Sam started putting together notes for the Giarri meeting. Meanwhile, Isabelle called her cousin Christina. The two of them put together a dinner plan for Thursday evening when Sam would be meeting with Tony Giarri.

*****

On Tuesday, still the week before the trip to New York City, Sam met with Midwest Insurance. He was assigned

129

four claims in the Northern Minnesota cities of Duluth, Hibbing, Grand Rapids and Bemidji. Sam figured these claims would take less than two days to investigate. There would be at most four hours of meetings with claimants and local officials. But there would be about twelve hours of driving. In the spirit of being inclusive, Sam asked Isabelle if she wanted to ride along. The big smile confirmed that this had been a smart idea. Sam was figuring things out.

*****

Isabelle and Sam departed for northern Minnesota early the following Monday morning. The trip turned out to be uneventful, but fun. On Monday, Sam had brief meetings with claimants, agents and officials in Duluth and Hibbing. Sam and Isabelle spent the night at Hibbing's Androy Hotel, a once-classy, now almost empty 1920s small-city hotel.

A Hibbing insurance agent recommended that Sam purchase Cornish pasties for dinner from Hibbing's Sunrise Bakery. The agent added, "Pasties are a tradition in mining towns like ours. In the old country, miners worked the mines from sunrise to sunset. But in the middle of the day, somewhere a half a mile down in a cold and wet mine tunnel, each miner could unwrap and enjoy a hot, nourishing and tasty pasty."

Sam and Isabelle bought two Cornish pasties to go. Each pasty looked like a large turnover—a folded over circular pastry crust stuffed with a meat, potato and vegetable filling and crimped along the rounded side. They stopped at a small grocery store on their way back to the hotel to buy a six-pack of Schlitz. Then they carried their dinner back to their hotel room where they ate the pasties washed down with Schlitz Beer in front of a television. They had a fun evening watching Lucille Ball and Andy Griffith.

The next morning, they made stops in Grand Rapids and Bemidji before returning home. Tuesday evening, Sam wrote reports on the claims while Isabelle packed for the trip to New York. After stuffing her bag, she focused on the *All About New York City* guide book she had purchased in a Duluth book store.

*****

The Boeing 707 landed at JFK around 5 PM on Wednesday afternoon. It was raining cats and dogs. Traffic was a nightmare. Sam and Isabelle's swerving, jerking and bumping taxi ride into New York City seemed to have come right out of an amusement park. They didn't get to their large and comfortable room at the Roosevelt Hotel until after eight. The room had old fashioned mahogany wood furniture that probably had been new when the hotel opened more than forty years before. In the twenties, The Roosevelt had been a world class hotel. Larger and fancier than the Hibbing's Androy, it was more on the scale of Minneapolis' Nicollet Hotel. But in the 1960's, all three hotels were coping with the same challenge. The Roosevelt had become tattered around the edges and needed more than just a little preservation. Still, Sam had never stayed in such a classy hotel and was hardly disappointed.

From the window of their hotel room, Sam and Isabelle looked down onto Madison Avenue and watched a moving stream of rush-hour pedestrians carrying black umbrellas scurrying to buses or subway stations while avoiding, as best they could, being soaked by speeding automobiles splashing through pond-like puddles.

*****

Isabelle said, "I'm hungry, Sam. I read about Keen's Steakhouse in my guidebook. The dining room opened almost a hundred years ago as a hangout for actors and theater goers. Let's go there for dinner. It's not too far away."

They shared an umbrella as they took the ten-block walk to Keen's. While waiting in the restaurant's lobby, they looked at a display of long-stemmed clay pipes that had belonged to famous men. There were pipes from Teddy Roosevelt, Babe Ruth, Will Rogers, Albert Einstein and "Buffalo Bill" Cody. Sam worried they wouldn't be seated without a reservation. But because of rain cancellations, they were soon led to their table.

Their waiter told them about the pipes in the lobby. "People who wanted to smoke purchased a clay pipe. Each time they returned to the restaurant, their pipe was retrieved for their use. Now the pipes are just used as a display."

They ordered a couple of beers while looking at the menu. Isabelle told Sam, "The guidebook said Keen's used to not serve women. But after they refused to admit King Edward's lover—an actress named Lillie Langtry—she sued them. It went all the way to the Supreme Court. She won her case sixty years ago. And as a result, I can eat here. So, here's to Lillie Langtry."

She lifted her glass of beer. Sam raised his and they toasted Lillie Langtry.

Sam ordered a New York steak. It was excellent, but too big to finish. Isabelle had a filet mignon. They split an order of creamed spinach and another of boiled baby potatoes with parsley and butter. It was not a cheap meal. But it was a fun evening. When they left the restaurant, stuffed and happy, the rain had stopped. They agreed that the walk back to the Roosevelt—looking at fascinating storefronts, smelling foods from diverse cultures and listening to the sounds of the big city—was an absolute pleasure.

Sam was glad he was not alone.

11. Dinner in Little Italy

Thursday morning was sunny. It felt like spring. Isabelle had assembled an itinerary for their one day in New York City that realistically would take three days to complete. Her goal was to see every famous landmarks in the city.

Isabelle and Sam walked and walked and walked. They rode the elevator to the observation deck of the Empire State Building, explored the Theater District, and strolled through Times Square. They wandered through Central Park where they bought chestnuts roasted over a charcoal grill from a street vendor. Then they moved on to the Museum of Modern Art, the Metropolitan Museum and the Guggenheim where they marveled at the continuous spiral of Frank Lloyd Wright's architecture.

By the time they exited the modern cork-screw-like building, Sam's feet were killing him. "Let's sit down and take a break, Isabelle."

"Sorry Sam. We have already taken more time than I planned. We need to hustle to meet my cousin Christina at the Algonquin Hotel. Afterwards, Christina and I are going to go out to dinner at a small Yugoslavian restaurant and you can go meet with Rosaline's old boyfriend."

The Algonquin was on 44th street. The Guggenheim was on 89th street—three miles away. Sam breathed a huge sigh of relief when Isabelle announced that they had to catch a cab in order to get to the Algonquin by five. The traffic in front of the Guggenheim was intense. But Isabelle flashed a large smile at a Checker Cab driver and the large square cab pulled over and picked them up.

As the spacious Checker Marathon dodged through traffic to the Algonquin Hotel, Isabelle told Sam about the bar's history which she had learned from her guidebook. "At the end of World War I, a group of famous New York writers and critics met there for lunch once a week. They always sat at the same round table. That's why they were called the *Algonquin Round Table.*"

*****

Christina hadn't arrived at the dimly lit Algonquin when Sam and Isabelle took a table at the back of the large cocktail lounge. Their table was in front of a painting of group of ragtime era characters seated at a round table. Isabelle explained, "The guidebook said that this is a group portrait of the *Algonquin Round Table.* That lady with the big hat and scowl on her face—that's Dorothy Parker."

After listening to Isabelle's stories about the group's drinking habits and the bar's history, Sam told her he would honor Dorothy Parker by ordering her favorite drink, a martini. Isabelle had never had a martini. She wanted one as well. A moment later, Christina joined them. Their waiter suggested they stay true to Dorothy Parker and order Tanqueray instead of the house gin and go light on the vermouth.

Minutes later, martinis were served to them in three chilled crystal stemmed cocktail glasses each of which sported a couple of stuffed green olives on a pick. The gin mixture was cold and strong. Sam, Christina and Isabelle agreed that the drinks were perfect.

*****

Christina's accent was as rich as Isabelle's. Sam sat back and listened to the music like banter of the two Cuban American women as they laughed and shed tears recalling

135

their childhoods. As kids in Havana, they had played together often. Then, they renewed their relationship in Miami. But the cousins hadn't seen one another for four years.

During their phone conversation before the trip, Isabelle had told Christina that Sam was a private investigator—and that he was going to be in New York City on a case. Christina had been impressed. Now, at the Algonquin, after chatting with Isabelle about memories of their childhood, Christina turned to Sam and said, "So, you're the PI, eh? Sort of like Sam Spade?"

"I'd be lying if I said no one has ever thought of that cute name for me before."

Christina bent her head to take a sip from her martini; looked up at him and asked, "Can you tell me about your case?"

"I really can't say much. You know, privacy of clients and all. The case is about a missing teenager. I'm just trying to figure out if there has been any foul play."

All of a sudden, Sam got an inspiration. Maybe Christina could give him some insight into the dynamics he was up against. "I do have a question for you, Christina—related to my case—something you might be able to give me some insight into."

Christina said, "OK. Shoot, Mr. PI."

"Do New York Cubans have the same sort of anger toward the revolution as Cuban Americans who live in Miami?"

Christina laughed. "This is fun. I not only have the chance to observe a real detective in action, I get to play expert witness. So here is your answer. *The New York Cubans* was a Negro league baseball team that played ball around here in the 1930s. Now you know about New York Cubans. Does that help?"

Christina cackled at her joke, then responded to Sam's question. "Most Cubans who came to Miami. Over time, some moved to other places in the US including to New York. So, Cubans here are not really that different from the ones who still live in Miami. The older generation longs for the good old days and the wealth they accumulated in Cuba before Castro. The second generation—they're younger— more open to change—most of them realize that before the revolution the vast majority of Cubans were dreadfully poor. So, my answer is that the older a Cuban American is, the more likely it is that they resent Castro. That's true in Miami, New York or anywhere in the States."

"Are there Cubans who have made alliances with the Mafia?"

Christina rolled her eyes. "You really like to ask the easy questions—don't you, Mr. Detective?

She took the pick from her glass and ate the olives. Then she eyed Sam directly and said, "We have our Cuban criminals—same as every nationality. But Cuban criminals tend to have their own gangs. They're not part of the Mafia. When Castro came to power, he nationalized assets of many small businesses and wealthy Cubanos at the same time that he outlawed the Mafia's whorehouses, casinos and other criminal operations. So, some Cubans have made alliances with the Mafia based on shared loss of wealth and power."

What had started as a light-hearted response was getting serious. Christina took another sip of her martini and then a deep breath. "Some Mafia-Cuban friendships go back to the fifties when the mob ran Havana—and owned Batista. Yes. Some of those friendships continue today.

Other Mafia Cuban friendships are newer. But they are all based upon the dream that the good old days will come back."

She paused, looking as if she was trying to figure out how she would finish her response. "What I just said, Sam— it is based on common knowledge—not personal experience. I don't know too much about the Mafia and I stay as far away as I can from those Cubanos who fled our homeland with dirty wealth."

As she finished, Christina eyed Sam closely. He realized she wasn't just responding to a stranger's questions. She was judging her childhood cousin's partner. He wondered if Christina, for some reason, was suspicious about why he was asking questions about the mob. Sam had now experienced that sort of judgmental spotlight twice; once with Rosaline and now with Christina.

*****

While not offering any unique new perspectives, Christina's answers had prepared him for dealing with Tony Giarri. After a second round of martinis (enjoyed by all), Sam announced he needed to head off to the dinner meeting. Christina and Isabelle, whose dinner reservations were not until seven, remained at the Algonquin.

*****

Sam had spent the whole day on his feet. Nevertheless, he decided to walk to Angelo's. He needed one more opportunity to think through his strategies before meeting with Giarri. As he walked to Little Italy, the river of people he passed was mesmerizing. There were businessmen in three-piece suits and fancy overcoats; hippies wearing worn blue jeans and pea jackets; tall stylish women in tailored outfits looking as if they had stepped out of Vogue Magazine; and old women lugging bags of groceries.

It took an hour to get to the Mulberry Street restaurant. By the time he arrived at Angelo's, he was prepared to pay attention to the nuances of having a conversation with a gangster.

*****

Sam entered the Italian restaurant and said to the maître d', "I am meeting a man named Tony Giarri for dinner. Has he arrived?"

The maître d' asked Sam to wait a moment and went to the back of the white table-clothed restaurant where he spoke with a tall thickset man in a black pin-striped suit, dark blue dress shirt and no tie. When the maître d' returned, he said, "Mr. Erickson?" Sam nodded. "Mr. Giarri asks that you join him at his table. Please follow me."

Giarri stood up and extended a large hand and said, "Welcome to Little Italy."

Sam shook his hand and sat down facing Giarri, his back to the restaurant's entrance. Giarri was a large man—a couple of inches taller than Sam—probably outweighing him by fifty pounds. He had black, combed-back hair and a dark five-o'clock shadow.

Giarri spoke first. "This evening, we will talk as much business as you like. But first, let's enjoy some fine cuisine. Angelo has a great antipasto and I ordered a fine bottle of Montepulciano d'Abruzzo."

Sam was hungry. The idea of deferring any serious discussions until after eating sounded good. A waiter in a white coat with a black bow-tie brought a dusty bottle of wine from which he poured a small amount into Tony's thick-walled no-stem glass. Tony tasted it and nodded to the waiter who promptly filled both diners' glasses. Sam glanced at the bottle. It was a 1959 vintage and there was a gold medal sticker above the label.

After Sam tasted the wine, he said, "Tony. This may be the best glass of wine I've ever had."

Tony offered a grunt of agreement.

The waiter reappeared with a basket of crusty Italian bread and a large plate of stuffed peppers, prosciutto, stuffed mushrooms, olives, tomatoes and fresh mozzarella. The bread was still warm and the antipasto was fresh and richly flavored. After watching the intensity with which Tony devoured the wine, antipasto and bread, Sam understood why Tony wasn't thin.

The waiter returned a few minutes later. Were they ready to order? Since the menu was entirely in Italian, Sam had no idea what entrees were available. He told the waiter he would let Tony order first. Tony ordered the *pappardelle campagnole* pasta and the *scaloppine di vitello piselli e prosciutto* main course.

Sam asked the waiter if he would describe what Tony had ordered.

The waiter responded in a thick Italian accent, "Mr. Giarri ordered the *primo* of homemade long, flat and wide ribbons of egg pasta with oyster mushrooms. His *secondo* will be veal cooked with baby peas and prosciutto—that's thinly sliced dry-cured ham. Both dishes are prepared in a Madeira wine sauce. I might add that Mr. Giarri has an excellent palate and our restaurant is famous for these dishes."

Sam told the waiter he would order the same dishes. He thought to himself, "When in Rome—or more appropriately—when in Little Italy...."

*****

They finished the bottle of Montepulciano and Tony Giarri order a bottle of 1958 Bertani Amarone della Valpolicella Classico. After the waiter left the table, Giarri said, "If you liked the Montepulciano, you will fall in love with this Amarone. Amarone is the patriarch of Valpolicella—made from partially dried grapes. This results in an intense and full flavor. 1958 was Bertani's first year for this *bel vino*. You will not forget it."

After their antipasto plates were cleared, Tony leaned forward, put his elbows on the table and said, "Now—we can talk about Fidelia. I knew Fidelia when she was about ten. She was a sweet kid. I found great joy in taking her and her mother out to dinner and the movies. Sometimes, I would take Fidelia to a playground or we would just go out for a pizza—the two of us. But I have not seen the *ragazza* since 1960. I am married now and have no children of my own. My memories of this little angel are special."

Sam gave no indication that Tony had just contradicted his letter to Rosaline in which he told her he did have kids. He just made a mental note that Tony could be flexible with the truth.

Tony went on. "A couple of years ago, I asked if Rosaline would allow Fidelia to visit me or if I could visit her in Chicago. While Rosaline is a beautiful woman, she has a cold heart. So, I accepted that I would not see that little angel again. A couple of months ago, a Chicago business associate of mine who knew of my affection for Fidelia called to inform me he had seen an article in the paper about her being missing. The newspaper article listed the precinct and phone number for an Officer Miller. I called Miller—asked how the case was proceeding—if there was anything I could do to help. He said they had no leads and told me he wasn't in a position to ask for assistance."

Giarri took a drink from his wine glass and slowly savored it as he looked at his wine glass. Then he looked back at Sam. "So that is what I know about Fidelia's disappearance. I wish I had information that could assure all of us she is doing well. Unfortunately, I do not have that or any information about her. I will gladly do anything I can to help find this kid. When you called, I could have just told you to *shove it* since I am sure you called because Fidelia's paranoid mother is afraid I stole her baby—which is not the case. I decided to meet with you because I care about Fidelia and maybe I can help you find her. But at this point, I know nothing."

Giarri stopped speaking, tore a piece of bread, dabbed it in olive tapenade, put it in his mouth, started chewing and then interrupted his chewing to casually ask, "Have you found any leads? What have you learned?"

The serious look on Giarri's face told Sam he wanted a response. Sam collected his thoughts, then said, "I didn't know who Fidelia was until a few weeks ago when I was introduced to Rosaline and her husband Luis. They told me about Fidelia's disappearance and asked if I could help find her. Your name came up among other interested parties."

Sam described the brief meetings he had at the school and precinct. "So, Officer Miller agreed with the school officials—she probably ran away with a boyfriend."

As he spoke, Sam watched Giarri closely. Giarri must have been a good poker player. He sat back with a blank, dispassionate look as he listened to Sam.

Sam continued, "In other words, nobody has given me any useful leads. I don't know where Fidelia might be or why she might be gone. I don't even know that she is alive. Her mother and step-dad are heartbroken. They asked me to check out every possible connection to Fidelia's past. So, I'm meeting with you and I will go to Miami to interview her grandfather and anyone else who might have known her. At this point, it's likely that I will come up with nothing. That's what I told her parents. But they wanted me to explore all avenues and I am doing it."

The waiter brought their dinners and the bottle of Amarone. After their glasses were filled, Tony lifted his. Sam reciprocated. Giarri said, "*Chi he sano e da pie del Sultano—* How does it profit a man if he gains the world—and loses his health?"

All business conversation stopped as Tony and Sam focused on the food and the wine which was as extraordinary as Tony Giarri had promised. As Sam tasted his meal, he had no regrets he'd ordered the same dinner as his host. This was the best Italian meal he'd ever tasted. But as he savored the delicate veal, Sam was also digesting all that had occurred and was wondering about the ominous message delivered within Giarri's toast.

When the waiter returned to ask if they were enjoying the food, Sam complimented him profusely. Tony just grunted his approval. He appeared to be not only enjoying the meal. He was clearly lost in his own thoughts.

*****

Sam did not trust Tony at all. He had been careful not to mention the possibility of a trip to Havana. If Giarri knew that Sam might visit Cuba, he would certainly notify federal authorities which would create huge conflicts for Sam. Sam was also careful not to mention the Miami street address he had found in Fidelia's notebook. He didn't know where that address would lead. But he preferred to be the one to find out. He didn't want Tony—for whatever reason—to anticipate and interfere with any of his next steps.

Sam was sure Giarri was not being upfront. Still, he asked him, "What am I overlooking? When I was an investigator for the Air Force, I learned that cases without any clues do not exist—just cases where you overlook the obvious. What is obvious that I am missing here, Tony?"

Giarri said nothing until their plates were cleared. Then he looked Sam in the eye and said, "I don't know Sam. It appears that you, the private dick, know less than me—who knows nothing. Maybe you should ask the girl's mother if there might be something she is not telling you—something you need to know."

Sam had no response to that. Still, he went ahead and asked one last question, "Is there anyone else in Miami who you think I should meet with—I mean other than the grandfather?"

Again, Tony sat in silence. Then he said, "Like I said, you're the detective, Mr. Erickson. I assume you're getting paid. Maybe you should start figuring this thing out yourself."

Then, Giarri seemed to catch himself and sweetened his delivery. "Look, I have some connections in Chicago and Miami. I'll put the word out—that we're looking for Fidelia. If I hear anything, I'll let you know. And Sam, I expect the same from you."

Giarri said this last sentence slowly, head bent down, but eyes drilling in on Sam. And Sam hadn't missed the fact that Giarri had used *we* when describing who was looking for Fidelia.

"Thank you, Tony. But of course, I'll have to respect my clients' confidentiality. I will stay in touch and hopefully, we will be able to help one another—and have a success to celebrate in the future."

The waiter brought dessert menus. Sam had eaten his fill. But he just gave a look at the desserts—and there it was, tiramisu. Sam loved tiramisu—the layered combination of lady's fingers, espresso, dark rum, mascarpone cheese, and dark bittersweet chocolate shavings. No desert came close—when it was prepared well. But there are many ways to screw it up. The most common method of failure ended up turning this delicate exotic delight into a mediocre mixture of sweet pudding and cake.

But Sam was stuffed. What to do? Sam said to himself, *I might never again have such an opportunity to taste the quality tiramisu available at Angelo's.* He looked up at the waiter and ordered the desert.

And tasting the tiramisu was like taking a brief voyage trip to a distant land. The distinctly diverse flavors had retained their individuality, but still complimented one another. The flavor was both delicate and forceful. Ordering it had definitely not been a mistake.

A moment later, the waiter brought two small glasses of sambuca, an anise flavored digestive. In addition to the liquor, each glass held three coffee beans. Tony explained, "The coffee beans, Sam, represent health, happiness and prosperity. *Alla sua salute, signor Erickson.*"

When the waiter brought the bill, Tony signed it and handed it back to the waiter who said, "*Grazie signor Giarri. Buona salute a voi.*"

Tony glanced at his impressive gold wristwatch. Then he stood up and offered a large hand to Sam. "Sorry Sam.

Gotta run." Sam shook his hand, thanked him for the advice and wonderful meal. Then he watched as Tony exited the restaurant through a back door.

*****

As Sam walked out of the restaurant, he looked at the menu in its storefront window. There he saw that all of the entrees were listed in English as well as in Italian. Someone had either assumed Sam spoke Italian well or a move had been made to establish control from the outset. Sam had no doubt which was the case—or why.

Sam had consumed a lot of wine—on top of two martinis and a full dinner. As he left Angelo's, he focused on walking in a straight line as he headed east towards Broadway. A couple of young men were heading toward him. As they passed Sam, one of them, a man with a trimmed full beard wearing blue jeans and a black leather jacket, bumped Sam's shoulder. The man spoke to Sam in English with a heavy accent, "Heh man—watch it! You just ran into me. Who the hell do you think you are?"

Sam recognized the accent. It was Cuban. He quickly apologized even though the physical contact was clearly not his fault nor any accident. The contact had been initiated to provoke a conflict and Sam understood he was not in condition to fight. The second guy was clean shaven, wearing blue jeans, a pea coat and a stocking cap. He reached around from behind Sam and pinned both of Sam's arms behind his back. The first guy slugged Sam in the stomach twice, then said—again in English with a thick Cuban accent, "You think you are so goddamned smart. I think you would be a lot smarter if you spent your time minding your own business. Stop messing into Cuban affairs."

The bearded man drove several additional powerful punches into Sam's gut. He finished with a hard shot to Sam's chin. After that, his partner let go of Sam's arms and Sam fell forward onto his hands and knees. He covered his head with his arms and hands—a defensive posture he had learned in military training—as the two men proceeded to kick him several times in the ribs. Then the clean-shaven tough guy said to his bearded partner in Spanish—also with a Cuban accent, "The old guy said he wanted us to send a message—nothing permanent. I think it has been delivered. Let's get out of here." The two men each kicked Sam one more time; then turned around and briskly walked away.

Sam's gut and ribs ached. But he was no longer feeling drunk. He picked himself up; made a quick inventory of what hurt and how much; then slowly made his way towards Broadway—three painful blocks away. He stopped once before he reached the thoroughfare and threw up a good portion of that evening's dinner.

When he got to Broadway, Sam flagged down a cab. Ten minutes later an exhausted Sam staggered into the safety of the Roosevelt Hotel's plush lobby.

*****

Isabelle had been back in their hotel room for a while. She was watching an old Kirk Douglas movie on television when Sam entered the room. She looked at his face and the way he carried himself and said, "Oh God—you're hurt! What happened?" She rushed up to him, put her hands softly on his face and kissed him on the forehead. Sam stumbled over to the bed and lay down. Tears on her cheeks, Isabelle ran into the bathroom and returned with a cold wet washcloth which she placed over Sam's eyes, across his forehead.

"We need to get you to a hospital."

"No. I'm OK. I just need to rest."

Later, Sam told Isabelle about the men who had beaten him up. Then he recounted his dinner with Tony Giarri. He asked Isabelle what she made of the comment from Giarri that Sam should ask Rosaline for more information.

"I don't have a clue, Sam. You have to ask Rosaline. But I am worried. Maybe taking this case wasn't such a good idea. These men are dangerous. I like you a lot and I don't want to see you hurt. And I know that Luis and Rosaline will be upset that you are in danger."

Sam didn't respond. He would have to chew on all that had transpired. He rested on the bed, replaying the meal with Giarri and the attack that occurred afterwards. Finally, he pulled the covers over himself and fell into a troubled and painful sleep.

*****

The following morning, Sam was very sore. His ribs hurt. His jaw hurt. And he had a black eye. Isabelle ordered a late room service breakfast for them. Sam just had oatmeal. He wasn't about to test his jaw with anything that required much chewing.

After breakfast, Sam looked in the mirror. He was taken aback by the damage to his face. But then, he thought to himself, "What're you going to do?"

In spite of the pain, Sam decided that before they left New York, he needed to give Tony Giarri a call. He had learned that communication with a suspect shortly after a crime's commission, can give a lot of insight about whether the person was involved in that crime—and how deeply.

He dialed Tony's number. The phone rang six times. Sam was about to hang up when Giarri answered. "I wanted to call you Tony and thank you again for the dinner. But, as it happens, I have one more question. Last night, after I left the restaurant, a couple of Cuban guys beat me up. They told me to mind my own business and stay out of Cuban affairs. Do you have any idea who they might have been?"

Tony responded, "Sam—there are a lot of tough guys in New York—a lot of gangs. If they were that violent, I doubt they were Cuban. They were probably Puerto Rican. But my advice to you is the same in any case. You just need to learn to be careful."

Tony was clearly not surprised that Sam had been beaten up. In fact, his statement about being careful seemed like a personal endorsement of the message *stay out of this affair*. Sam was not going to say anything more to Tony. Might as well leave well enough alone. He thanked Tony for his input and repeated how much he'd enjoyed the wonderful dinner at Angelo's.

*****

After a delicious lunch of Fazolová, a traditional Czech bean soup, at a Czechoslovakian restaurant on 41st Street, Sam and Isabelle caught a cab to JFK for their return flight to the Twin Cities.

The trip to New York City had provided Sam with a lot of to consider. He had confirmed Tony's interest in finding Fidelia. And if there had been any doubt that Tony Giarri was dangerous, that had been cleared up. Sam was now sure that there was some sort of Cuban-Mafia link. Finally, Tony Giarri's asking to be kept in the informational loop told Sam that Giarri probably did not know more about Fidelia's disappearance than he had shared.

12. Healing

Sam and Isabelle got home late Friday evening. Sam was in pain. His ribs were sore and his back ached when he bent over—even a little. He spent Saturday and Sunday taking it easy, hoping that a couple of days' rest would reduce the pain. Sunday evening, he realized he needed to see his doctor.

First thing Monday morning, Sam went into Dr. James Nolan's clinic in St. Paul. He had received medical care from Dr. Nolan since he was ten and he trusted him. Nolan was able to fit Sam into his schedule at noon. He listened to Sam's brief description of the beating, shook his head and said, "Sounds like those guys don't like you a whole lot."

Nolan prodded, then probed Sam's black and blue torso. Sam groaned as his tender injuries were explored. Nolan told Sam he needed a few x-rays. He would meet with Sam at three that afternoon—after the x-rays had been taken and were available.

*****

After being x-rayed, Sam had a couple of hours to kill. Cecil's Delicatessen was about a mile from the clinic. Sam went to the deli and ordered his usual—half a hot corned beef sandwich and a cup of matzo ball soup. While he waited for his order, Sam jotted down a few questions in a notebook,

- *Who beat me up? Were they Tony's associates or Rosaline's father's friends?*
- *Who else might have sent them?*
- *Who is "the Old Guy" that the assailants referred to? Is it Rosaline's father?*

- *What did they mean when they said "Stop messing into Cuban affairs"? Why refer to Fidelia's disappearance as a Cuban affair?*
- *What was Tony's real reason for being so interested in Fidelia?*
- *Was Tony telling the truth when he said he didn't have any information about where Fidelia might be?*
- *What was Tony referring to when he said, "Ask the mother if there is something she is not sharing with you."*

Sam realized that answers to these questions would explain most of what had transpired in New York. It was also possible that they could put him well on the way to finding Rosaline's daughter—or maybe not.

Sam looked up from the list of questions. Not only had his soup and sandwich been delivered, but as he pondered his questions, he had consumed half of each. For the remainder of his lunch, Sam carefully directed his attention to the rich, tender thinly sliced corned beef, the freshness of the rye bread and the satisfying aroma, texture and flavor of the matzo ball and its savory chicken broth.

*****

A couple hours later, Dr. Nolan's nurse called Sam back into one of the small clinic exam rooms. After Nolan joined Sam, he spent a couple of minutes looking at the x-rays. Then he turned to Sam and said, "These guys really gave you a beating. There will probably be no permanent damage. But for the next few months, you are going to have to leave the fighting to Sonny Liston and Cassius Clay. The good news is that there doesn't seem to be any hematoma or internal bleeding. You're pretty lucky there. But you do have two rib fractures on your right side; one rib fracture on your left. They may be painful, but they're not severe. You will heal in a few months."

Nolan showed Sam the x-rays, pointing out the areas that had been injured. Sam was quiet.

Nolan went on, "My concerns are primarily for your lower back. You have a fractured vertebra. That's where one of these assholes planted a solid kick. It should heal over time. But you are going to always have to take care not to put too much stress on that area. In a couple of months, you can begin some gentle exercises. But for now, just rest it. Ice it to reduce the pain. I'll give you a prescription for Darvon. Take it easy on the Darvon. You can get hooked on this stuff. After popping one of these tablets, it won't be safe to drive for six or seven hours. And you gotta keep in mind, the vertebra may heal, but it will always be vulnerable to reinjury."

Nolan paused, looked directly at Sam and said, "You are dealing with some tough people here, Sam. You're lucky not to be nursing severe internal injuries in a hospital bed right now—or even worse. Take it easy. And more important— realize that people like this can kill you."

Sam got up to leave, but Nolan wasn't done. "And Sam, you told me how much you love your bike—you said it was a 1950s BMW. I have bad news for you. You should never ride that motorcycle—never again—not ever. Riding that bike in the next few months would be very damaging. But even if you wait a year or two, that BMW could cause serious re-injury to your back. Sam, you're going to have to get rid of your motorcycle."

*****

Sam drove home in a daze—totally lost in thought. "This case is tough. But giving up my bike? That's about the worst thing that could have happened. I love that bike. Now I have to sell it."

When he got home, Isabelle was waiting for him at the door. He filled her in on his visit with Nolan; told her everything— except what Dr. Nolan had said about his bike. He knew Nolan was right. But he couldn't bring himself to repeat the ugly words *sell the BMW.*

Sam went to their bedroom, took a Darvon capsule and lay down with an ice bag on his back. Two hours later, Isabelle woke him for dinner. The Darvon had pretty much knocked him out. As Sam walked down to dinner, he felt shaky and cautiously held onto the banister. Nolan had been right. Sam was going to have to be careful with these painkillers.

*****

The following day as Isabelle was leaving for class, Sam told her he would stay home and catch up on paperwork. He did that, but he had another plan for the day. Nolan had been right about getting rid of the BMW and Sam knew it. If he kept the bike, he would eventually ride it. That had to be avoided. The sooner he sold the BMW, the quicker he could move on.

Sam posted a want ad in the Minneapolis Star.
Classic Rare 1953 BMW R25 Motorcycle. 250 cc. Less than 4,000 KM on total rebuild. Full-width brakes, front fork sliders, air pump, chromed front fender. This is a dream bike. $1200 firm.

Sam had often heard how painful it was for a cowboy to shoot his horse after it broke a leg. Selling his motorcycle seemed about as close Sam could come to that.

He took another pain pill and went to bed.

*****

When he awoke, the pain in his ribs was overwhelming. But he could smell dinner. Something good was being cooked. He hobbled downstairs. Isabelle was in the kitchen making Cornish pasties!

"I went to the University library and found a fabulous recipe for pasties. Its crust will be richer and flakier than the pasties we ate in Hibbing. And, my sweet injured boyfriend, I also picked up a six-pack of your favorite—Guinness Stout.

An hour later, Sam told Isabelle, "I am eating what must be the best meat pie in the world. You need to be careful because if you continue to cook like this, I am going to be a fat man."

Isabelle smiled. After turning away, she inauspiciously wiped away a tear.

Sam had a lump in his throat. "Now, I'm going to tell you about something really painful. Something I didn't tell you yesterday."

Isabelle stopped eating, took a deep breath, exhaled and looked at him with anxiety in her eyes. She waited for whatever he was about to say.

"Dr. Nolan told me I have to stop riding my cycle. I'm gonna sell it."

The look Sam received was not one of sympathy. Isabelle stood up, walked over to him and gave him a big kiss. Sam was a little amazed. After the kiss, he felt better— less pain in the ribs—less sadness. Sam laughed and said, "What a powerful drug a kiss is, Issy. Darvon—eat your heart out!"

Sam asked for another kiss. Before giving it to him, Isabelle gave a big smile and said, "Well—I guess I will have to make Cornish pasties for you more often!"

This was clearly the time to share his plan for what he would do after the cycle sold. "First of all," Sam began, "selling the cycle is very hard for me. But I need to move on—and I need to find a way to ease its loss. I figured out how to accomplish that. I've never purchased a car, Issa. One car for the two of us—even a cool car like the Rocket—it's not working—it's not going to work. We need a second car."

Isabelle interrupted him and said, "But you have a car and I cannot afford to buy one. It's not fair that you have to buy a second car because I live with you."

"Listen Isabelle—I want to do this and I'm excited about it. The car I buy needs to give me the sort of joy I experienced when I rode the BMW. Since I'm not going to let you stop me from buying it, you ought to just kick back and hear my plan. I'm going to get a car that will be fun to drive on country outings—a car that lets me feel the road and the rush of the wind through my hair. For some time, I have been watching advertisements for the new Ford Mustang convertibles. These cars have so much class, Issa. They are a combination of sports car and hot rod. Making this purchase is going to make me happy. And Mustangs are not that expensive. If I sell the cycle for $1200, I am half way there. I can afford this and I want to do it! That's the way it is."

*****

Saturday, Sam's motorcycle advertisement appeared in the Minneapolis Star. His phone was ringing off the hook by seven in the morning. Two hours later, Sam held twelve crisp one-hundred-dollar bills and his beautiful BMW R25 was history. By noon, he and Isabelle were at a Freeway Ford's showroom looking at Mustang Convertibles. Sam told the salesman he wanted the four-speed manual transmission and 289 cubic inch V-8 engine with a four-barrel carburetor. The dealer had four vehicles that met the criteria. Isabelle told Sam she liked the yellow Mustang, a color the salesman had referred to as *Springtime Yellow*.

Now, yellow was not Sam's favorite color. Sam liked red. At Ford, it was called *Candy Apple Red*. But the yellow looked pretty nice too. And Isabelle had never bought a new car either. So, Springtime Yellow it was. The new convertible was christened *Mr. Mustang*. Mr. Mustang had a black ragtop, black interior and black bucket seats. It cost a few hundred dollars more than Sam had anticipated. But, oh—it was so eye-catching and so much fun to drive.

The next day was sunny, but still pretty cool. Sam and Isabelle didn't mind the weather. They jumped in Mr. Mustang, put the top down, cranked up the heater and drove down to Owatonna for lunch. Sam enjoyed the power of the car—how quickly it accelerated; how tightly it held the road. As he shifted gears on the curves and hills, he couldn't help but smile. Isabelle had a scarf over her head and was wearing her warm winter coat and mittens. She was cold. But her smile was just as broad as Sam's. As they drove, Sam turned up Mr. Mustang's radio. They both sang along with the Troggs' hit song *Wild Thing*. The words felt like a tribute to the car.

Wild thing
I think I love you

*****

Sam and Isabelle were both shivering by the time they arrived at the Old Mill Restaurant. But they each wore a grin. After a satisfying lunch of bean soup and splitting a meatloaf sandwich, they headed home. As they left the restaurant, Sam told Isabelle what he had learned that morning, "No matter how nice your car is, if you drive around with the top down in early April, you freeze your ass off."

On the way home, Sam had just as much fun shifting gears, but he kept the convertible top up. They listened to rock and roll and watched the countryside pass them by. The Beatles' *In my Life* came on the radio and Sam found himself singing along happily.

Though I know I'll never lose affection
For people and things that went before
I know I'll often stop and think about them
In my life I love you more.

When they got home, Isabelle fixed them cups of hot chocolate topped with small marshmallows. As she sank onto the couch beside him, she sighed and said, "I am so happy Sam. It was such a wonderful day. I think Mr. Mustang is perfect."

*****

Monday morning, after Isabelle headed off to the University, Sam once again pulled out his list of questions about the Tony Giarri dinner and the assault that followed. He didn't know who had beaten him up. But it certainly wasn't a coincidence that the beating occurred right after the dinner. He decided he would just treat as a fact that his assailants had learned about Sam from Tony. Beyond that, he had no answer to the first question in his list: *Who beat me up?*

And *the old guy*—who was he? If Sam could figure that one out, he might be able to answer several other questions including why Tony was so interested in Fidelia. *The old guy* could be Rosaline's father—but that really didn't ring true. Rosaline's father didn't seem like a person who would have any sort of power.

What bothered Sam more than anything else was Tony's statement that implied Rosaline had important information she hadn't shared. If Rosaline and Luis were holding something back, well, Sam might have to drop the case. The best course of action was to go ahead and call Rosaline and Luis; update them; then ask if anything had been withheld.

Sam made a fresh pot of coffee, poured himself a cup and made the call. Luis answered the phone. After pleasantries were exchanged, Sam asked, "When would be a good time to update you and Rosaline on my trip to New York?

Luis said, "Rosaline isn't home. But if it works for you, you could update me now and I'll relay the information on to Rosaline when she gets back from the hairdresser."

That wasn't what Sam had hoped for, but it would work. Sam started out by reviewing his conversation with Giarri. Luis said nothing during Sam's report until Sam described leaving the restaurant and seeing the menu in English and Italian. "That's interesting, Sam, I mean about the menus. It may be as telling as anything else that you told me about from the meal. It seems Giarri works hard to make sure everything is on his terms. He has to be in control. I suppose in the world of Mafia machismo, a woman who resists that control has committed a terrible sin."

Luis paused, then added, "And I think I can tell you what Giarri was referring to when he said Rosaline knows something she is not telling you. Rosaline saw a lot of Fidel

Castro before she met Miguel. While that's no secret, some people in Miami speculated about their relationship wondering if Rosaline and Castro were lovers and could Fidelia be Castro's illegitimate love-child."

Luis had all of Sam's attention, now. Where was this going?

"You don't have to be a rocket scientist to know that *Fidelia* is the female adaptation of the name *Fidel.* What these creeps don't know is that long before Castro dated Rosaline, he and Miguel were very close friends. Miguel once told Rosie he wanted to name his first child after Fidel. She agreed—and that was that. But in Miami, there is no knowledge of this. The vicious rumor that Fidel is Fidelia's father; well, it's just plain wrong. It has always been a source of embarrassment for Rosie. I apologize for not sharing that—it's just that it causes Rosaline so much embarrassment—and the rumor is not true. We should have told you. I promise there's nothing else—I know of—that we haven't told you. I'll ask Rosaline if there could be anything else? But I'm pretty sure she'll concur. This is what Giarri was getting at."

The explanation rang true. Sam felt compassion for Rosaline. Then Sam told Luis about the beating in Little Italy. As he described the attack and remembered the kicks and punches he had endured, it was like a cue for his ribs to begin to ache once again.

There was silence. Sam was thinking the conversation was about to end when Luis said, "The connection between the Mafia and Cuba goes way back, Sam. Long before Batista became president, corrupt Cubans were selling out the Cuban people. They were taking bribes, allowing the Mafia to freely run Cuba's whorehouses, gambling, drug dealing and money laundering. But there was a third partner in all of that—the US government. It allowed the corruption while protecting American corporations which profited from the Cuban people's poverty. Later on, the CIA worked with the Mafia and Cuban-Americans who wanted to try to overthrow Castro at the Bay of Pigs. Their goal was to return the old corrupt system."

Sam was surprised with Luis' intensity. Luis was an American citizen who had become very successful after leaving Cuba. Sam had no idea that Luis was so critical of the corruption or supportive of the revolution.

Luis continued. "So, who do I think *the old guy* is? Could it be Rosaline's father? Is it some Mafia kingpin? Maybe someone else? I don't know. Was Fidelia taken by the Mafia and bitter Cuban-Americans to threaten or embarrass Castro? I don't know. What did those young gang members mean by *affairs*? They could be being cute—referencing Fidel and Rosaline. They might be telling you not to look at anything with a Mafia Cuban connection. Again, I don't know. It could be more bravado than anything else. But I remember an old saying my grandfather used to use, *If a snake has bitten you once, stay away from it.* Sam, I feel terrible that working for Rosaline and me has put you in danger. This investigation might be too risky. If you decide to quit the case, we will respect your decision. But we don't have anyone else to turn to, Sam. You have shown much bravery. We trust you. We appreciate your work. We hope you are able to continue."

Sam was touched by Luis' candor. No wonder Isabelle thought the world of them.

Luis finished up. "You are probably wondering how a retired baseball pitcher who has become a successful capitalist and owns a Cadillac dealership, could feel as I do about pre-Castro Cuba. Let me tell you, Sam, if it weren't for my strong right arm, I would have been just one more body working in the fields—harvesting sugar cane—along with my father and brothers. My family was dirt poor—I was dirt poor. I have benefited tremendously from America's wealth. But I will never forget the cruel poverty of my youth or how my friends and family suffered under the criminal dictatorship of Batista—and all of Batista's immoral partners-in-crime."

Sam realized that Luis probably rarely shared these feelings about Cuba. He also knew that while this case was more complex than he had anticipated, he in no way was tempted to back out.

"Thank you for your openness, Luis. I can tell you I'm royally pissed off at those sons-of-bitches. They beat up the wrong guy! I'm more committed to solving your case than ever. I just need a few days to heal a little from the beating. I'll get back to you and Rosaline in a couple of weeks with a plan for visiting Miami and later, if necessary, Havana."

"Thank you, Sam. I do have some good news for you. Rosaline sent her letter to Castro the day you left Chicago—you know—through our friend in Mexico. On Saturday we got a response. Castro's letter was quite warm. You will receive visa authorization to visit Havana—and the visa will include Isabelle. Castro wrote that he looks forward to meeting you. He promised his assistance in your search for Fidelia. We should be receiving a letter from a government official soon. It will serve as your visa when you travel to Cuba. Yesterday I mailed you a Xerox copy of Castro's letter. I will send you the letter from the Cuban official once we receive it. Thank you, Sam, for your courage. And don't forget to send me another invoice."

Sam laughed. "Don't worry my friend. Sending you that invoice may be the only thing in this case that I can absolutely guarantee will happen."

*****

Sam poured himself another cup of coffee. Even that simple, small movement caused pain in his ribs. He slowly sat down on the living room couch. He considered all Luis had shared with him and decided he was more confident than ever in his trust for Luis and Rosaline. After speaking with Luis, he could appreciate even more fully that he was their best chance of finding Fidelia.

That being said, Sam had to admit that the information he had assembled did not fit together into any meaningful pattern. Once more, the lines from Weldon Kees' poem flew through his brain.

Small wonder that the case remains unsolved,
Or that the sleuth, Le Roux, is now incurably insane,
Sam sat quietly. He was not feeling confident.

13. Next Steps

During April, Sam made overnight trips for Midwest Insurance and completed a couple of small investigations for a local law firm. While he enjoyed taking Mr. Mustang on the road and was pleased that his detective agency was prospering, he found that he was too often in a rush. Sam's grandfather had once told him that his great regret in life that he spent too much time working at Lucky's; that he had not taken enough time to slow down and enjoy small sweet moments of quiet. Sam was determined not to repeat his grandfather's error. He made an effort to slow his pace—to create those quiet moments. During the last week of April, other than quick trips around town in Mr. Mustang (on sunny days with the top down), Sam stayed home.

Sam was so intimidated by Isabelle's skill; he had stopped playing his guitar after she moved into the house. Having committed to play for her, he practiced the guitar when she was in class. He had forgotten how satisfying it was to pluck the instrument's strings; to hear soft resonant sounds emanate from his red cedar and rosewood guitar.

And Sam started going for regular morning walks—pushing himself to notice the beauty of his neighborhood. As spring progressed, Sam marveled as buds formed on the fruit trees and the daffodils and crocuses emerge from snow-covered flower beds. As he walked, he often thought about the many changes that had had occurred in his life over the past few months. He realized he was a lucky man.

*****

It was time to plan the trip to Miami. Isabelle's final class before spring break was on May 12. While Sam didn't like the idea of flying on a Friday the 13th—he was superstitious—seats on flights for Saturday the 14th were not available. So, Sam ignored his superstitions and booked tickets for the 13th. If they stayed in Miami through Tuesday, the 17th, he would have time to meet with Rosaline's father, check out the address found in Fidelia's room and follow any other leads that developed. He took Luis' recommendation and booked a room at Miami's National Hotel for that time period.

Sam put off planning any trip to Havana until June at the soonest. What he learned in Miami would probably determine if there even was a need to go to Cuba. And in any case, Isabelle's spring term classes didn't end until late May and no trip to Cuba could be planned until the visa letter from Cuban officials arrived.

Sam shared his plan to put off the Havana trip with Isabelle using his best southern belle imitation quoting Scarlet O'Hara from *Gone with the Wind*, "I can't think about that right now. ... I'll think about that tomorrow."

*****

A new baseball season was beginning. Sam did not buy 1966 Twins' season tickets. His busy schedule meant he would miss too many games. Instead, he planned on buying individual game tickets as the season progressed. He bought his first pair of tickets to the second game of the season against the Kansas City Athletics.

As Sam drove Mr. Mustang to Metropolitan Stadium, Isabelle told him about her favorite baseball memory. "Baseball was the national game of Cuba. Havana had a team in the American minor leagues and they played home games at Havana's Grand Stadium—a beautiful and sunny place. I remember begging Papa to take me to one of their games. One day, Papa told me he had a surprise. He held both of his hands behind his back. He said, 'Pick a Hand.' I told him I didn't know which hand to pick. So, Papa showed me both hands. Each hand held one baseball ticket. Papa and I were going to see the *Havana Cubans*!"

Isabelle stopped speaking and looked out the window for a moment and smiled. "That day, the Cubans played a team from Charleston, South Carolina. I don't remember a lot about the game—just that Papa bought me caramel corn and a Coca Cola. The Cubans won the game. That is one of my most special memories. The game, it was fun, yes. But more important was going with Papa. That was the last time I saw a baseball game."

Sam and Isabelle arrived at Metropolitan Stadium. To honor Isabelle's memory, Sam bought her a box of Cracker Jacks and a Coca Cola. He had a Hamm's beer and some peanuts. It was a cool sunny day. Camilo Pascual pitched for the Twins. Isabelle had known Pascual for four years. She laughed when Sam told her that Twins' radio commentator, Halsey Hall, always referred to Pascual as the *curve-balling Castilian*. Including Pascual, four Cuban Americans started that game for the Twins. Two of them—Sandy Valdespino and Tony Oliva—hit home runs. Minnesota won the game 5 to 3.

The Twins didn't do very well during that first month of the 1966 season. Still, Sam was happy that baseball was back regardless of whether that meant reading about the games in the Minneapolis Star or Tribune, going in person, watching them on TV or just listening to them on Mr. Mustang's radio.

*****

On Tuesday, May third, Sam was practicing guitar in his living room. Isabelle was at the university. There was a knock at the door. Sam put down his guitar and went to the door. There were two men in suits and ties. One of them, wearing a grey suit, dark red tie and brown fedora with a little red feather in it, asked Sam if they could come in and speak with him for a few minutes.

Sam replied, "Before I invite you into my home, I'd like to know who you are and why you're asking to speak with me."

The man responded in an emotionless monotone. "Mr. Erickson. My name is Wozniak. I work for the Federal Bureau of Investigation. We have a few questions about your involvement in a missing person's case. If you would take five minutes with us, it would be worth your while."

As he was saying this, Wozniak reached inside his suit jacket breast pocket, pulled out his wallet and flashed a badge. Next to the badge in the opened wallet was a card. It simply said, *Special Agent Wozniak, Federal Bureau of Investigations.*

Wozniak did not introduce his partner, a taller thin man dressed in a dark gray pinstripe suit. The partner didn't say a word and did not remove his sun glasses.

Sam hesitated, then told the two men they could enter his home.

"We understand you are looking for a young girl who's been missing from her parents' home in Chicago. Is that correct?"

Sam simply said, "Yes."

Wozniak continued, "Would you please update us on your progress—by that I mean the information you have turned up during the investigation?"

Sam answered, "No." Then he added, "But I really appreciate your interest."

Wozniak paused, giving a cold look at Sam. "As you know, the missing girl is Cuban American. Are you aware of the federal government's laws regarding communications with Cuba and with Cuban nationals?"

Sam took a deep breath, exhaled and said, "Would you be so kind as to tell me all about those laws?"

Agent Wozniak clenched his jaw. He continued—still in a monotone. "I think you may wish to consult with an attorney on the subject. Suffice it to say, any communication you have with any person representing the government of Cuba will be—most likely—illegal."

Sam didn't like being pushed around. He decided this was purely an intimidation visit. "Thanks for the public service visit, gentlemen. You are so thoughtful. I remember when I worked in the Air Force doing investigations, I always used to travel around Spain advising citizens that they should talk to their attorney. It makes it such a more wonderful world—doesn't it—when everybody talks to their attorney?"

Sam was beginning to wonder if Wozniak's silent partner was even in the FBI. "By the way, Mr. Wozniak, can you please introduce me to your quiet friend here? You know, your buddy with the sun glasses? And I want to see his identification as well."

Sam's request was ignored. Instead, Wozniak's monotone added a level of intensity. "You need to realize that you are living with a woman who is a Cuban immigrant. She may have citizenship papers, but the United States government expects her demonstrate her patriotism—that she is honoring her oath. If you believe that you—and she— have no responsibility to respect our country, then you better think again. If you are under the illusion that the

United States government has no power over your actions, well, you are awfully naive."

Sam was normally a peaceful guy. But he was losing his temper. He doubted Officer Miller would have taken the time to follow up with the FBI or anyone other than Tony Giarri. More than likely, this was a pressure tactic initiated by Tony Giarri and the Cubans. Sam said nothing, but was silently amused, thinking to himself, *Tony Giarri and the Cubans—now doesn't that sound like the name of a lousy rock and roll group?*

Sam decided to up the ante. "By the way," he said, "since I want to make sure I can follow up with you on the legal advice I receive. Can I have your business card? You know, maybe my attorney will have a few questions for you. I also want the business card for your silent buddy, Harpo here. I imagine he would be a fountain of useful information—if he knew how to talk. And while you are at it, can you let me know under which federal authorizing statute you have come to my home to give me this caring advice? I am sure my attorney will be deeply interested in that. Perhaps, this is a new program of the Federal Government to teach citizens international relations? And, by the way, could you clarify who is so concerned about me? Is it the President, the Congress, the Supreme Court—or maybe—just maybe, could it be Tony Giarri?"

When he said *Tony Giarri*, the second guy winced and glanced at Wozniak.

Wozniak stood up. "If you choose not to cooperate, Mr. Erickson, I can promise you you're going to regret it."

The two men in their grey suits started toward the door. As Wozniak reached for the doorknob, Sam said, "I asked for your cards—may I have them—now?"

Neither Wozniak nor his buddy responded. As Wozniak opened the door, he turned to Sam and said, "Thanks for your time. Erickson. You appear to think this is a joke. If I were you, I'd think carefully about my behavior. And a bit of advice—people like you who think they are tough sometimes discover that they've seriously overestimated themselves."

Sam watched as they walked out the door and away from the house, Sam called after them, "Hey—I want those business cards."

Normally, Sam had a lot of common sense. But he had become angry and followed the two men with the intent of writing down their license plate number. But the two men in grey suits did not get in a car in front of his home. They walked down the sidewalk. Sam followed them. His ribs still hurt from the last time someone had given him advice. But Sam understood that getting a license plate number might be the only means of identifying who these guys really were. Sam stayed half a block behind them as they walk away. When they reached the street corner a block and a half from Sam's home, they climbed into a late model blue Chevrolet Impala, started it up, hit the gas and drove off too quickly for Sam to make out anything except that the car had Minnesota plates.

As Sam walked back to his house, he chewed on the fact that the car did not have federal license plates. It had to be a rental. Sam was willing to bet that these men were not federal agents.

Sam went into his living room, took out his phone book and looked up the telephone number for the office of the local FBI. He called that number and asked to speak to Agent Wozniak. The operator told him there was no one with that last name assigned to that office. He asked if the person might be temporarily there from another FBI office.

Sam waited for a moment. The woman responded. "I'm sorry sir. There is no FBI employee named Wozniak—regular or temporarily assigned—working for the FBI in Minnesota." She paused and added, "And I just looked at our national directory. It includes all current Federal Bureau of Investigation agents. It lists no one with that last name. Would you like to speak with someone else in our office?"

Sam declined and thanked her.

He sat down on the couch. Sam couldn't remember being so angry. He considered calling the Minneapolis Police. But he decided that if he reported the interaction, the police would require information that Rosaline had not wanted to be made public. Anyway, Sam strongly doubted that the police could help. It might be a crime to impersonate an FBI agent, but without any evidence or trail to identify Wozniak, the police would be unable to help.

What really fried Sam was that Wozniak had threatened Isabelle. Even though the whole episode would upset her, Sam realized he was going to have to tell her about the meeting.

Sam needed to calm down before she got home. With that in mind, he picked up his guitar and began to play *Recuerdos de la Alhambra*—a turn of the Century Spanish composition that literally translates to *Memories of the Alhambra*. As Sam plucked the strings, the haunting sounds that emanated from his guitar released tensions from inside him—tensions that was a direct result of the meeting with the fake FBI agents. As he lost himself in the peaceful tones of *Recuerdos*. Sam closed his eyes. But in the back of his mind, he was analyzing and considered a whole range of alternative actions that might be useful in responding to Wozniak—or whatever the hell that imposter's real name was.

For a half an hour, Sam bathed in the soft tones of his guitar. When he stopped playing and put the guitar down on the couch next to him, he looked over at the door. Isabelle was standing in front of the doorway. He had been so focused on playing *Recuerdos* that he hadn't heard her enter the house.

"That was beautiful, Sam. That is the first time I have heard you play guitar. You play with such feeling—your guitar has such a beautiful resonant tone. I did not mean to interrupt you—but listening to you play, Sam—it was inspiring. Thank you."

Playing *Recuerdos de la Alhambra* had restored Sam's nerves. He was ready to tell Isabelle about the meeting. "Isabelle, I need to speak to you about something that just happened."

"Can I fix myself a cup of mint tea first? I will get a cup for you too—if you like."

*****

A half an hour later, Sam had finished telling Isabelle about his conversation with Wozniak. As she listened, Isabelle silently shook her head. For five minutes nothing was said. Then, Isabelle spoke. "You know, Sam. I have heard stories about people in this country—going around frightening Cubans. The men who do this are no better than Batista. We cannot afford to be afraid of such cowards. If we do, we lose everything. I would be lying if I said that these threats don't frighten me. But I know that being bullied into silence would be worse. If I allow intimidation to occur, I might as well be living in Cuba—under Batista."

She stood up, went into the kitchen and returned with the teapot. Isabelle poured each of them another cup of mint tea. Then she continued speaking. "We knew you needed to be careful. Now, it appears I must be careful as well. I grew up in one dictatorship, Sam. I refuse to begin to behave like I live in another. I am a citizen. I have rights too! We must contact the police. We don't need to tell them anything about Rosaline."

There were tears in Isabelle's eyes, but her face offered a look of determination Sam hadn't seen before. He was inspired—by Isabelle's passion for life, her courage and, most of all, by her integrity! "You're right, Issa. We need to have this episode on the record—in case this Wozniak and his dumb buddy return."

Sam reached over and picked up the phonebook.

*****

An hour later, two officers from the Minneapolis Police Department sat with Sam and Isabelle in the living room.

Sam described the encounter. Then he added, "Due to client confidentiality, I cannot share the names of my clients or of their missing daughter. But the local office of the FBI confirmed by phone that no one named Wozniak is in their employ—locally or nationally. I know that lying about being an FBI agent is a crime. The guy who called himself Wozniak was not just trying to intimidate me—he was clearly threatening Isabelle because of her Cuban birth. My objective today is to make a formal record of their actions. I know I haven't given you sufficient information to do anything other than document what happened. But if they come back, I will contact you immediately and there will be a record."

The officers were polite and professional. They asked a few questions while taking notes and seemed relieved they were not being asked to do anything other than document the incident. As they left, one of the officers told Sam, "I think you're right. These two men—Wozniak and his buddy—I'm certain they weren't FBI. They broke too many legal protocols. Thanks for reporting the incident. Be cautious and definitely let us know if you get any more communications of any sort from Wozniak."

*****

That evening, Sam and Isabelle went out for pizza and beer. Sam told her, "I'm sorry you're being dragged into this whole affair just because I took a case."

Isabelle responded, "I feel bad you are being threatened; getting beaten up just for trying to help my friends." Isabelle paused, then laughed and added, "Heh Sam—aren't we supposed to be blaming one another rather than each of us trying to take sole responsibility for something that neither of us could have foreseen?"

They both laughed. When they got home, Sam gave Luis and Rosaline a call. Luis answered and Sam asked him when would be a good time for them to have a longer phone conversation.

Luis responded, "I intended to call you this evening to ask if Rosaline and I could visit you this weekend. I've got good news. Rosaline received your Cuban visa authorization. We wanted to deliver it to you by hand rather than send mail it. Can our conversation wait until then?"

"Sure, Luis. That would be great. Issa will be thrilled to get together with Rosaline again."

Luis and Rosaline planned to drive to Minneapolis that Friday. They would spend the night with Sam and Isabelle, then return to Chicago on Saturday.

*****

It had been an upsetting day. After the phone call with Luis, neither Sam nor Isabelle was ready for bed. Sam poured a couple of glasses of Rioja and they sat in the living room sipping wine, talking, relaxing and laughing.

"You know Isabelle, I like living together—not just from a relationship standpoint, but also because I didn't like being alone all of the time."

"Yes. Being alone all the time is difficult. But I'd rather be alone than be with someone who didn't make me feel comfortable. And Sam, I am comfortable living with you."

For a while, nothing was said. Then Sam asked, "Have you had ever thought much about getting married?"

Isabelle laughed softly. "What little girl doesn't imagine she will be married someday. Yes. I dreamed I'd get married, that it would be by a priest—in a church. I even fantasized about having a couple of kids someday. Your father died before you were born. My mother died when I was a newborn. Neither of us had siblings. I last saw my father when I was thirteen—he died when I was fifteen. My fantasy was—it is—that I someday will have some sort of normal family."

They were silent for a few minutes, then Isabelle turned to Sam and asked, "How about you? Have you ever thought about getting married?"

This time it was Sam who took some time before responding. "Lately, I have been thinking a lot about my childhood—about my life. I was a loner, Issa. My mom was a nice person, but the restaurant took most of her time and energy. I mean I know I was important to her. But even with my grandparents living with us, it was never much of a family."

Sam took a sip of Rioja, savored it, then took a deep breath and said, "I haven't been alone recently. When that guy—that Wozniak—threatened your safety, Issa, it made me angry—really angry. It hit me how important you are to me. I know we haven't known one another long. But I've been happier during these last two months than, well, than I ever have been."

Again, there was a long silence. Then Isabelle asked, "Are you asking me to marry you?"

Sam nodded.

Isabelle gave a mischievous smile. "Well. Aren't you supposed to get down on a knee or something—and give me a ring?"

"I'll be back in a moment."

Sam went up to their bedroom, opened the bottom drawer of his dresser and pulled out a memory box. When Sam wanted to keep something small and special for the future, he would put it in that box. Each item had a special story behind it. When Sam opened his memory box and saw the ring, a chill ran through him.

In a back corner of the memory box, he found what he was looking for. When his grandparents had married, they didn't have more than a few dollars. Sam's grandpa told Sam they purchased simple silver bands for their wedding. But by 1925, they owned a home and Lucky's had become a successful diner. For their tenth anniversary, Sam's grandpa had surprised his grandma with a platinum art deco diamond ring. His mom inherited the ring when Sam's grandma died. When his mom passed, it went to Sam who put the ring away in his memory box. He had not looked at it since that day.

Sam took the ring out of its box. This was what that glittering ring was for. He returned downstairs to Isabelle and got down on one knee in front of her. Then he opened his hand, showed her the ring and said, "Will this do the trick?"

A slightly shocked Isabelle smiled. She asked, "Aren't you supposed to—uh—put it on my finger or something?"

Sam slowly, and awkwardly, put the ring on her finger. It fit. Then he said, "Will you marry me?"

Isabelle bit her bottom lip. She did not look at Sam. Instead, she quietly viewed the ring on her finger. Sam saw the intense emotion on her face—and then the tears. A moment later Isabelle began to weep, her body shaking as she buried her face in her hands. Then Isabelle stood up and went to the bathroom. She returned a few minutes later— red-eyed, but composed.

"Just to clarify," she said. "That was a *yes*."

*****

When Sam awoke the following morning, Isabelle was already up. As he walked down the stairs, he smelled the fragrances of coffee and freshly baked cinnamon rolls. Sam was greeted in the kitchen with a big kiss.

They ate hot buttered cinnamon rolls and drank fresh rich coffee in silence. Isabelle kept holding her hand up— looking at her ring—and smiling.

"Where did you get this beautiful ring?" she finally asked. "It is very pretty. The setting is incredible—and the cut of the diamond—well, it is totally amazing."

She listened as Sam told the story of the ring. He finished up with, "When do you think we should get married? I have never given much thought to a wedding ceremony. I'm clueless."

"I always wanted to get married in a church, Sam. But it doesn't have to be. I dreamed that it would be a big occasion. But it doesn't need to be. The only person who needs to be there, other than me, is you. I am just happy to be marrying you."

Sam suggested calling Father Tom to ask for advice. Isabelle had never met Father Tom, but she encouraged the call. Sam had spoken a lot about Tom and she understood that Father Tom was about as close to family as anyone in Sam's life.

Sam and Tom spent about a half hour on the phone. After the call, Sam returned to the kitchen where Isabelle was finishing cleaning up the mess after making the cinnamon rolls. "Father Tom was happy to hear from me, happy I was in love. He wants to meet you, Issa. He was pleased we want to include him in the ceremony and suggested we stop by and chat with him this morning."

Isabelle's face flushed. "You know Sam, that was the first time I've ever heard you use the word *love*."

*****

Father Tom welcomed them with cups of coffee and congratulations. The meeting lasted about an hour and a half. Tom listened with a warm smile on his face while Sam told him how he and Isabelle had met. Then Isabelle told Father Tom about her life.

"Sam," Tom said when they finished, "you have always had more than just a touch of loneliness. I see none of that in you today. I am so happy for both of you. Together, you seem to have found something special. Ordinarily, I'd suggest you meet with me for a few months—get counseling about what marriage means. But since you are already living together, I think I should forgo that step in the process. When would you like to get married?"

Sam and Isabelle looked at one another waiting for the other to respond.

Finally, Sam said, "We want to be married in the church—if we can. But we are not planning on having a lot of guests." He paused, looked at Isabelle, and added, "I prefer to get married as soon as we can. What do you think, Isabelle?"

Isabelle just said "Yes, Father. We should move ahead."

Father Tom took over. "Well, I have nothing planned for Saturday morning or Saturday afternoon. I could perform the marriage sacrament for you then. You will need a couple of witnesses and you'll have to get your marriage license today or tomorrow. But if that works for you, we may have a plan."

Isabelle said nothing. Tears were flowing down her cheeks again.

Father Tom asked, "Is there anything wrong?

Sam replied, "No Father. I'm just starting to get to understand her. I believe her tears mean she is happy with your plan. We will be here on Saturday morning. Isabelle has two good friends who will be visiting this weekend. We'll invite them as our witnesses. And thank you, Father Tom. You are making—well, you continually make—a great difference in my life—and now in both of our lives."

*****

On their way home, Sam and Isabelle stopped at the Minneapolis City Hall and purchased a marriage license. When they got home, Isabelle called Luis and Rosaline to inform them of the plan. Rosaline answered the phone. Sam was nervous and left the room and let Isabelle update her friend.

Afterwards, he asked Isabelle how it went. "It went great. Rosie is happy for me. But she made a couple of small changes in our plans. She and Luis will arrive on Thursday instead of Friday. Her gift to me will be a wedding dress. She told me that when she and Luis get here on Thursday, she will call a few of my friends and invite them to our wedding. She absolutely insisted that on Saturday evening, she and Luis host a little party to celebrate our marriage. She suggested we have the party here, at our home. Rosie was not to be denied on any of these changes to our wedding plans. So, I just had to say *yes*—for both of us."

After saying that, Isabelle smiled at him, then went into the kitchen. Moments later, Sam was pleased to hear her singing the Dean Martin song, *That's Amore*. He remembered his grandfather singing that song to his grandmother. He had always loved the chorus.

When you walk in a dream
But you know, you're not dreaming, signore
Scusa mi, but you see
Back in old Napoli, that's amore.

14. Getting Together

Wednesday was a long day that started out with Sam phoning Rosaline's father. Hector Diaz didn't seem at all surprised that Fidelia was missing or that Sam was contacting him regarding her disappearance. He agreed to meet with Sam on Monday morning, May sixteenth.

It was also the day that Sam and Isabelle went shopping for wedding bands. Based on the labeling of the ring box, Sam knew his grandfather had purchased his grandmother's ring—Isabelle's engagement ring—at Bergstrom Jewelers. Sam and Isabelle decided it would be fun to buy their wedding rings at that same store.

After returning home with their new rings, Isabelle was beaming. She said, "My new wedding band goes perfectly with your grandma's ring. I love art deco! And in case you hadn't noticed, Sam, you have made your fiancée happy."

Sam grinned. This was the first time Isabelle had used the term *fiancée*. It sounded good.

*****

That evening and the following morning, Isabelle gave the house a thorough cleaning. She said, "Samuel, this is my house now too. I don't want Rosa and Luis thinking we live like pigs."

She vacuumed, dusted, cleaned the bathrooms, straightened up throughout the house and then went out to purchase a bouquet of red and yellow tulips for the dining room table. Upon returning, she opened all of the house's windows and doors to, as she put it, *refresh the air*. It was still cool outside. Sam considered complaining, but decided that for this week, discretion would definitely be the better part of valor. He put on a warm sweater, made a cup of tea with rum and honey and relaxed.

*****

Luis and Rosaline arrived in the early afternoon. Rosaline and Isabelle immediately went upstairs to plan the wedding. The men folk stayed downstairs and drank Hamm's beer. Luis said, "Rosaline is excited about planning the wedding and told me in no uncertain terms not to interfere. She and Isabelle are going to have a good time and we should not interfere with them in any way! I have not seen Rosie this animated since she planned our wedding."

An hour later, two giggling Cuban-American women headed out of the house on their way to purchase Isabelle's wedding dress. Sam went to the kitchen and returned with a couple more cans of beer. Then Luis finished lamenting the problems with the Chicago Cubs. He concluded by saying, "I am afraid that this bunch of over-the-hill ballplayers is going to be even worse than last year's."

The conversation moved into Sam's search for Fidelia. Luis handed Sam the signed letter from Fidel Castro authorizing Sam's visit and a clearly worded letter from a Cuban governmental official that would serve as Sam and Isabelle's Cuban visas. The letters hopefully would minimize the bureaucratic challenges Sam and Isabelle would face should they end up traveling to Cuba.

Sam told Luis about his meeting with Wozniak and his silent partner.

Luis gave Sam a serious look. "I like the way you handled it. Somebody is getting awfully nervous with your investigation and it's gotta involve Giarri. I worry what else they might try."

Then Luis took a big swig of beer and turned back to Sam. "Rosie and I have another big concern. If you locate Fidelia—say you find her in Miami—how are you going to protect her? This isn't a small issue, Sam. If Fidelia was pressured into leaving by Giarri or anyone else, she might be in danger if she tries to leave. And, if she is in hiding, finding her could blow her cover. She'll be vulnerable. It worries us a lot."

Sam was quiet for a moment. Then he simply said, "I've worried about that as well."

The two men spent the better part of an hour discussing how, if Sam were to find Fidelia, he would keep her safe until she was returned to Luis and Rosaline.

*****

The phone rang. Sam answered. It was Rosaline.

"Isabelle and I were successful in our wedding dress hunt. And she found a lovely pair of shoes! Would you tell Luis that the clothing selection at Donaldson's is simply marvelous? Isabelle and I were able to find an outfit for me—a wonderful Valentino Garavani dress and a color coordinated pair of Dominic Romano Pumps. The dress and shoes will go beautifully with my wide-brimmed hat—the Saint Laurent Luis likes so much. He will absolutely adore them!"

Isabelle got on the phone. "You'll just love my dress, Sam. It is the most beautiful shade of yellow. Oh, I am so happy! And now, Rosa and I are now going to have our own small bachelorette party at Murrays'—just the two of us—martinis and maybe a filet mignon."

"Have a great time."

Sam knew Murrays' Restaurant well. His grandparents—friends of the Murrays—had taken him there several times. Isabelle and Rosaline would have a ball.

But now, Sam and Luis were also free. They could have a bachelor party! Sam pulled two man-sized *Swanson's* fried chicken TV dinners out of the freezer. The chicken legs would go well washed down with a six-pack of Hamm's. And timing is everything. The Minnesota Twins were playing the Yankees that evening—and it was televised. What luck!

A couple of hours later, they sat down in front of the TV with their dinners. Sam turned down the TV volume and instead listened to Luis' commentary. It would be far more informative than the TV's normal play-by-play guys.

Camilo Pascual was pitching for the Twins that evening—and he struggled. Luis pointed out that Pascual's curve ball just wasn't cutting as sharply as it had in the past. Pascual was taken out of the game in the sixth inning for a pinch hitter.

During one commercial, Luis and Sam got into a discussion of who had been the best baseball player of their generation, Mickey Mantle or Willie Mays. Sam argued for Mantle. "I've just seen 'The Mick', with his heroic bat, glove and arm, defeat the Twins too often."

Luis disagreed. "It's true that as a young ballplayer, Mantle showed more potential than Mays. But his knees have given out, Sam. He just isn't the same ballplayer he was only a few years ago. But the 'Say Hey Kid'—he continues to play at the same stellar level."

Then Luis added an insight that Sam couldn't have had. "Mays was the toughest batter I ever faced, Sam. I used to dread pitching against the Giants. I knew Willie was going to feast on my pitching. That man doesn't have a weakness.

High, low, inside or outside; fastball, curve or change-up, I had no insight into how to get him out."

The Mickey Mantle they saw that evening was still a good player. But Sam had to agree he wasn't the dominant athlete he had once been. In the top of the ninth with two outs, Bobby Richardson got a single. Mantle came to the plate representing the winning run. Sam was nervous. In the past, Mantle had regularly beaten the Twins in similar situations. However, the baseball gods smiled on the Twins that night. Mickey Mantle took a third strike looking. In fact, Mantle didn't have a hit in the game.

Luis gave Sam his due. "If this had been 1962, I don't care who was pitching, Mantle would have hit it out of the park in the ninth. The Yanks would have won. But tonight, there is no joy in Mudville. Mighty Mantle has struck out."

The Twins won the game 4-3. Pascual was the winning pitcher and Sam's bachelor party had turned into a memorable success.

*****

Friday was a blur. Rosaline was on the phone much of the day telling friends about the wedding and catching up on local Cuban-American community gossip. Isabelle also spent time on the phone updating friends. Both women were excited about the evening wedding reception and party at Sam and Isabelle's home.

Sam and Luis tried to keep a low profile, hoping to avoid being assigned to any wedding preparatory task. But they also discussed strategies that Sam might employ in his search for Fidelia—if he found her in Miami or in Havana. Luis knew both cities well and also suggested hotels and good restaurants for each city.

That afternoon, Sam asked Rosaline if there were other relatives or friends he should try to meet with while in Miami. At first, Rosaline couldn't think of anyone other than her father. Then she remembered her father's neighbor, a woman who had been sympathetic to her situation when Tony Giarri had been pushing his marriage proposal.

"She is not Cuban. Her name is Betty She lived just a couple of doors down the street from my father. When I met her—almost ten years ago, Betty had already been in her house for twenty years. While I haven't heard from her since I left Miami, if she's still alive, I bet she lives there. And if you do see her, Sam, give her my love. She's a good soul and can definitely be trusted!"

****

Rosaline and Luis hosted Sam and Isabelle for dinner that evening at the restaurant of their choice. Without a moment's hesitation, Isabelle suggested the Waikiki Room. Sam eagerly seconded that proposal.

The meal was every bit as delicious as had been their first meal at that restaurant. Toasts over mai tais for a good life and many healthy babies were offered by Luis and Rosaline. That evening, Sam chose not to have a second Mai tai. He had already been educated on how generous the Nicollet was with rum in the drinks.

Toward the end of the meal, two Hawaiian singers serenaded their table accompanied by their ukuleles. They sang the *Hawaiian Wedding Song*.

This is the moment
Of sweet Aloha
I will love you longer than forever
Promise me that you will leave me never

Of course, the gentle music and sweet sentiment soon had tears in Isabelle's eyes. But on this night, Sam also shed tears. He wiped them away in a casual manner so as to not allow the others to know he was crying. Isabelle, Rosaline and Luis were respectful enough to not let on that they had each seen Sam's attempt to hide his tears.

*****

Saturday, Sam and Luis arrived at Our Lady of Lourdes Catholic Church at one o'clock in the afternoon. Isabelle and Rosaline had not yet arrived. Sam was wearing his still almost new charcoal grey pin striped suit and French cuffed shirt. He wore his grandfather's gold cuff links again and this time he had the yellow tie that Isabelle and Rosaline had purchased for him during their Thursday shopping trip.

Sam had anticipated being greeted at the church by Father Tom and maybe a couple of Rosaline and Isabelle's friends. When he arrived, however, he was surprised to see more than a dozen people. By the time Rosaline and Isabelle got to the church, the number of well-wishers had swelled to over thirty. The word had been put out and the Cuban-American community had responded.

When Rosaline and Isabelle arrived, they were not alone. Isabelle's cousin Christina had flown in from New York. When Sam expressed surprise that she had been able to join them on such short notice, she responded in English, with her thick Cuban accent, "What you think, Sam? I was about to miss this festivity? Issa needs family here—to give her away to the groom! You think I don't love my Issa?"

Isabelle was grinning from ear to ear as she walked down the aisle escorted by Christina who was beaming with joy. Sam did not see Isabelle's dress until the processional. Rosaline had described the dress as a "yellow and white crepe double strapped Vicky Vaughn party dress with a yellow pillbox hat that had a birdcage veil." Sam had had no idea what that meant. But as he watched her walk with Christina to the forefront of the church, he realized how lucky he was.

The ceremony was brief and moving. When Sam kissed his new wife, the congregation that was now over forty people, applauded. All of the attendees were invited to Sam and Isabelle's house for the reception that evening. Guests were encouraged to bring their favorite Cuban dish and perhaps a bottle of their favorite drink.

*****

That evening, the house was packed. Sam was especially pleased to see Father Tom had joined the celebration. The dining room table was covered with a wide array of Cuban dishes. There were corn tamales; yucca topped with garlic, red onions and chicken scallions; deep fried pork; empanadas; ropa vieja; plantain chips; flan; and another half dozen dishes with which Sam wasn't familiar. The counter in the kitchen had been set aside for beverages and was packed with drinks for every taste.

At about seven o'clock, five Minnesota Twins showed up with their wives or girlfriends. The Twins had just completed a 5-1 home game victory over the Boston Red Sox. The group of ballplayers included Twin stars Camilo Pascual, Harmon Killebrew and Tony Oliva. Two Boston Red Sox players also joined the party. One of them was Jose Tartabull, Luis' childhood friend. And Tartabull had brought along Carl Yastrzemski. It was like an All-star Game in Sam's living room! Carl Yastrzemski, Camilo Pascual, Harmon Killebrew and Tony Oliva—all in his home—all celebrating his marriage to Isabelle. Oh, what a party!

*****

About eight o'clock, the guests began to chant "Música, Música, Música, Música!" Sam quickly learned that they didn't want to hear just any music. They wanted to hear his wife sing. Until that moment, Sam hadn't understood how much Isabelle's singing was cherished by the Cuban-American community.

Isabelle brought down both her guitars and sat tuning them for a couple of minutes. Then, everyone applauded and she began to sing some of the ballads Sam had already come to appreciate. Someone picked up her other guitar and began to accompany her. Soon Sam's guitar was taken from its stand in the corner of the living room and was passed to Minnesota Twins shortstop Zoilo Versalles who had just arrived at the party. Many of the guests joined in on the chorus as Isabelle sang *Chan Chan, Guantanamera, Choco's Guajira* and other Cuban classics.

Isabelle announced she had one more song she'd sing before turning her guitar over to someone else. "It is time for me to enjoy my wedding celebration. I thank you all for coming. But after this song, I will rely on my much loved friends for Música. I close out with a moving American song—Johnny Mathis' *It's not for me to say.*"

She sang it soulfully, slowly, putting extra emphasis on the last verse.

"Perhaps the glow of love will grow
With every passing day
Or we may never meet again
But then it's not for me to say."

There was silence in the room after Isabelle finished singing. She put down her guitar and walked over to Sam. He took her hand and the two of them walked out the front door to sit down together on the porch steps. They said nothing to one another; just enjoyed seeing the stars in the clear nighttime sky and breathing the fresh air of the warm spring evening.

*****

But the music was just starting. Guitars were passed from one person to another and a variety of guests took their turns leading in the singing of traditional songs. Someone brought in a couple of batá drums. The music turned from ballads to the traditional dance music of son and cha cha. Furniture was moved to the outer edges of the living room and Sam was given another wonderful demonstration of Cuban dance.

Then it was Isabelle and Sam dancing in the center of the room. Sam displayed a few of his more challenging *cha cha* moves to the raucous laughter and applause of his guests. Party-goers stood around the dancing newlyweds singing and clapping to the beat of the batá drums.

The ballplayers and their wives left the party before eleven. There would be another ballgame the following day. But the party did not break up for several hours. The music slowly got softer. Gradually, one couple after another left the party. When Sam and Isabelle turned in at 1:30 in the morning, there were still more than a dozen people dancing, laughing and singing.

*****

The following morning, Sam and Isabelle slept in. When they awoke at eleven, all of their guests were gone. The dishes had been washed and the living room furniture moved back into position. And when Sam looked, he found that the refrigerator was packed with many wonderful leftovers. It had been a fabulous party.

15. Miami

Sam and Isabelle decided that in addition to moving his investigation forward, the trip to Miami would serve as their honeymoon. After arriving in Miami on the following Friday afternoon, they went directly to Hertz's airport rental office where Sam collected the keys to a 1966 Ford Thunderbird convertible. Thunderbird had been the only other model Sam had considered before he purchased Mr. Mustang. But a stripped-down T-Bird cost twice as much as Mr. Mustang.

However, renting a Thunderbird convertible in Miami for five days while being reimbursed for the cost was just too good an opportunity to pass up. They settled themselves into the white leather bucket seats of the maroon T-Bird. with a powerful V-8 engine and smooth automatic transmission. As Sam drove away from Miami's International Airport, he put the pedal to the metal, turning briefly to grin at Isabelle. Driving this little baby around Miami was going to be a lot of fun.

*****

Two hours later, Sam and Isabelle arrived at the National Hotel on Miami Beach. As they walked into the hotel's marble floored lobby and saw its stylish furniture and fixtures, Sam turned to Isabelle and said, "Ain't this the life?"

After exploring the hotel and viewing its narrow two-hundred-foot-long pool, Sam and Isabelle walked down Ocean Drive in search of dinner. They passed art deco hotels, high-end designer clothing stores, sidewalk cafes and bars that throbbed with the beat of Latin music. Eventually they reached a sidewalk café Luis had recommended and were seated under an umbrella. Their waiter suggested mango rum punch drinks and the restaurant's dinner special—Cuban roast pork with garlic mashed yucca, Creole pepper salad and black beans. They took the waiter's advice and didn't regret it. Sam and Isabelle finished their meal by sharing a piece of *tres leches* cake.

During their walk back to the National Hotel, Isabelle offered a non-stop commentary on the shops, hotels and cafés they passed. "Look at that hotel's beautiful neon lights. Don't you love the pastels of South Beach architecture? And it feels so good to hear the Latin music coming out of each bar we pass."

Just before reaching their hotel, she turned to Sam and said, "Let's walk in the water." They took off their shoes and socks, and walked through the shallow surf enjoying the warm breeze and the sound of waves rolling onto the shore.

It really did feel like a honeymoon.

****

The next morning, they woke up refreshed and ready to enjoy Miami Beach. Isabelle put on green pedal pushers, a white t-shirt and a bright yellow head scarf. Sam said, "You look like an orchid in bloom."

Their plan for Saturday had been to take it easy and enjoy South Beach. Isabelle said she just wanted to rest by the pool. But Sam told her he wanted to drive by Rosaline's father's home that morning. "I want to be confident I can find his place before going to meet with him on Monday. I also need to identify the home of Rosaline's friend Betty. It might even make sense to visit with her today."

Isabelle hesitated, then agreed to go along. That morning, they drank coffee and ate croissants with strawberry jam in the hotel dining room while Sam studied a street map of Miami, marking the location of Hector Diaz's home. Sam looked up at his wife and asked her for the address of her uncle's home.

Isabelle gave him the address. "But I do not want to see or speak with Uncle under any circumstances."

Sam turned the map over to look at a much less detailed map entitled *Greater Metropolitan Miami*. There was Hallandale Beach—the site of the mystery address he'd found in the journal in Fidelia's room. The suburban city was about twenty miles north of their hotel. Sam had no idea what they would find, but he decided they should drive up there on Sunday morning to check out the address.

*****

An hour later, Isabelle and Sam were cruising through the Buena Vista neighborhood of Miami. Isabelle, who was energized by seeing the stylish homes and gardens gave a running commentary on the area's colorful vegetation and architectural influences. She compared many things they saw to sites she remembered in Havana.

"Sam—you see all these homes with red tiled roofing. The roofing material is called *barrel clay tiles*. And those homes with textured stucco walls painted soft pastel colors—their architecture style is called *Mediterranean Revival*. The houses we went past a little while ago—you know, the ones with the flat roofs that look like scaled down versions of old Spanish missions—they are *Mission Revival*. And oh my God, Sam—look at all of the colorful bougainvillea, the hibiscus, and other flowering bushes— and see that—all of those palm trees are of different ages, sizes and shapes—how beautiful! Oh Sam, this is truly fabulous."

They were getting close to the Buena Vista neighborhood where Rosaline's father lived. The landscaping around many of the homes was overgrown, but Sam was able to imagine how beautiful it had been in its day.

As the Thunderbird turned down an avenue lined with tall palms, Sam said, "Rosaline's father lives around here." He paused and added, "In fact, I think that one there is Betty's—and down there—see—that must be Hector Diaz's home."

Both houses were Mission Revival. Betty's was the smallest house on the block. Its blue paint had faded, its stucco cracked and its picket fence had fallen into serious disrepair. Diaz's home was the largest on the block. But it looked as worn-out as Betty's and all of the others.

Sam drove around the block and parked the car at the far end of the street. He and Isabelle walked up to the faded blue home to check if Betty still lived there and find out if she would be willing to speak with them. As they approached the house, Sam saw an older woman sitting in the living room looking out at them. After he knocked on the screen door, the woman, a grey-haired Black woman in a plaid shirt dress came to the door.

"Can I help you?" she asked.

"Yes, you can—if you're Betty." Sam responded.

She nodded, but looked quite apprehensive. "Yes. I am Betty."

"My name is Sam. This is my wife, Isabelle. We're friends of Rosaline Garcia—Hector Diaz's daughter. Rosaline has fond memories of you from when she lived here. When Rosaline heard we were coming to Miami, she asked if we could stop by and pass her greetings on to you. So, here we are."

Betty relaxed and smiled warmly. "Rosie? How is she doing?"

"She is doing well. She lives in Chicago. Her husband is a former major league baseball pitcher."

At that point, Betty opened up to a big smile and she said, "How nice. I liked that girl. She was always so sweet—so different from that dried up goat of a father of hers. She would stop by my house. We would visit. She was always so polite; never had a mean thing to say about anyone or anything. And how is her little baby? I haven't seen either of them since they moved up north. That little girl—Fidelia I think her name was—she was always such an angel—spitting image of her mother."

Sam jumped on the opportunity. "Fidelia still is the spitting image of her mom. But there is a problem. Fidelia has gone missing. Rosaline doesn't know if she ran way or has run into foul play. That is why I am going to speak with Hector Diaz on Monday—to find out if he can help locate Fidelia. And Rosaline is—uhm—how shall I say this—concerned that Hector might—uh—be somehow involved in Fidelia's disappearance. In that context, I was wondering if maybe you could give us some help. Have you noticed anything strange—I mean Hector having any unusual visitors—in the past couple of months?"

At first, Betty did not respond to the question. Instead, she offered Sam and Isabelle tea. They declined. Then, Betty returned to Sam's question. "Hector doesn't mix much with his neighbors—especially not with an old Black lady like me. He is just too damn high and mighty for that!"

Betty looked at Sam, then at Isabelle, maybe sizing them up regarding whether she could trust them. Then she said, "I don't pay no attention to other people's business. But

I also don't have a whole lot that I need to do. So, I often sit here—in my living room— minding my own business— listening to the radio—sipping my tea. Sometimes, I take a look-see out the window. I notice stuff. A few days ago, Hector had a visit from three white men in a big black shiny automobile. It was driven by a young kid."

"Can you describe Hector's visitors?"

"One of them was an old guy in a baggy white short-sleeved shirt. You could see the others treated him like he was the big shot. Another one was a tall guy in a grey suit, sun glasses. He had a brown hat and looked almost like a business man—but I wouldn't buy anything from any business he owned. Wouldn't trust him at all. The third guy had a black sport shirt. He was tall, stocky, built like an ape. I wouldn't want to get that fellow mad at me. The young kid driving the car was in jeans and a t-shirt. He looked like he might've been Cuban. I don't remember more about them than that."

Then Betty smiled and said, "But I do want to hear more about Rosaline. She was such a dear. Tell me about her. Is he nice—I mean the fellow she married? Is she happy?" Then she paused and added, "But what you said about Rosaline's little darling—that concerns me a whole lot."

Isabelle answered a series of questions Betty had about Rosaline. Sam and Isabelle ended up staying another fifteen minutes. When they left, Sam wrote Hotel National on the back of his business card and gave it to Betty—in case she thought of anything else.

As they walked away, Isabelle said to Sam, "Rosaline was right. Betty is a nice lady."

Sam and Isabelle returned to the Thunderbird. The sun had become intense. Isabelle was already wearing an orange wide-brimmed sun hat. Sam put on his Minnesota Twin's baseball cap and dropped the convertible's top. They each put on Ray-Ban sunglasses.

Sam turned to Isabelle. "Do you want to go by any of your old haunts on the way back to the hotel? Or maybe, do you want to reconsider and visit your uncle?"

"No, Sam. My memories of Miami are just too painful. Uncle never liked Papa and he always spoke about my mother as if she had wasted her life by marrying Papa. Uncle would say, *your mom could have married an attractive or successful man. Instead, she ended up choosing a loser.* Uncle took his resentment out on me. He once said, *If your mother hadn't gotten pregnant with you, she would never have married your father. Her life might have become something better than the failure it turned into.*"

Isabelle just looked out, away from Sam. Sam looked at her and did not start the car. Then she spoke again. "When I think back to high school, Sam—how hard it was being in the United States, missing my Papa so much—waiting for him to send for me—then finding out...finding out...."

Isabelle stopped speaking. She collected herself. "Uncle married an American woman with money. She was one mean bitch. She seemed to resent me a lot. They had two kids—a boy and a girl—both a lot younger than me. I used to have to babysit those spoiled little monsters. I have no love for them. I don't want to ever see Uncle again. While I lived here, with the exception of Christina, my father's niece, there were no family or friends in Miami who cared about me—who I care to remember."

Isabelle looked out across the street without saying anything for a couple of minutes. Then she vented a large sigh and said, "I am sorry for whining, Sam. Those years were so awful. I do everything I can just to try to forget them. I know you're curious to see where I lived. Go ahead. Drive by the place."

*****

Isabelle gave Sam directions to her uncle's home in Coral Gables. As they drove into the development in which the home was located, Sam quickly understood where Isabelle had learned about the *Mediterranean Revival* home style. All of the houses in her uncle's neighborhood met all of the criteria Isabelle had used in describing that style. But they were also larger, better landscaped and in better condition than any home Sam and Isabelle had passed in the Buena Vista neighborhood.

They drove past her uncle's house. Its lot had to be half an acre. There was a tall iron bar fence surrounding the property. A four-foot hedge grew inside of that fence. Gates to the driveway hung off of tall stone gateposts and a cobblestone driveway led up to the house. The white two-story home had green awnings and was landscaped with flowering bushes and tall palms. A red Porsche convertible and a white Jaguar sedan were parked in the driveway. Sam caught a glimpse of a swimming pool in the backyard. Isabelle's uncle obviously had money.

Isabelle said, "That's Uncle's Porsche. I used to have to wash the damned thing."

Isabelle grimaced, then looked down and said to Sam, "That was Uncle—walking by the pool. Can we just get out of here, Sam? Seeing all of this—it just brings back so many hurtful memories."

Sam felt badly he had suggested going by the home. He turned north and headed back to the hotel. They stopped for a hamburger and fries at a small stand Isabelle remembered. They ate their burgers and fries in silence. The lunch did not reduce Isabelle's sadness.

The couple spent the rest of the afternoon relaxing by the hotel pool. Dinner was at a nearby seafood restaurant. Isabelle had a Shrimp Louis salad; Sam, a Jamaican seafood soup. They shared a piece of key lime pie for dessert. The food was good, but the memory of driving by Isabelle's uncle's home had left a damper on the day.

*****

Sunday morning, they ordered breakfast from room service—coffee, fresh fruit and muffins. They dressed in summer casuals and headed down to the T-Bird, their plan being to drive by the address Sam had found in Fidelia's notebook.

Hallandale Beach was difficult to navigate because the development had been built on a series of canals—each street became a dead end. They wandered through the suburban city for a while before finding Hibiscus Drive; then headed down the street to the address which turned out to be a residence.

Its tan cobblestone driveway led to an upscale mid-century modern single-story house surrounded by tall palms. As Sam slowly drove by the home, he was taken aback. A young man was polishing a late model black Lincoln Continental Coupe in the driveway. He was almost certainly the clean-shaven tough guy who, with a partner, had pummeled Sam in Little Italy. A hundred yards down the street, Hibiscus Drive ended at a canal. Sam stopped the car and informed Isabelle who it was they had just seen.

"We have to drive by that address again—just to get out of here. You can check out the house, the car and the jerk in

198

the front yard. But be careful. Don't look too obvious. Given my prior meeting with him, I don't want to test my luck."

Sam raised the top of the T-Bird, pulled his baseball hat down further over his forehead and headed back on Hibiscus Drive. As they passed the house, the black Lincoln and the tough guy, Sam kept looking straight ahead.

A short while later, Sam drove into a Phillips 66 service station. The T-Bird's gas tank was almost full, but Sam wanted to learn whatever he could about whoever lived in that house. A teenage gas station attendant came out to the car. He was wearing a dirty white t-shirt, worn blue jeans and a bright blue baseball hat with a green and orange Florida Gators logo.

The teenager asked, "Fill her up mister?"

Sam said, "I don't need gas. But could you check the car's oil?"

Sam held out a dollar bill. The kid gave a big grin and said, "Yes sir!"

Sam had decided that in a small town like Hallandale Beach, a home owner with a Lincoln Continental might turn out to be a well-known big shot. A couple of casual questions might be productive.

After the kid had checked the oil and cleaned the windshield, Sam said, "I'm looking for a friend who lives on Hibiscus Drive. He has a black Lincoln Continental Coupe— you know—a big shiny car with suicide doors. Do you know where Hibiscus Drive is?"

The kid gave a big grin and said, "Sure do. You must mean Mr. Lansky. Boy is that car ever a mean machine! I can tell you how to get there."

He proceeded to give Sam directions.

Meyer Lansky! Sam kept a poker face, but was stunned. He thanked the kid and drove off—back to the hotel—and, in a sense, back to the drawing board.

As they rode back to the hotel, Isabelle asked, "Who is this Meyer Lansky?"

"He is a big-time gangster—I mean really famous—high up in the mob—very dangerous. I didn't even know Lansky was still alive until Rosaline mentioned that Giarri worked for Lansky when Giarri was trying to marry her."

*****

Monday morning, after a light breakfast, Isabelle went to catch some sun by the pool. Sam got into the T-Bird and headed out, by himself, to meet with Hector Diaz. It was nine-thirty when Sam rang Diaz's doorbell. A short thin man with wire rimmed glasses and thinning combed back hair came to the door. His short-sleeved white shirt and black bowtie seemed like an odd way to dress on a hot day.

Diaz introduced himself, shook Sam's hand and invited him into his home. He led Sam into a living room that looked like it might have been in style ten years before. But fashions change and the lime-green shag carpet and 1950s furniture seemed shabby. Diaz suggested they sit on the couch which had a coffee table in front of it. On the table was a porcelain blue-flowered coffee pot, two matching cups and saucers and a cream and sugar set. A blue-flowered plate which held several small stacks of Oreo cookies completed the arrangement.

Sam started the conversation. "Thanks for meeting with me, Mr. Diaz."

"Please call me Hector. I guess my daughter must have told you horrible things about me."

Hector carefully poured a cup of coffee for Sam, then put two Oreos, one on top of the other, on a saucer beside the cup.

"No. Actually, Rosaline said very little about you. She just wants to find her daughter. She thought perhaps Fidelia might have contacted you or someone you know in Miami."

Hector's face relaxed. "I would be glad to offer any help I can. But I haven't heard anything from Fidelia. Can you share—uhm—any information about Fidelia's disappearance—I mean what you have learned? It might—uh—help me—uhm—."

Hector didn't finish his thought. Sam thought this was starting out a lot like the meeting with Tony Giarri—the *I don't know anything but could you tell me everything you know* approach. He decided he would have to do some serious fishing if he wanted land anything from this guy. Sam asked how Hector had learned about Fidelia's disappearance. Hector sincerely explained that the first he had heard of it was when Sam called to set up the meeting.

Sam thought about asking if Hector had been in touch with Tony Giarri. But he could almost imagine Hector's response of, *Why no. I haven't heard from Mr. Giarri in years. I didn't know you knew him? How is Mr. Giarri doing?*

So, Sam decided to take a more indirect approach—to cast his line upstream, so-to-speak. "Hector—when Mr. Giarri and Mr. Lansky visited you recently, did they say anything about Fidelia's disappearance."

This visibly jarred Diaz. He was probably trying to remember if he had been told by Giarri or Lansky that Sam knew about their meeting. Diaz took what he must have thought was a very cunning and low-key approach. "Why no. I don't recall that being mentioned."

Diaz was obviously too smart to be tricked into sharing anything that he shouldn't share.

Sam jerked the fishline a little bit. "How well do you know Mr. Lansky?"

Hector began to look uncomfortable. "I've met him once or twice over the years. They just stopped by—uh—to visit—uhm—because they were in the neighborhood."

Sam decided he needed to give the fish a little more line before setting the hook. "Hector. One of the theories we have is that all of this relates to the rumors that Rosaline had had an affair with Fidel Castro—and that Fidel was the father of Fidelia. Do you think that rumor could be a factor?"

Hector looked lost with the directness of the question. "I don't know Sam—that rumor has always been around—but I have no idea. Do you think it could be the issue? Might Castro be involved in this? I mean, I wouldn't put anything beyond Fidel Castro."

Sam was still working the fish. "I don't know why Castro would be involved. It was a shame that rumor ever started. As you know, Hector, logistically it just couldn't be the case."

Hector found Sam's response interesting. Sam could see he wanted to ask why it couldn't be the case—what the *logistics* were. But Hector held back from asking.

Then, Sam put his cup down and gave Hector his card. "Well thank you and if anything comes up, would you give me call?"

Hector warmly agreed and said, "You will tell me if you find any news of Fidelia. I'm worried about my granddaughter."

As Hector led Sam to the door, Sam jerked the line and set the hook. "Oh by the way, the third guy who came to your house with Lansky and Giarri—I forget his name—did he leave his hat here?"

Hector bit. "Oh no. I am certain Mr. Hunt didn't leave his hat here. I would have found it."

As Hector finished saying that, looked uneasy, perhaps realizing he might have let something slip. But by then, Sam and Hector were shaking hands at the door; Sam thanking Hector and telling him what a nice home he had; and Hector returning the warm goodbye while wishing Sam a safe journey back to Minnesota.

*****

Sam decided there was no upside in trying to approach Meyer Lansky. Such a meeting would not be one where Sam would come out on top. Lansky—or more precisely his henchmen—had already demonstrated no bashfulness in the use of violence and Sam didn't want to get beaten up again.

On the drive back to the hotel, Sam reviewed what he had put together in the last few days.

- It seemed that a Mr. Hunt was Agent Wozniak—Sam needed to find out who the hell Hunt was.
- The address in Fidelia's room belonged to the gangster boss Meyer Lansky.
- The Cubans who beat Sam up in New York were working for Lansky—and Lansky was *the Old Guy*.
- It was clear that Giarri, Lansky, Diaz and Hunt were all on the same page—probably working together with a common goal.

- The group had no more knowledge about Fidelia's whereabouts than did Sam.
- The rumor about Castro being the father of Fidelia might turn out to be an important factor in her disappearance. Sam wondered about that rumor.

The trip had been productive. Now the thing that Sam most wanted to do was get out of Miami while he was still in one piece. He arrived at the hotel well before noon and with the help of the front desk was able to move their return flight reservations to later that day. Isabelle and Sam packed quickly and checked out of the hotel. When Northwest Orient's Miami flight to Minneapolis departed at four that afternoon, they were on it.

As the Boeing 707 went airborne, Sam let out a deep sigh.

16. Havana

Isabelle finished her final exams on June eighth. The next morning, she and Sam boarded a flight to Mexico City. There, they purchased Cubana Airlines tickets for the following day's flight to Havana and checked into a nearby hotel where they spent the night.

The next morning, their fixed-wing propeller-driven DC3 took off at seven with stops in Vera Cruz and Cancun. As the uncomfortable and noisy flight made its way across the Gulf of Mexico, Sam wondered whether he could justify continuing to work on the case if his visit to Cuba produced no clues.

Once again, the search for Fidelia—all of its nuances combined with no real progress in finding the missing girl— reminded Sam of Weldon Kees' poem *The Crime Club* and the sleuth Le Roux. The words from the poem that kept coming back into his thoughts were, *clues lead nowhere, or to walls so high their tops cannot be seen.*

*****

Sam reread the letter from Castro to Rosaline authorizing their visit and the one from the Cuban official that they were using as a visa. He tried to anticipate every bureaucratic hurdle that might be put in front of them and to formulate a strategy to address that hurdle. He had their American passports, their birth certificates, Xerox copies of Isabelle's citizenship papers and their marriage license. Sam hoped he wouldn't be required to produce any other critical documents.

The plane landed near Havana at 9:15 that evening. At 10:30 they were sitting in front of a customs and immigration clerk. The clerk shook his head after reading the letters from Castro and the Cuban official. Minutes later, the clerk looked even more troubled after he reviewed Isabelle's American citizenship papers and their marriage certificate. He sucked in some air, paused, then under his breath said in Spanish, "This one is very complex."

After a few minutes of staring at the letters and paging through a regulations book, the clerk excused himself and left the small interview room. Moments later, he returned with his supervisor. Sam watched the clerk and the supervisor reading and rereading the letters—then consulting with one another about next steps.

The supervisor left the room and the clerk told Sam and Isabelle they would have to wait in there until his supervisor was able to clarify "appropriate protocols". Sam was concerned, but not totally surprised. He had learned in the military that bureaucracies are always complex, if not utterly convoluted; and that low level officials, even from vastly different governments, behave similarly. Red tape is red tape is red tape and regardless of whether an official is from the United States, Spain or Cuba, he or she lives in mortal fear of doing something wrong—particularly on high profile cases.

Shortly after midnight, someone at a high level in the government must have broken the bureaucratic stalemate because the supervisor returned to the interview room, warmly shook hands with Sam and proudly announced, "I have worked out all the issues. A taxi is waiting outside the customs office. It will take the two of you to the Hotel Nacional de Cuba. I sincerely hope that the wait has not been frustrating."

He paused, then added quietly, "You have very good friends in extremely high places."

*****

It was a huge relief to have passed that first hurdle—entry into Cuba. But Sam and Isabelle were totally exhausted.

Minutes later in their taxi, the driver chattered as he drove them into Havana. "The Hotel Nacional de Cuba has been off limits to most tourists since the revolution. It is used to house visiting diplomats and officials of friendly foreign governments. So, you two must be very important indeed to be sent there by the customs and immigration office."

The driver paused speaking has he maneuvered the taxi pas a large truck. Then he continued to speak. "The hotel's history is full of celebrities. In its heyday, its guests included Frank Sinatra, Marlene Dietrich, Rita Hayworth, Gary Cooper, and Winston Churchill. Even the Duke and Duchess of Windsor stayed there."

During all of this, Sam was looking out the window, amazed that he was in Cuba and appreciating the beautiful 1950s cars they passed.

Meanwhile, the taxi driver continued his monologue, "Batista was close friends with Mafia kingpin Meyer Lansky. In fact, Lansky was Batista's minister of gambling—talk about an unusual government minister! In 1946, Lansky hosted a meeting of American mobsters at Hotel Nacional. *The Havana Conference,* as it is now called, was run by Lansky and his crime buddy Lucky Luciano. Representatives of crime families from throughout the United States came to the meeting. It was like a convention called to discuss American mob business interests. In 1955, Lansky moved into Hotel Nacional and became its manager."

As Sam listened, he couldn't help but think with some irony of how, throughout this case, he continually crossed Lansky's path.

*****

As Isabelle and Sam walked into the Hotel Nacional, Sam appreciated its unusual magnificence. Its architecture was some sort of cross between the art deco of the Nicollet Hotel and a Spanish style mission. Minutes later, both he and Isabelle were thankful when they got into their well-furnished, if a little dated, hotel room. Its worn set of matching Sheraton mahogany furniture had certainly been in the room for decades.

After they got in bed, Sam turned to Isabelle and said, "We're going to be sleeping in front of ghosts of important people who stayed in this room in the past."

Isabelle just gave Sam a dirty look and said, "Not funny."

Within minutes, they were both fast asleep.

*****

The next morning, Sam opened the drapes of their sixth-floor bedroom and looked out at a picture-postcard view of the hotel's swimming pool and gardens and its backdrop of Havana Harbor and the Gulf of Mexico. At breakfast, Sam and Isabelle sat at a table under an umbrella next to the hotel pool enjoying café con leche, grilled buttered bread and a shared bowl of melon, papaya and mango.

An hour later, Sam was trying to figure out how he could contact Castro when a desk clerk walked up to their table and said, "Mr. Erickson?"

Sam nodded and the desk clerk handed him an envelope with his name typed on it. Sam nervously opened the envelope and read in English:

Senor Erickson,

Welcome to Havana. We were informed you arrived yesterday evening and hope that you and your wife are enjoying your accommodations.

I understand you wish to meet with the Prime Minister to discuss a personal matter. The Prime Minister has asked me to set up a meeting for the two of you tomorrow evening, June 11, over dinner.

Fidel Castro is eager to hear about his friend Rosaline. He also anticipates having an in-depth discussion of the issue about which you have inquired.

Unfortunately, this invitation is for you alone. The Prime Minister has many enemies. In preparation for the meeting, security officials have fully reviewed your background. However, since we were not aware until recently that you would be traveling with your wife, no similar security review has taken place on her background. Thus, Signora Erickson will not be able to join the Prime Minister and you for dinner.

A vehicle and driver will meet you in front of Hotel Nacional at five in the afternoon on Saturday, June 11 to take you to the dinner meeting.

If you have any questions, please call me at the Office of the Prime Minister.

Sincerely,

Ricardo Cruz, Special Assistant to the Prime Minister

Sam was taken aback. This was more attention from Castro than he had expected. Dinner with Fidel Castro—maybe even just the two of them? Incredible!

Sam passed the letter to Isabelle. She read it silently, then shrugged. "I am disappointed, but not surprised. Castro has many enemies. I am pleased for Rosaline that you will speak with him. I hope the meeting is constructive; that it somehow helps us find Fidelia."

It was Friday morning. Since the meeting with Castro was not to occur until Saturday afternoon, Sam suggested that they try to contact Miguel Garcia's father Carlos and his sister Maria.

Moments later, Sam was looking through a phone book in the hotel lobby.

When he returned to Isabelle, he reported on what he had found. "There are fifteen listings for someone named *Carlos Garcia*, twelve for *Maria Garcia*, eighteen for *C. Garcia* and *fourteen for M. Garcia*. None of these listings show the return address on the letters to Rosaline. Calling all of the listed individuals would be a wild goose chase. While there is no guarantee that Miguel's father and sister still live at the address they had written from several years before, I think our best strategy would be to take a taxi to that address."

Isabelle rolled her eyes and responded, "You're the detective."

*****

Sam and Isabelle decided to enjoy the flavor of Havana by going for a walk before they tried to find a taxi. Sam also realized that if they got their cab at an unanticipated location, the probability that the cab driver would be an agent for the Cuban government who had been assigned to track them—or any other interested party trying to do the same—would be reduced.

There was a warm soft breeze coming off of the harbor as they headed west on the Malecón—the boulevard and walkway built above the seawall to protect Havana from ocean storms. They watched old men fishing off of the seawall and mothers walking with their small children. Sam looked across the roadway at very old, neglected structures. He told Isabelle those buildings seemed older than any he had ever seen.

Isabelle stopped and looked at the buildings. "The Malecón stretches out for five miles. Buildings with forgotten histories line the entire boulevard. But Sam, if this section impresses you, you will be knocked out by the architecture in the old section of the city."

She took a deep breath, gave a satisfied smile and exhaled, saying, "My heart is so full, Sam. Being in Havana; being here on the Malecón; sharing it with you; it all gives me so much joy; it represents so many special memories."

*****

They got on with the business of the day. Sam flagged down a cab. It was 1953 Chevrolet Bel Air with a dark blue body and white roof. Rust around the wheels disclosed that the Chevy's had seen better days, but its interior was pristine.

The cab driver's name was Esteban. As Esteban drove them to the address where they hoped to find the Garcias, he asked Sam and Isabelle where they were staying, where they came from and why they were visiting Havana.

Sam wanted to keep his response simple. "We are staying at the Hotel Nacional. We're from Minneapolis—it's in the center of North America—right next to Canada. While we are here on a business trip, my wife is sharing her memories with me. Isabelle lived in Havana as a child."

Esteban responded in a cool manner. "That is good. Cuba gets very few business visitors or tourists from the United States." He paused and added, "However, those business people are rarely invited to stay at Hotel Nacional."

They rode silently for a while. Finally, Isabelle broke the ice by telling Esteban that her father had died in the revolution—fighting for Castro. She shared memories of Havana including that Ernest Hemingway had been a good friend of her father. After that, Esteban showed some warmth. He asked Isabelle questions about the famous American writer.

Isabelle did her best to answer Esteban's questions. Then she asked, "Can you tell me how life has changed for Cubans since the revolution?"

Sam wondered how candid Esteban would be, particularly in view of how he had responded to Sam's lie about being a businessman. He wondered if Esteban might actually be a government agent. And even if he weren't, how comfortable would Esteban be sharing personal reflections on Castro and the revolution?

For a while, Esteban said nothing. Sam wondered if the cab driver might just choose to not speak with them anymore. But after several minutes, Esteban began to share his thoughts.

"Life under Castro has included some good—and some bad. I am old enough—I have driven a taxi for a long time— that I have a clear memory of life under Batista. Some people became quite wealthy under Batista. I was not among them. After the revolution, businesses that belonged to Batista's friends were nationalized—their wealth taken from them.

Those people—they hate Castro. Many of them have gone to Florida. But those who were impoverished before Castro came to power, they forgive the controlling behavior of Castro's government. Today, they have food, shelter, education and healthcare. Those were unknown to many of us under the previous regime."

The simple, eloquent straightforwardness of Esteban's response told Sam that the cab driver was not a government agent. Esteban appeared to relax and became even more open.

"Cuba is poor. The common people here have always had great poverty. But many of our current problems can be traced—at least partly—to the United States' trade embargo. Our economy cannot use its main product—the sugar we produce—as a resource to fund the purchase of things we need from the United States. For example, an impact of the embargo on me is that I cannot buy replacement automobile parts to repair my vehicle. I must always be innovative in my repairs. I rebuilt the clutch on this Chevrolet using one I salvaged from an old broken-down Ford."

Sam was intrigued. "Do you have confidence in Castro's economic decisions?"

"I would be lying if I didn't admit that our economy suffers because the government has done a poor job of running many of the businesses it nationalized—and of managing the economy. My wife complains there is too little to choose from at the market—too little food, too little clothing, too little of everything. She must line up at a store without knowing if the store has what we need on its shelves. She must buy what the store has—when it has it—or buy nothing at all. The supply of most everything is too small. But the prices are fair. Under Castro, each family has a home. They are able to feed themselves. And while even an engineer gets paid a small salary, every Cuban has a job."

"Is there corruption?"

Esteban smiled. "Officials high up in the government enjoy a kind of luxury I can only imagine. For example, I have heard that Fidel eats and drinks quite well. But in my family, rice and beans are the staple. Occasionally we get a chicken or a fish. But I don't even remember what beef tastes like. When I was young, there were many nights I went to bed hungry. In today's Cuba, no child goes to bed without a meal."

Esteban stopped speaking while he navigated around an ancient tractor pulling a trailer piled with manure. Then he continued. "Those of us who live in Cuba must live thriftily —we have much less than you do in the United States. But it is not like it was before Castro came to power. My kids go to school—something I didn't do. They receive health care when they are sick—something I didn't get. They have clothing. And as I said, my children do not go to bed hungry."

The cab ride continued without conversation for some time. Then Sam asked, "Is the government repressive?

Esteban was silent for several minutes. Then he spoke. "There isn't political freedom in Cuba. Anyone who publicly disagrees with the regime is arrested. They often disappear- - the same as under Batista—just under a different set of rules. But politics is not my thing. I just want to live my life, have a roof over my head and put enough food on the table for my family. If I wanted to publicly criticize Fidel, I have no doubt that it would be another story."

"So, what do you think of Castro."

"My friend. You ask many questions. If I felt you were with the government, I would be full of fear, now. But I listen to my heart. I will speak the truth—as I see it. It is no secret Fidel likes the ladies. Any fool can see he does not live at the same basic level as the rest of us. But I can easily forgive him those things. The Cuban people did not need a saint. They needed a leader willing to throw out the criminals who forced most of us to live in hunger—without any hope for the future. The Cuban people wanted a leader who would treat common workers with respect. Fidel Castro has given us this. We are eternally grateful."

*****

It took less than half an hour to get to their destination—a small faded green stucco house in an older residential area. Isabelle stayed in the taxi while Sam walked up to the house and knocked on the front door. Isabelle watched him speak with a woman before returning to the cab and asking Esteban to wait for them—they would only be at the house for a short while.

As they walked up to the house, Sam told Isabelle, "Miguel's father, Carlos, passed away. The woman I was speaking with was Miguel's sister, Maria. Maria is no longer a Garcia. She is married and has taken her husband's last name."

Maria welcomed Sam and Isabelle into her home. "I have never met Rosaline or Fidelia. But they are family and I am pleased to meet their friends. In particular, I am interested in hearing about my niece Fidelia."

As Sam told Maria about Fidelia's disappearance, he could see she was interested—but not upset. Sam said, "I am hopeful that I will find Fidelia. When I do, I will ask her to write a letter to you. I have a question, though. Can you tell me about the letters you and your father sent to Rosaline? When I read them, I wondered if there was a backstory to why you wrote them."

"Papa had a friend, someone who worked high up in the government. This man gave him Rosaline's Chicago address in 1962. He encouraged Papa to write her and to ask how Fidelia was doing. Papa wrote a letter. Then I wrote a letter. But we received no responses and I assumed we would never hear from my brother's wife or child. I let it go. Life goes on."

After visiting with Maria for a little while longer, Sam told her that he and Isabelle had to return to their hotel. Maria did not seem disappointed and wished them well.

On the way back to the car, Sam said to Isabelle, "I think Maria told us the truth. But it was worth the trip to out here just to learn that they had been asked to contact Rosaline by someone high up in the Cuban government. It seems like someone high up in the government cares an awful lot about a dead soldier's daughter."

*****

Shortly before arriving at the Hotel Nacional, Isabelle brought up her childhood home. "Papa and I lived in the town of San Francisco de Paula—nine miles outside of Havana. I told you before that our home was only two blocks from Ernest Hemingway's compound and how I would walk with Papa to Ernest Hemingway's home. Could we go to San Francisco de Paula tomorrow morning?"

Sam liked the idea. Esteban agreed to pick Sam and Isabelle up at the hotel the following morning at nine.

Sam and Isabelle had a light lunch of white gazpacho soup in the hotel restaurant. Afterwards, they returned to the Malecón—this time heading east towards old Havana. Classic American cars, some of them belching smoke from their exhaust, sped past them as they walked along the harbor.

Isabelle reminisced. "Papa was so proud of his black fifty-one Ford convertible coupe. Its whitewall tires were always so clean; its black paint and chrome detail so shiny. I recall how happy I used to be to sit next to him as he drove us into central Havana for dinner with friends. The convertible top would be down—the wind from the harbor would toss my hair—it was glorious."

After walking for about forty-five minutes, Sam and Isabelle turned south into *Habana Vieja*—Old Havana. For a while, they walked silently—admiring the marvelous architecture from a different era. Isabelle began to recount the history of this old city that was founded by the Spanish in 1519 as a stopping point for treasure laden ships crossing between the New World and Spain.

They stopped at a coffee shop in the Plaza de la Cathedral. They sat at a sidewalk table across the street from the majestic Cathedral of the Virgin Mary of the Immaculate Conception, each had with a cup of Cuban coffee—a dark, intense espresso-like shot sweetened with raw cane sugar.

Isabelle spoke as she looked up at the church. "The history of this city—of its architecture—it is so amazing. Papa told me once that the cathedral was constructed from blocks of coral cut from the Gulf of Mexico's ocean floor. The cathedral was completed about the same time as the America's Declaration of Independence was signed."

It was already seven o clock. Isabelle suggested they dine at a small restaurant she remembered going to with her father. A moment later, they found it. Sam ordered pork and black bean stew. Isabelle had Cilantro Citrus Chicken. After tasting one another's dishes, they ended up happily sharing their two dinners, washing them down with Bucanero Beer.

Afterwards, they took a taxi back to the hotel.

*****

Saturday morning, Esteban was waiting for Sam and Isabelle when they walked out of the hotel. Within half an hour, they were in San Francisco de Paula sitting in the taxi in front of Isabelle's childhood home. The pale-yellow, single-story adobe house was narrow and had a small front yard. After sitting in the cab for several minutes—not knowing what to do—Sam suggested he knock on the door of the house and inquire if they could look around inside.

Isabelle shook her head. "I feel uncomfortable asking for such a favor from strangers. I would rather just walk around the neighborhood. We could go up to Hemingway's old house."

Sam agreed. Esteban would pick them up in front of Isabelle's childhood home in two hours.

As they walked through the quaint San Francisco de Paula neighborhood, Isabelle pointed out homes of people she remembered. "My best friend Jana lived in that small pink house. Papa was friends with a man who lived in that pale blue stucco home. This empty lot—there used to be a sweet little cottage here. It had a garden that was always full of colorful flowers. A gentle old woman spent her days there, working in that garden. Whenever I walked by, she would smile and greet me. Once she gave me a rose."

Even though Isabelle was describing happy memories, a sense of sadness pervaded the walk. "Right now, I miss Papa—more than I have in years. The familiar surroundings—they make me feel like I should be able to run up to him—that he would pick me up in his arms, hold me high in the air and tell me I was his wonderful sweetheart."

Isabelle looked around and sighed. "But I know feeling that way...it is just empty nonsense."

*****

When they got to the top of a hill, they saw the Hemingway House. It was a crème-colored stucco home with white trim. Hemingway had named it *Finca Vigia,* literally *Lookout House*. Its nicely landscaped yard was full of bird of paradise plants, ginger and bougainvillea in addition to a number of coconut and palm trees. The house was empty—its doors locked.

Isabelle and Sam walked around the home's exterior gazing through the windows into the empty house. Isabelle said, "Papa and I would sometimes walk over here for dinner—but only when Hemingway's wife was out of town. Papa and old man Hemingway would sit in the great room, drinking, talking, laughing and smoking. I played with my dolls—out there on the sun porch. I remember those off-white floor tiles so well."

Isabelle described dinners enjoyed on the wooden dining room table; how after the meal, Hemingway and her father would often remain at the table for hours exchanging stories, drinking dark Cuban rum. She laughed and said, "One time Papa got so drunk, that we spent the night here. Walking the two blocks home that evening had just seemed too challenging."

As Isabelle and Sam left *Finca Vigia* and returned to the street of her old home to meet Esteban, Isabelle was silent. Sam saw there were tears in her eyes. He understood she was far away—lost in memories of her childhood. When they arrived back in front of the pale-yellow adobe house, they saw a short old woman in a dark skirt, white blouse and red head kerchief who was tending flowers in the house's small front yard.

Isabelle walked up to the woman. In a very tentative voice, Isabelle said, "Ireneo? Is that you?" The woman stood up, turned around, looked at Isabelle and they fell into one another's arms and wept. Soon, they began to speak to one another.

After a couple of minutes, Ireneo asked, "Isabelle—who is this man?"

Isabelle flushed, "Ireneo—this is my husband Sam. Sam, this is Ireneo. She took care of me when I was a child. Ireneo is as close to being my mother as anyone ever has been."

There were more hugs and tears.

Ireneo invited Sam and Isabelle to have lunch with her. As they were accepting her invitation, Esteban drove up. Sam told Esteban they wanted to stay for lunch. Could he hire Esteban and his taxi for the day? If so, could Esteban return at three that afternoon to pick them up?

Esteban had no problem with that plan.

*****

Ireneo, Sam and Isabelle went inside. While Ireneo fixed lunch, Isabelle and Sam meandered through the home. "Sam, these are many of the same pieces of furniture and paintings I grew up with. This was my bedroom. Late on some evenings, when Papa thought I was fast asleep, I would climb out of that window to play with kids in the neighborhood."

They went into the hallway. Isabelle walked up to a photograph and touched it. "Sam, that is Papa with Ernest

Hemingway. And you see that sweet little girl there? That is me!" She shook her head and said, "So many memories."

Lunch was plantain soup. The savory dish—ground plantain chips in a chicken broth flavored with cumin and a touch of lime—was dusted with chopped cilantro. Ireneo served it with a fresh loaf of home baked Cuban bread.

Isabelle was focused on her lunch. At one point, she looked up at Sam and said, "I'm sorry to ignore you. But I haven't had plantain soup in more than a decade. Each spoonful brings back such comfortable, glorious feelings from my childhood."

The lunch was full of stories about Isabelle as a little girl; memories of her father; more tears; and then more laughter. During the meal, Isabelle learned that her father's will had left the home to Ireneo and her as tenants-in-common. Ireneo wanted to somehow give Isabelle her share of the property.

Isabelle shook her head. "Ireneo—I am certain it would have been Papa's wish that you own the home—that you continue to live a long, full and happy life in it."

They wept once more.

The afternoon went quickly. At three, Esteban arrived. Sam told Ireneo he had a business meeting. He suggested that Isabelle and Ireneo spend the evening together—a plan quickly endorsed by all. Esteban would return to pick up Isabelle and deliver her to the hotel later that evening.

As he rode off in the taxi, Sam looked back at Isabelle and Ireneo holding hands while walking into the house. This visit to a pale-yellow adobe house had made the whole trip worthwhile.

17. A Dinner Meeting

A black 1956 Cadillac Sedan Deville pulled in front of the Hotel Nacional de Cuba precisely at five that afternoon. It was driven by a young man in green military fatigues. He got out of the Cadillac and walked up to Sam. In English with a heavy accent, he said, "Mr. Erickson. The prime minister has requested I drive you to meet him for dinner."

The young man opened the Sedan Deville's rear door, Sam took a seat and they were off. Five minutes later, the car stopped in front of a large apartment building. The driver got out of the Cadillac, opened the door for Sam and said, "Please follow me to the prime minister's quarters."

Inside the building, a door to an apartment was opened by another young man in green fatigues who led Sam down a hallway to a large office. Fidel Castro, wearing military fatigues similar to those Sam had seen on the young man who had brought him to the apartment, sat reading a document at an elaborately carved desk.

Castro looked up from his document and said, "Mr. Erickson. It is a pleasure to welcome you to our beautiful land. I trust you are enjoying your visit?"

"Mr. Prime Minister. Thank you for finding the time to meet with me. I am truly humbled. And yes, my wife and I are thoroughly enjoying our visit."

Sam had been told by Rosaline that Castro spoke English well. But this meeting with the revolutionary was conducted entirely in Spanish.

Castro stood up slowly—studied Sam for a moment— then said, "We have a mutual friend who is dear to me. I look forward to hearing about Rosaline. Later on, we can speak about the disappearance of her daughter. But first, I suggest we have a drink and a cigar. I trust you will accommodate me in this regard?"

Castro walked across the room, leading Sam to a pair of leather wingback chairs. An antique inlaid mahogany coffee table was in front of the chairs. On the table, on a circular engraved silver tray, was an unopened bottle of Chivas Regal scotch. Next to the bottle were two cut crystal highball glasses, a cut crystal ice bucket and a carved teak humidor.

That Fidel Castro was living the good life was not lost on Sam. But Sam remembered what Esteban had told him was of importance to the Cuba—that common people no longer experienced the poverty or suffering they had to endure during under Batista.

In any case, Sam realized he wasn't here to judge Castro, but to get information about Fidelia—if he could. He was brought back from his philosophical musings when Castro asked, "On the rocks?" Sam nodded. Fidel fixed two sizeable drinks and handed one of them to Sam. Then the Cuban leader opened the humidor, pulled out two long dark cigars, snipped the ends off of each with a small silver tool, and passed one to Sam.

"Mr. Erickson—You are about to smoke a *Cohiba Corona Especial.* These cigars are my favorite. Years ago, I had a bodyguard who used to smoke cigars that smelled very good. One day, I asked him about his cigars. He gave me one. I smoked it and liked it very much. He told me a friend of his—Eduardo Ribera—made the cigars."

Castro struck a wooden match and reached across to light Sam's cigar. Then he lit his own. "We contacted Ribera. He agreed to make cigars for me. Following Ribera's methods of outstanding tobacco leaf selection, fermentation and his process for cigar assembly, Cuba's state-owned tobacco company will soon begin producing similar quality cigars in mass at our Havana factory. Cohibas will one day be recognized and respected by knowledgeable cigar smokers throughout the world."

Sam took a strong draw from his cigar. He reflected on how fortunate he was that Luis had taught him how to smoke one properly. This cigar's taste was full flavored—almost earthy. A moment later, a sip of ice-cold scotch provided the perfect counter-balance to the Cohiba.

Castro spoke again. "I see you are familiar with how to treat a fine cigar."

Sam responded, "My wife Isabelle has introduced me to many of her Cuban-American friends. They have taught me how to taste and appreciate quality cigars. But I have never smoked a cigar of this extraordinary quality."

Castro smiled and quipped, "I suspect that some of those people who taught you about cigars would prefer that I was in a coffin."

"Perhaps one or two of them feel that way. But I have met very few. My friends have described the extreme poverty that existed in your land before the revolution. Those who are bitter were not among the poor. In fact, Rosaline's husband Luis Martinez is the person who was my primary mentor on how to properly smoke a cigar. Luis's father and brother worked in the sugar cane fields. Luis shared with me the devastating poverty his family—and most Cubans—experienced prior to the revolution."

Castro's eyes lit up. "Did you know I knew Luis? He was a very good ballplayer. After he went to the States, I followed his career—as I follow many Cubanos in the big leagues. But of course, before Luis played baseball in the States, he played here in Cuba. He pitched to me twice! I will not give you details of those at bats—I did not do well. But I was quite the ballplayer. In 1949, the New York Giants offered me five thousand dollars to sign a contract to play professional baseball in their organization. While I loved baseball, my destiny was in other fundamentally more important areas."

Sam had not known that Castro had played baseball. He found it a little hard to believe. But Sam knew better than to question a statement from Fidel Castro—to his face, anyway.

Castro must have read Sam's facial expression, because he added, "You wonder if I exaggerate? Ask Luis when you see him. He will tell you! I was a good ballplayer."

Castro refilled their glasses. They sat quietly for a few minutes—tasting their cigars and drinking the scotch. Sam finally broke the silence. "The Cohiba's flavor seems to have grown slightly sweet. It actually tastes better with each puff!"

Castro said nothing, but took a drag on his cigar. Then he smiled and nodded assent.

*****

There was a knock on the door. Castro said to Sam, "Our dinner is ready. I hope you brought your appetite. We are about to have a fabulous Cuban dinner."

Castro led Sam into the next room—a wood paneled dining room with a table and a sufficient number of chairs to easily seat a dozen people. But the table was set for only two. Castro sat at its head. Sam was seated to his left.

Castro picked up a corkscrew and opened a bottle of Spanish Rioja that was sitting on his right. He filled two carved crystal wineglasses; then proposed a toast. "To the day when the United States government is more interested in being friends with the people of Cuba than in assassinating Cuba's leader."

A young woman brought in several serving dishes and placed them on the table. Castro and Sam served themselves from those dishes.

As they ate, the conversation focused on the food. Castro said, "This first dish is called shrimp ceviche. It is my favorite—and very popular throughout Cuba."

Sam liked the refreshing, light and clean taste of the ceviche. The other dishes—an avocado and pineapple salad and black beans and rice—complemented it nicely. And Castro kept their wine glasses full.

The same woman who had brought the food to the table returned. She asked, "Mr. Prime Minister—may I clear your plates?"

Castro thanked her. As she removed the dishes, Castro asked her to bring another bottle of Rioja. After the table was cleared and the wine delivered, Castro filled each of their glasses one more time and pulled out two more Cohibas from his shirt pocket.

Sam commented that he had heard John F. Kennedy loved Cuban cigars. After making that statement, Sam was uncomfortable. He did not know exactly how Castro would respond to a statement about the man who had been the president of the United States when the Bay of Pigs invasion was staged.

However, Castro showed no irritation. "Yes. Kennedy did love his cigars."

Castro took a puff and watched as his exhaled smoke curled toward the ceiling. Then he continued. "I will share something only a few people know. Kennedy and I were negotiating removal of the trade embargo shortly before he was killed. If he had lived another month, the embargo would have been lifted. In return, I would have initiated actions within Cuba that Kennedy had requested. That agreement would have made many Cuban-Americans very angry."

Castro took a deep breath and inspected his still lit cigar before continuing. "But finalizing the agreement was not to be. It was a shame he was murdered. He was an intelligent and thoughtful man—just not prepared for the intrigues of the high government position he attained. I don't believe it was ever Kennedy's desire to invade Cuba. The Bay of Pigs was instigated by others. It was not something he wanted. The fact that Kennedy did not bring the United States military in to support the invasion created anger in Miami's Cuban American community—and in the CIA—and in the American Mafia as well."

Castro leaned forward, drew briefly on his cigar, exhaled, then went on. "I believe that that anger—from those groups—and the fact that we were successfully negotiating a resolution to the embargo is what led to his assassination. I don't exactly know what happened in Dallas. Some people have made accusations that the Mafia was working with me to kill Kennedy. What a joke."

Castro laughed quietly. "The Mafia has always wanted to see me dead and have tried to accomplish this many times. How absurd that some fools believe they conspired with me. But the Mafia does work with the CIA and I would give you good odds that the conspiracy to assassinate your president was formed by the Mafia, the CIA and some old friends of Batista."

Castro looked directly at Sam, keeping his cigar in his large hand as he gestured while speaking. "I share this insight with you today because it relates directly to the issue we are about to discuss—the disappearance of Fidelia. A good starting point on that discussion—for me—would be for you to share what you have learned during your investigation. Rosaline did not relate much of this in her letter."

Sam opened his notebook and took out a photo of Rosaline and Fidelia. He handed it to Castro. Castro looked at the photograph. Then Sam began to tell him what he knew about Fidelia's disappearance and recounted his search for her. Sam's narrative was detailed and Castro listened attentively. Sam described his meetings in Chicago—at Fidelia's school and with Officer Miller; his dinner with Giarri in New York; how he had been beaten up by a couple of Cuban-American tough guys; and how one of his assailants had referenced someone called *the old man*. Sam told Castro about Wozniak's visit to his home; about his trip to Miami and learning that the address from Fidelia's room was for Meyer Lansky's home. Sam chuckled as he explained how he got Diaz to admit he had been in contact with Giarri, Lansky and Wozniak—and let Castro know that Wozniak's real name is Hunt.

"I've pulled together a lot of information over these past few months, Mr. Prime Minister. Still, I fear I am no closer to finding Fidelia then I was at the beginning of my search. My heart goes out to Rosaline. She loves her daughter a great deal—and my respect for her husband Luis has grown and grown. Luis loves both Rosaline and Fidelia so much. And while it is a distinct honor to meet with you, I am not confident that you will be able to assist me."

Sam stopped speaking. He took a big drink from his glass of Rioja, then looked directly at the Cuban leader and added, "And I have no idea at all how I should proceed after I leave Cuba."

*****

Off and on through Sam's narration, Castro had puffed on his cigar. But through most of the narrative, his eyes were fixed on the photograph of Rosaline and Fidelia. When Sam finished, there was silence for several minutes.

Castro studied the photograph of Rosaline and Fidelia. "I look at this picture of mother and daughter. Fidelia is as beautiful as her mother. In fact, she looks like Rosaline did when I first met her. I regret I have not seen Rosa in all of these years—that I never got to know her lovely daughter. I appreciate your dedication to Rosaline—and how you have diligently pursued the leads you were given. You have been tenacious."

Castro placed the photograph back on the table, took a drink of Rioja, looked at Sam, then continued. "The backdrop for this story—the backdrop for my entire life—has been the historic poverty of the Cuban masses—and the wealth of a very few. The challenges my people faced go back to the occupation of our land by Spain. When our people finally were able to win independence from Spain—fulfilling the vision of José Martí, then the Americans came in. They made us a colony!"

Castro took a long drag from his cigar, exhaled it and shook his head sadly from side to side. "We had struggled for so long to rid ourselves of one imperial power—only to have another imperial power come in and treat us as its spoils of war! Sam, you cannot imagine the poverty and abuse my people have endured. When I was born, two-thirds of the farmlands in Cuba were owned by North Americans! Cuban families were hungry—living in conditions similar to those endured by America's slaves. In fact, for the vast majority of Cubans, my country has been a huge plantation—growing wealth for foreigners."

Sam listened quietly. The passion with which Castro spoke about the hardships of his people was remarkable.

"Then the Mafia discovered what a rich opportunity Cuba was to peddle drugs, gambling and whoring. American gangsters created great wealth and power for themselves at the expense of my people. The partnership that Batista and others forged with the mob—it was sinful. Criminals from the United States had more power over the Cuban government than the Cuban people! It is true that some Cubans prospered under Batista. And I do know that some of those people were honest professionals. But most of those who prospered during that time did so by making deals with the devil. They had much in common with the criminals and imperialists for whom they worked."

For a while, Castro and Sam sat saying nothing. Sam realized that while Castro had been open with him about his intense love for Cuba and his belief in the revolution, he had not yet addressed the purpose of their meeting—finding Fidelia.

Almost as if he were reading Sam's mind, Castro turned his comments to Sam's search. "I asked a few friends in the States to explore what might have happened to Rosaline's daughter. Their reports confirmed the involvement of those you believe tried to inhibit your search. One of those is the devil Meyer Lansky. After the revolution swept out Batista and his cronies, Lansky moved to Miami. Enter Tony Giarri. He became one of Lansky's most trusted lieutenants. Lansky asked Giarri to build an alliance with Cubans who benefitted from Batista's regime and then fled to Miami. At the same time, the CIA was trying to create a partnership between

American corporations that had lost investments, Cuban expatriates and the mob. One of the primary CIA organizers was an adjunct employee of the CIA named Howard Hunt."

Castro chuckled for a moment. He gestured with his right hand which held his smoking cigar as he said, "Hunt's tendency was to come up with complex and convoluted plans—then royally screw them up. We believe he was the key organizer of the Bay of Pigs invasion. He was building alliances with many of the same Cuban expatriates that Giarri was courting. And yes, I think your FBI Agent Wozniak was really CIA Agent Hunt. Here is a picture of the bastard Howard Hunt."

As he said this, Castro pulled a snapshot out of his shirt pocket and handed it to Sam. Sam looked at it. There was Agent Wozniak—complete with hat, sunglasses and dark suit. In the photograph, Wozniak had a lit cigarette sticking out of the corner of his mouth.

Castro had stopped speaking as he watched Sam react to the photo.

"The CIA, the Mafia and Cuban expatriates continue to work incessantly to undercut our revolution. One of their primary objectives has been to assassinate me. As you see, they have not been successful. Part of the reason for their failure is that the Central Intelligence Agency lacks any intelligence. I call them the Central Idiot Agency. Howard Hunt is the CIA's Chief Idiot Agent."

At this point, Castro looked down at his cigar and smiled. Then he drew deeply from his Cohiba Corona Especial. After watching the cigar smoke curl to the room's ceiling and then disappear, he went on. "Since you have Rosa's complete trust, I am going to trust you too. Rosaline was well known before I met her—one of the most beautiful and gracious women in all of Cuba. We became close—quite close—years before she met Miguel Garcia, another dear friend of mine."

Castro looked out across the room, almost as if he was seeing the past. He gave a deep sigh, took a sip of Rioja. A moment later, he looked back to Sam. "Rosaline and I never had a falling out. It just was not to be. I was married. She was not. And as you have surmised, I care deeply about Fidelia. I am more than aware that some people believe she is my daughter. As things turned out, naming her Fidelia—whether it was in my honor or because she was my daughter—well, naming her Fidelia was an unfortunate decision. But one can never go back in time—to try to change what happened, to explain it, to deny it or to conceal it."

Castro leaned forward, putting his elbows on the table with his cigar in between the ring and middle fingers of his hand. He looked seriously at Sam. "Whether Fidelia is my daughter or not is totally irrelevant. Facts do not matter to hyenas. If these animals find a way to hurt me—or to embarrass Cuba, they will do so—regardless of whether they have a basis for what they say—or not. No matter how painful it may be for others—how much it could hurt Fidelia and Rosaline—they will do whatever they can to cause embarrassment for me—and for Cuba."

Castro shrugged. "So that is where we are today. As you might imagine, in addition to enemies in the United States, I have many friends. There are networks across the country—people who are supportive of our cause. They are not my agents—or spies for this country. They understand what Cuba's revolution has accomplished. Even in Minneapolis—I have friends—even some friends who enjoyed your recent wedding."

Castro gave a warm smile, lifted his glass up and held it out towards Sam. "I offer my hearty congratulations to you and your lovely Cuban wife Isabelle! May your love last long. May you both prosper. And may you have many beautiful and healthy children."

Castro drank from his glass. "Some of my friends were not surprised at my request that they be on the lookout for Fidelia."

Sam sat forward—not at all certain what was coming next, but aware that he had never before been involved in such an incredible conversation.

"Danger exists if you find Fidelia while being followed by those who wish to cause pain to me and to Cuba. Your life would be in danger. Fidelia's life would be at risk. You have already seen these people are not afraid to use violence to achieve their purposes. I can tell you where you can find Fidelia. But you must first offer a plan for assuring she will not be in danger as a result of your discovery. The Central Intelligence Agency is fully aware you are in Cuba. I will assist you in departing Cuba without their knowledge. Once you are gone, you must go directly to Fidelia. You must protect her."

Castro paused, letting what he had just said sink in. "If you can come up with a plan for achieving her safety, I will share her location with you."

Sam was dumbfounded. But he knew Castro's concerns were legitimate. When and if Sam found her, Fidelia and he would both be in danger—until and unless Sam was able to insulate them from the perils that would follow. Ever since he had learned of the connection between Lansky, Diaz and Giarri, Sam had known that a plan to protect Fidelia from danger was necessary. He had laid awake nights putting such a strategy together. And Sam did have a plan. He proceeded to share it with the prime minister of Cuba.

After listening to Sam, Castro said, "Pretty good. We both know there are never guarantees. But I like the way you think. You just need to never lose sight of the fact that the CIA is no more your friend than it is mine."

So, Fidel Castro told Sam where he could find Fidelia. He told Sam that he would pass on to a contact that Sam would be coming. Fidel Castro's contact would let Fidelia know a friend would be touching base with her soon—a friend who could be trusted. Castro also assured Sam that if he was not successful in meeting with Fidelia; if something went wrong; Sam could rely on the contact for help. Castro told Sam to use an assumed name. The contact would know that name as well as the hotel at which Sam would be staying. If things did not go smoothly, Castro's contact would find Sam.

"So, Mr. Sam Erickson. What name shall I tell my contact you will use?"

Sam thought for a while. Then he turned to Castro, smiled and said, "I have chosen the name *Mr. Jim Wormold.*"

Castro gave a hearty laugh. "You thought I wouldn't catch the subtlety—didn't you? I know who the hero was in the book *Our Man in Havana.*"

*****

That evening Isabelle arrived at the Hotel Nacional at about the same time as Sam was returning in the black Cadillac from his dinner with Castro. They walked up to their room together. Isabelle was glowing. She had had a wonderful evening with Ireneo.

Before asking about Sam's evening, her eyes glistening, she began to unwrap a small package and said to Sam in a voice full of emotion, "Ireneo has given us a wonderful wedding present."

She carefully removed the string and newspaper in which the gift had been wrapped. Sam looked at the framed photograph of Isabelle, her father and Ernest Hemingway.

****

Isabelle wanted to hear every detail of Sam's dinner with Fidel Castro. She rapidly fired off a series of questions, "How were you treated? What was Fidel Castro like? Where did you meet him? What did you have for dinner? Did you learn anything about Fidelia's whereabouts?"

Sam told her he would tell her almost everything—and that was a lot—but he could only answer one question at a time. Then he went on to recount almost all of the details of the evening.

Isabelle shook her head in wonder as Sam described the openness of the conversation between the Cuban leader and her husband. She listened intently as Sam told how he was greeted with Scotch and Cohibas. He described—in as detailed a manner as he was able—the furniture and furnishings in Castro's office and dining room. Sam tried to recount every detail from the dinner—both the food and the conversation.

"Sam," she said. "This is so amazing. I have never known anyone who was allowed to come so close to Fidel Castro! He must have an awful lot of fondness for Rosaline—and for Fidelia as well, I guess."

Sam thought about her statement for a moment, then just said, "Yes."

But Sam wasn't done telling her about their conversation. Isabelle's eyes opened wider and her jaw dropped when Sam told her that Castro's sources had located Fidelia. After Sam had finished recounting the conversation with Castro, Isabelle agreed that there would be danger in trying to safely retrieve Fidelia. Then she listened closely as Sam described much of his plan for leaving Cuba, for contacting Fidelia and for hopefully protecting both of them from those who stood in their way.

*****

Sam and Isabelle's original itinerary had been to leave Havana on Thursday, June sixteenth flying out on Cubana Airlines to Mexico City and then on to Minneapolis. Isabelle would retain that schedule. But Sam would not. Castro had offered passage on a Cuban Military Transport to Mexico City—on June fifteenth—a day earlier. The advantage of flying ahead of schedule on the military transport was that the CIA would not be aware of Sam's arrival in Mexico City. Hopefully, he would not be followed to his next destination—which he did not share with Isabelle in order to protect her in case she was questioned by anyone seeking to stop him.

Sam gave Isabelle the phone number for a trusted colleague of Luis at Luis's dealership. She must call that number once she had safely returned to Minneapolis. She had to make the call from a pay phone and should not, under any circumstances, tell the person who answered the phone who was calling. She should just have him fetch Luis. If Luis wasn't available, the colleague should set up a time when Luis would be available for Isabelle to call again. Odds were that Luis' home and office phone line were both tapped by the CIA. Sam stressed how critical it was for Isabelle to be careful.

Once Isabelle had Luis on the line, she should bring him up to speed on Sam's progress. But she was not to use any names or specific locations. Isabelle had to understand there was real danger. Caution needed to guide her every action.

*****

After that evening, for the next few days, Sam and Isabelle celebrated. They had a real honeymoon—forgetting about the CIA, the mob and even Fidelia. They focused on the sun, the food, the music, the dancers and Cuba's extraordinary culture. They enjoyed one another and reveled in the intimacy of being together.

One evening, while sitting in a small café listening to a trio play a Cuban salsa, Isabelle laughed and said, "It was really sly how you manipulated this whole missing person case—just so you could take me to Havana for our honeymoon."

Tuesday evening, Sam and Isabelle had a wonderful dinner in old Havana before walking back to Hotel Nacional on the Malecón. They arrived at the hotel shortly before sunset. Isabelle suggested they go down to the beach and get their feet wet one last time in Havana Harbor before Sam had to fly out the next day.

It was a warm evening. They were walking on wet sand, hand in hand, enjoying the waves as they rolled onto the beach. Isabelle, inspired by their mood and the beautiful evening, began to sing a song Sam hadn't heard in years—*Twilight Time*. She only remembered the first and last verse, so it was a short performance. But against the backdrop of the Havana beach on a tropical evening, the song was magical.

> *Heavenly shades of night are falling, it's twilight time*
> *Out of the mist your voice is calling, it's twilight time*
> *When purple-colored curtains mark the end of day*
> *I'll hear you, my dear, at twilight time*

18. A Flower in her Hair

The young Cuban diplomat—he'd said his name was Cesar—woke Sam by shaking his shoulder. Sam removed the Kleenex wads out of his ears. Cesar let him know that the Ilyushin Il-12 had already passed over Vera Cruz and would land in Mexico City in about an hour.

Sam was groggy, but pleased to learn that the noisy airplane ride was about to end. He spent that final hour of the flight reviewing the strategies he was about to implement—trying to anticipate what could go wrong—and hoping it wouldn't.

The Cuban military transport moved into its final approach to Mexico City's Benito Juarez International Airport and minutes later bounced in for a landing. Sam would fly out the next day. Cesar suggested the two of them travel together by cab to a local hotel. Sam was about to decline when Cesar explained that the prime minister had asked him to stay with Sam until Sam boarded an Aeromexico flight to the United States the following morning.

Then Sam discovered one of the advantages of flying on the Cuban diplomatic transport. He did not have to go through normal customs. An hour after landing in Mexico City, Sam was at a good, small Oaxacan restaurant polishing off an excellent meal of mole chichilo with chicken, rice and black beans. He washed the spicy dinner down with two Dos Equis beers. After dinner, Cesar had to talk Sam into ordering a cup of the restaurant's Oaxaca hot chocolate. Sam agreed in order to be polite, but discovered that the rich, thick hot chocolate with strong cinnamon overtones was one of the best deserts he'd ever had.

Two hours later, Sam was fast asleep in a hotel room at Hotel Faja de Oro.

*****

The next morning, Cesar hired a taxi for their short trip to the Airport. Sam's reservation with Aeromexico for a flight to San Francisco was in the name of *Stan Ericksen*. Sam explained to the clerk that the misspelling of his name must have been a clerical input error. As he was about the board the airplane, he thanked Cesar and asked him to pass his deep appreciation on to Fidel Castro for all of the assistance that had been provided.

A couple of hours later, Sam was in the air on a four-engine McDonnell Douglas DC-8 jet airliner. He noticed—and appreciated—the comfortable, quiet, and smooth ride of the airplane as compared to the Ilyushin Il-12. The uneventful flight landed at San Francisco's International Airport in mid-afternoon. After collecting his bag and passing through customs, Sam caught a taxicab to the Fairmont Hotel.

*****

The Fairmont Hotel was at the top of Nob Hill, right across from the Mark Hopkins Hotel. As the cab pulled up to the Fairmont's grand entrance, Sam felt like he had arrived at a nineteenth century European palace.

As he entered the hotel, Sam surveyed the ornate lobby. He wasn't looking at its marble columns, impressive fixtures or furniture fit for royals. He was scanning the room for anyone—CIA or Mafia in particular—who might be on the lookout for him. At the front desk, he asked for the reservation for Mr. Jim Wormold. Once in his room, an exhausted Sam laid down for a nap. He fell into a deep sleep waking at seven that evening. Sam ordered a hamburger, fries and milk shake from room service. He ate dinner in front of the television watching a San Francisco Giants baseball game in which Willie Mays had three hits. After the game, Sam turned in for the night.

*****

The next morning, Sam ordered breakfast from room service and read the San Francisco Examiner—beginning with the sports page. How were the Twins doing?

Damn! The Twins' record was now twenty-eight wins and thirty losses. Last year, the Twins had gone to the World Series. This year, it looked like they were going to the dogs. *Well*, Sam thought to himself, *there's always next year*.

*****

One of the Fairmont's restaurants—The Venetian Room—was a night club in the evenings when it featured performers like Ella Fitzgerald, Nat King Cole and Vic Damone. But during breakfasts and lunches, it was a quiet, five-star restaurant offering excellent soups, salads and sandwiches.

The Venetian had recently hired a new busgirl—a young Hispanic woman—named Felli Garcia.

Sam went to the Venetian for lunch. He ordered a tomato soup and BLT combination. When a young Hispanic woman—the spitting image of her mother—walked past his table, he asked if she would fill his glass and passed her a note he had written that morning on Fairmont Hotel stationary.

Dear Fidelia,

My name is Sam Erickson. I am here at the request of your mother. She is worried about you. I believe I understand the issues—and the people—you are concerned about. I will assist you in addressing those concerns.

When can we get together and talk? I would like to help you. I believe one of your friends has told you to expect my arrival.

I am registered at the Fairmont in room 410 under the name Jim Wormold. Can you either contact me at my hotel room or pass me a note here in the restaurant? I would like to know when and where we can meet.

Gracias,
Sam

Fidelia flushed a little when he handed her the note. She nodded at him, but said nothing and moved on to the next table, pouring water for the couple sitting there.

*****

Sam was worried that perhaps Fidelia hadn't been told to expect him. What if she just took off her busgirl jacket and ran away from the Hotel? What would he do then? He continued to slowly eat his lunch. But he was not focused upon the soup or sandwich's taste. He was just plain worried.

About five minutes later, Fidelia walked up to his table and asked if he needed more water. Sam said *yes*. As she poured the water, she put a note down on the table and then went on her way.

A moment later, Sam opened the note.

Dear Sam,
Yes. I was told to expect you. I am so glad you are here. I need help.

I will work until ten this evening. But I have the weekend off. I share a house with a few other people near Haight-Ashbury. Can you meet me at the Panhandle of Golden Gate Park tomorrow morning at about eleven? There is a large oak tree in the Panhandle just off of Oak and Central. I will meet you there.

Thank you. I have been frightened and I miss my mother.

I look forward to seeing you tomorrow.
Fidelia Garcia

Sam gave a huge sigh of relief. As he looked up, he saw Fidelia was watching him from across the dining room. He gave a small nod and smile. She made eye contact, returned the nod, then looked away.

Sam finished his lunch and went back to his room. He made a phone call to set up an appointment for Saturday afternoon. That appointment was a critical part of his strategy to insulate Fidelia—and himself—from the danger they faced. The call was successful. Sam began to feel that maybe, just maybe, things might fall into place.

Sam spent the rest of the day in his room. He was still tired from the flight on the Ilyushin Il-12. But more than that, he did not want to take the risk of going out. Someone might be looking for him. This was not a day for sightseeing.

*****

The next morning after a room service breakfast of bacon and eggs, Sam headed out for the day. He wore jeans and a white t-shirt. The last thing he wanted to do as he walked through Haight-Ashbury was to look like a cop.

Sam rode the cable car down Nob Hill to Market Street, then caught a streetcar to the Haight-Ashbury District. The Haight-Ashbury District was one great big happy festival. Sam had read about it in Life Magazine. It was the hippy center of the world—the home of San Francisco's flower children—a showplace for every imaginable anti-establishment style and behavior. As he walked through the Haight, he saw Hell's Angels in leather and chains, flower children in colorful outfits, junkies with rotting teeth and musicians playing Bob Dylan songs in front of guitar cases that were open to collect donations. Every street corner had Anglo-Saxon Buddhists chanting for peace and young poorly dressed pan handlers asking for a quarter. All of it was accompanied by an endless aroma of incense and marijuana.

The Panhandle is a narrow strip of Golden Gate Park located two blocks from Haight Street. Sam knew the Panhandle had turned into the gathering spot for San Francisco's flower children.

When Sam arrived at the Panhandle, he could see a bandstand had been set up. Colorfully dressed young people were sitting on the grass around the bandstand, smoking pot and visiting with friends. Sam quickly spotted the large oak tree Fidelia had referenced—and there she was—standing in blue jeans and a tie-died t-shirt with a red carnation in her thick black frizzy hair.

Fidelia was wearing granny sunglasses and looked like a classic flower child from a picture in *Life Magazine*. She gave a big wave and walked up to Sam. He was caught off guard and a little embarrassed when she gave him a big warm hug. Then, when he looked down at her, he understood. She was actually sobbing.

Sam asked, "Is there a quiet place where we can go—sit and talk—maybe get something to eat or drink?"

She wiped her eyes and nose with the back of her hand. "That sounds really nice."

Fidelia led him back to Haight Street to a small macrobiotic café called *Good Healthy Grains*. They each ordered a bowl of lentil soup which was accompanied by a thick piece of whole grain bread. Sam ordered a cup of mint tea and Fidelia had a blackberry banana smoothie. They took their lunches to a small table in the café and sat down.

Sam spoke first. "I met your mom and step-dad four months ago at a wedding of a Cuban couple in Minneapolis. My girlfriend—now she's my wife—she is originally from Cuba also. Anyway...."

And Sam proceeded to tell Fidelia about his efforts to find her. Fidelia listened intently as she hungrily ate her lunch. Occasionally, she gave a look of surprise or of agreement. Sam went light on the description of his conversation with Fidel Castro.

When he finished his story, Fidelia laughed and said, "I bet you're wondering how you ended up falling down this rabbit hole. I certainly have been trying to figure out how it happened to me. The whole thing began when I was contacted by my grandfather. He sent me a letter—at my school. In it, he asked me to meet with a friend of his—someone I would know."

"Did you write a response to your grandfather?

Fidelia blushed. "I found grandpa's phone number in mom's desk. I just called him. Grandpa said Tony Giarri was going to be in town and really wanted to see me. I didn't want to meet with him at first. I felt guilty sneaking behind my mom's back. But after Grandpa told me how much Tony missed me, I felt the least I could do was to meet him. So, I skipped a class and we met at a coffee shop. He was really nice; didn't ask for anything; just said he had fond memories of me when I was a kid and really missed me. I agreed to meet with him again."

Fidelia excused herself to go to the bathroom. Sam waited. Suddenly, he worried that she might skip out the back door for some reason.

Sam was relieved a moment later when Fidelia returned and continued speaking. "First of all, I've known for years that some people believe that Fidel Castro is my father. My grandpa used to bring that up when we lived in Miami. But I've never confronted my mom about that rumor and she never brought it up to me. I just thought it was better off left alone."

Fidelia laughed softly, then said, "You know, this is an awful lot of crap for one teen-ager to have to cope with. Anyway, in early December, I broke down and asked my mom about Tony Giarri. She told me about his connection to the mob—that he was the reason we moved to Chicago from Miami. She said my grandpa tried to talk her into marrying the creep—even though he had been accused of killing his last wife! So, I went to the library and read about the Mafia and Batista. I learned the Mafia had used Cuba for gambling, drugs and prostitution before Castro came to power. I read one article that claimed the Mafia and some Cuban-Americans were trying to kill Castro so things could go back to how they were before the revolution."

Fidelia gave a big-eyed look of wonder and said, "I mean really—the Mafia is just horrible! In January, I met one last time with Tony. He brought some other guy with him. I think it was the fellow you talked about—Hunt. The two of 'em wanted me to come live with my grandpa in Florida or maybe even with Giarri in New York. I asked them why they didn't just ask my mom. Tony just said that she had a closed mind and was not looking out for my best interests."

Fidelia gave a heavy sigh, then continued. "So, I put them on the defensive—I asked if the reason they wanted me to come live with them had anything to do with the rumors that Castro was my father. Tony said, *Of course not. That has nothing to do with it. I just want you to have a good life.* But the other guy twitched. I didn't trust that other guy at all. He made my skin crawl."

Fidelia finished her smoothie, wiped her lips with a napkin, then said, "The two of them wanted me to leave with them that day. I was afraid and didn't know what to do. I was afraid if I said *no*, they might just take me—by force—then and there. So, I told 'em I needed the night to think it out—and to pack a few things. I promised not to tell my mom or Luis anything about their visits or that I might be going with them. I would meet them early the next morning and either tell them *no* or be ready and packed to go."

Sam was impressed with Fidelia. She had been in a tough position and had to make some scary decisions. She was quite a girl.

"I just didn't know what to do, Sam. I was really scared. I didn't want them to hurt my mom—and I didn't want to get hurt myself either. That evening, after I packed my bags, I wrote the Miami address Tony had given me in the notebook you found. Tony told me in our first meeting that if I ever needed a place to hide, the old guy who lived at that address knew who I was and would protect me. I didn't know who lived there, but figured if anything happened to me, well, I was leaving a clue for my mom."

Fidelia teared up. "Early the next morning, I took off. I was so afraid. Looking back at it, I know what I did was dumb—I just plain panicked. I was really confused, really afraid."

She sat there and began to quietly cry. Tears ran down her cheeks. Sam figured he was seeing fear that had been repressed for months that now could be expressed. The tears and sadness lasted only a minute. Sam handed her his napkin and she wiped her eyes, regaining her composure.

Sam spoke. "I don't know what Giarri and Hunt's plan was—I mean if you'd gone with them. One thing I have learned is that these guys are not rocket scientists. They don't ever seem to think anything out completely. But whatever they had chosen to do, it wouldn't have been good for you. For example, if Giarri announced to the world that you were really Fidel Castro's daughter and that you hated Castro, it wouldn't make any difference what you said later on—or, for that matter, who your father really was. They would have embarrassed Castro. The fact that you would have been hurt, along with your mom and Luis—well, that wasn't their problem."

Sam paid for lunch and continued to update her as they walked back to the Panhandle. "In any case, my goal is to bring you home to your mom. I have a strategy that I think will protect you and your family. And, as a nice bonus, it will get Giarri and your grandfather to stop bothering you."

Sam looked at Fidelia and asked, "Have you ever had polio?"

Fidelia gave Sam a big-eyed double take and answered, "No. I received a vaccine that protected me. I don't see what that has to do with anything we're speaking about."

"A polio vaccine is similar to the strategy we're going to use. Our next step will be like an inoculation designed to keep Giarri and his pals away from you. We just need to deliver it."

Fidelia looked up at Sam quizzically and said, "I don't have a clue what you're saying. But I understand the principle you just described. If it'll do the trick, I'm more than game."

*****

They had arrived at the Panhandle. A rock band was playing. Fidelia and Sam walked into the crowd and listened to the music. Sam asked a young man with a broad-brimmed cowboy hat, long hair and an out-of-control beard what the name of the band was. The long-haired bearded guy said, "It's *Big Brother and the Holding Company*. They're pretty good. But I have no clue who the chick is who's singing lead."

The *chick* singing lead was a stocky brown-haired white woman with a voice that was rich and raspy.

Bye, bye, bye, baby, bye, bye
I maybe seein' you around
When I change my livin' standard and I move uptown
Bye, bye, baby, bye, bye

Sam told the guy, "I think she is pretty good."

The long-haired guy responded, "Oh—maybe she's ok. But I've never heard that chick sing with them before—and I'm willing to bet I'll never hear her again. She's not much to look at and I'm sure it's just a one-time gig."

As Sam and Fidelia moved through the crowd, enjoying the music. Sam was offered drags off of joints at least a dozen times. They just kept walking.

Sam turned to Fidelia, "We're going to catch a flight to Chicago tomorrow morning. You'll spend the night at my hotel. But just to clarify— in my room there are two queen sized beds. Uhm—uh—you needn't worry about any inappropriate behavior."

Fidelia giggled. "I am not worried. Are you?"

*****

Fidelia had been staying in a commune eight blocks from Haight-Ashbury. She shared the house with about a dozen young Latinos—half of them Cuban-Americans. At two that afternoon, Sam and Fidelia walked to the house. When they arrived, Fidelia told her housemates she was going to be going home. She thanked them for their kindness. They responded with affection. She didn't have a lot of stuff to pack—it all fit into an old backpack she had been given.

A half hour later, a taxi cab picked them up and took them to the Fairmont. Sam paid the cabby and the doorman opened the door to the hotel's opulent lobby. As they walked to the elevator, Fidelia stopped and looked in awe around her at the huge lobby's sparking marble floors, tall ceilings and elaborate grand salon furniture.

"This is amazing," she said. "I've worked at the Fairmont for three months, now. But this is the first time I've even seen the lobby. Employees are told they must enter the hotel through a small entrance off of Sacramento Street—right by the time-clock. My boss told me, in no uncertain terms, never visit any customer areas unless required by my duties. This lavish lobby blows my mind."

*****

Minutes later, Sam and Fidelia were in his room. It was 3:30. Sam said, "We're going to meet with Abe Greene at a lounge across California Street at 4:00. Abe Greene has a weekly column in the San Francisco Chronicle."

"Heh Sam, I live here. I know who the dude is. His column covers local politics, weird stories and how crazy life is in San Francisco. Greene wrote a bunch of stories about hippies. Why are we connecting with him?"

"It'll seem obvious to you later. He's going to help us. I called him yesterday to tell him about you and to ask if he would sit down with us to hear your story. Greene said he would *give it a go.*"

Fidelia gave Sam a questioning look and said "Ok. Can I take a quick shower before we go to meet with him?"

Sam was feeling time-pressed, but agreed.

Fidelia came out of the shower fifteen minutes later with a grin that seemed to go from ear-to-ear. "It's been like forever since I took a long hot shower—and with real shampoo! Oh man! I just loved it!"

*****

Sam and Fidelia walked across the street to the Mark Hopkins Hotel. The Mark Hopkins' lobby turned out to be just as grand as the Fairmont's—high ceilings, huge crystal chandeliers, ornate furniture and thick oriental rugs on marble floors. And there he was Abe Greene. Sam recognized him from his photo in the Chronicle. He was sitting in the middle of the lobby on a big plush chair, writing in a notepad. After brief introductions, Sam, Fidelia and Greene took the elevator to the Top of the Mark—the hotel's rooftop lounge. The views of San Francisco's skyline and the Golden Gate Bridge were extraordinary. But what pleased Sam—what relieved him—was that the lounge was almost empty. This was the privacy he sought.

They sat down at a table, ordered a couple of beers and a 7-up. Then Sam recounted the story of Fidelia's disappearance. He explained that her name—Fidelia—was a big part of the whole issue. Her mom had been friends with Castro. There had been rumors that Castro was her biological father. But Sam explained to Greene that Fidelia's father, who had died in the revolution, had been a close friend of Fidel Castro. Thus, her name! There was no basis for those rumors except that her name was Fidelia and her mom and dad had known Castro.

He told Greene all about his dinner with Giarri; getting beaten up afterwards; about the fake FBI agent whose real name was Howard Hunt; about his meeting with Diaz and his drive by Lansky's home. He explained that he had seen the young Cuban who had beaten him up at Lansky's. He described a portion of his meeting with Castro—but only a portion of what was said with the Cuban Prime Minister. Then Fidelia told Greene why she had left Chicago and about her three months in San Francisco.

Sam tied it together. "So, here's the deal: Fidelia is some kind of pawn here. These guys want to say Fidelia is Castro's daughter. And they probably want to say Fidelia hates Castro—or something like that. I don't want to embarrass Giarri, Lansky or Hunt so badly that they will retaliate against me. In fact, if you could keep their names out of your column, I'd appreciate it. I want to just get this story out to neutralize Fidelia's value to them."

Sam paused, then added, "And also, if you could avoid including in the article that I went to Cuba and met with Fidel Castro—well, that would probably keep me out of trouble with the State Department—or whoever the hell enforces that sort of stuff for the government."

Greene looked doubtful. "Sam, I gotta be honest with you. This is sort of a far-fetched story."

Sam quickly responded, "Call the Chicago and Minneapolis Police Departments—and call Rosaline and Luis for confirmation. Here are the phone numbers—theirs—mine and other phone numbers as well. They're all on this page and you can call them."

Greene took the list and looked it over. A moment later, Greene was smiling and his eyes were starting to twinkle.

"When I was hired," Sam said, "Fidelia's mother didn't know if her daughter was dead, had been kidnapped or had run away with a boyfriend. My search introduced me to the Mafia, the CIA and a Cuban expatriate population that is angry as hell. I got beaten up by Cubans with mob connections and threatened by a CIA operative. And the frosting on this cake was that I met the leader of the Cuban Revolution who is also U.S. public enemy number one. I mean—how incredible! And now, here I am—in San Francisco with Abe Greene and a beautiful flower child who I hadn't met until yesterday."

Greene laughed and said, "What a shame. I'd love to have at least that Castro bit in there. But I understand you don't want to piss off the royal bureaucrats in DC. We don't want to hurt the feelings of any federal stuffed shirts, do we?"

Greene turned to Fidelia and asked her a series of questions about her life, about Giarri, about her grandfather and about running away to San Francisco. "I am not just seeking information sweetheart. I'm trying to corroborate your Uncle Sam's story here."

He turned to Sam and laughed while saying, "*Uncle Sam*—that's pretty rich, isn't it?"

Greene was chuckling as he scribbled furiously in his notebook.

Then he looked up and said, "Well, I'll need to confirm your story with the Chicago and Minneapolis coppers. I am going to wait until Tuesday to call them—give you a chance to get out of Dodge and get this sweetheart home. I saw you have a number for Tony Giarri—ok if I call him as well? I doubt he'll be too forthcoming—probably'll plead the fifth—but it would be a gas to hear his patter. And I should call Diaz. He sounds like a naïve duck. It'll be interesting hearing how he screws up when he denies the whole story. And seriously—I understand your fears—and why you're contacting me. I like your *inoculation* strategy. More people should use it! This is my kind of story, Sam. I think it might end up taking most of next Sunday's column!"

Then he turned to Fidelia and took both of her hands in his. "Honey—you are a beautiful young woman. Your mother and step-father obviously love you a great deal. And to think—Luis Martinez—I've seen him pitch several times. That man could throw a curve ball! I will definitely give him a call—if only to talk baseball."

Greene finished up. "This all sounds good. Young lady—thank you. I wish you only the best! Mr. Erickson—Uncle Sam—it's been a real pleasure. If everything you said checks out, this story will be in my column next weekend. My write-up will suit your purposes quite nicely—and be an entertaining story for the average idiot who reads my column. Thank you so much!"

*****

About an hour later, Fidelia and Sam were in his Fairmont Hotel room. Sam had reservations to Chicago with Western Airlines at ten the next morning in the name of Stan Ericksen and his daughter Felli. Sam wanted to be in a taxi on the way to San Francisco International by seven-thirty.

Sam did not call up Luis and Rosaline to pass on the good news. That would have to wait until the next day. "Their home phone number is probably tapped. Maybe I am just being paranoid," he said to Fidelia. "But being paranoid and cautious is much better than being confident and having someone kick the shit out of me. I speak from experience."

They ate dinner in the hotel room. Fidelia was hungry. She devoured her hamburger, fries and milkshake as well as part of Sam's rib eye steak and baked potato. Fidelia had not watched television since she left home in January. So that evening, the TV was on until Sam turned off the lights at eleven. Fidelia had already fallen asleep while watching *Vertigo* on *Saturday Night at the Movies*.

*****

Sunday morning, when they arrived at San Francisco International Airport, Sam was nervous. He kept checking over his shoulder. Were there any men—with sunglasses in dark suits—watching their progress as they moved through the ticket line?

However, everything went smoothly. The check-in at the airport was fast. When Sam paid for his ticket, he explained, that a reservations clerk must have just misspelled his name. When the ticket agent found the reservation with the misspelled name, Sam told her, "This sort of screw-up has happened to me before."

She responded to him, "I can believe it."

He was thinking, *If you only knew.*

19. The Inoculation

After disembarking from the Boeing 707, Sam rented a light blue '66 Dodge Dart and drove to the O'Hare Airport Holiday Inn. Stan Ericksen had a reservation there and paid cash for two adjoining rooms. He and Fidelia ate bland room service dinners while watching the Ed Sullivan Show on the hotel room television. Ed's guests that night included Marvin Gaye and the Smothers Brothers.

The next morning, after breakfast in the Holiday Inn dining room, Sam called Luis's Cadillac dealership. The person who answered told Sam that Luis was in a meeting. Sam told her to interrupt the meeting—Luis was waiting for this call. A few minutes later, Luis was on the phone. Sam informed Luis that his package was safe—with him in Chicago and he was about to carry out the strategy the two of them had spoken about. Sam asked if Luis could meet them at ten-thirty.

Luis laughed. "Are you kidding? We've been updated by your wife. Of course, we'll be there. We'll see you at the station."

Sam cautioned him, "Be careful. Your personal phone line is probably tapped."

"Don't worry. See you soon."

*****

At ten-twenty, Sam and Fidelia arrived at the Halsted Street Precinct Station. A few minutes later when Rosaline and Luis arrived, Rosaline and Fidelia ran up to one another and fell into one another's arms. They each wept. While Rosaline and Fidelia embraced, Luis and Sam quickly shared nuances of their upcoming strategy.

Sam told the desk sergeant, "I would like to speak with both Officer Miller and Precinct Captain O'Malley related to the missing person's case of Fidelia Garcia. I am asking for Captain O'Malley to be included because some of the issues that my clients and I will explain to him are quite serious. We intend to make a statement explaining what has transpired on this case and to share our concerns. The captain will want to hear this statement."

Minutes later, Sam was informed that Miller was on vacation. But Captain O'Malley and Miller's backup could meet with Sam and his clients in fifteen minutes. Sam was pleased that Miller was out of the office. He thought to himself, *Just chalk this one up to being lucky.*

Once they had given a statement to the police, formally documenting all that had occurred—including the names of Giarri, Lansky, Hunt and Diaz—Sam believed that any future interference or intimidation from any of those four— or their buddies would be unlikely.

Sam, Fidelia, Rosaline and Luis were soon asked to step into Captain's O'Malley's office. In addition to Captain O'Malley, they were joined by Officer Joyce Middleton— Miller's backup.

After introductions, O'Malley spoke first. "I am pleased and relieved to see Fidelia is back with her parents. Officer Middleton is Officer Miller's colleague. She just reviewed the file with me. I understand you wish to make a statement."

Luis spoke first. "Thank you, Captain. I appreciate your willingness to meet with us on such short notice. When Fidelia disappeared, we were distraught. We had no idea where she might have gone or if she had been a victim of violence. Around the first of March, we hired Sam Erickson to investigate the case. Sam has worked diligently on it ever since. Today, Rosaline and I are thrilled that our daughter is back with us. We would like Sam to share the results of his investigation with you."

The Captain and Officer Middleton turned their attention to Sam who began to recount the events of the last few months.

"When I met with Officer Miller, he was helpful and responsive. He allowed me to review his notes and the official file. The only thing in that file that seemed odd was that Tony Giarri, a man who had dated Rosaline in the late fifties had inquired about Fidelia's location. Rosaline had dated Giarri for about six months several years ago. She broke up with him when she read a newspaper article that stated he was being investigated for the murder of his first wife. The article also reported that Giarri was a lieutenant to Meyer Lansky."

O'Malley looked up from the notes he was writing.

Sam said, "Yup—you heard me right—the head of Miami's organized crime syndicate. Miller's notes in the file stated that Giarri wanted to be kept up-to-date on the progress of the case. Since Rosaline had already informed me that Giarri had contacted her more than once asking for visitations with Fidelia, I felt it was worth exploring. Giarri became my primary suspect thanks to Miller's notes."

Sam reviewed his visits to New York and Miami. He included a description of the attack in Little Italy and the comments of his attackers. He shared finding an address in Fidelia's bedroom and described his drive past Lansky's home. He did not forget to mention that while they drove by the Lansky residence, one of his New York attackers happened to be washing Lansky's car. Sam also told the captain about the visit from two men who identified themselves as FBI agents. He gave the captain the names of the officers in Minneapolis to whom he had made a report at that time.

"The Minneapolis Office of the FBI informed me that they did not have an Agent Wozniak. I've since learned the identity of the person who impersonated an FBI Agent—an act which I believe is a felony. The fake agent's real name is Howard Hunt. I understand in the past that he has worked with the CIA. I happen to have a photograph of Howard Hunt. You can take a Xerox of it if you like."

Both the Captain and Officer Middleton leaned forward in their seats—listening while hurriedly taking notes. After Sam spoke of his visit with Rosaline's father, Hector Diaz, and the linkage of Lansky, Giarri and Hunt at Diaz's house, the silence in the captain's office was deafening.

Sam explained the baseless rumors that Fidelia's father was Fidel Castro—not her first common-law husband, Castro's close friend and Fidelia's real father Miguel Garcia who had fought and died in the Cuban revolution. Sam explained that those rumors had always been hurtful to Rosaline—but she had never imagined that someone would try to hurt her or her daughter by manipulating them.

Sam continued, "I concluded Lansky, Giarri and Hunt's objective was to get control of Fidelia and use her to somehow embarrass or blackmail Castro. I had no idea where Fidelia was. I received a tip last week on her location from a source whose identity I promised to protect—for his safety. I went to San Francisco, found Fidelia, and we returned to Chicago last night. Before Fidelia shares her story—which will align with what I just told you—I want to tell you that the Martinez family does not want to press charges. They just want their lives to return to normal. We are sharing this information with you out of respect for the Chicago Police Department. Luis and Rosaline sincerely thank you, Captain O'Malley, for your assistance."

Then Fidelia shared the events of the past six months with the Captain and Officer Middleton. Her parents were hearing her story for the first time. Fidelia told about the calls with her grandfather, the first visits from Giarri and the last visit with both Giarri and the man whose picture Sam had just shared. Fidelia remained calm as she relayed her story, only tearing up a couple of times. She concluded by speaking about meeting Sam at the Fairmont Hotel and how relieved she was to finally be returning to her home and her parents. At that point, she broke down in tears, leaning into her mother's arms. Needless to say, Rosaline also wept.

It was the captain's turn to speak. "I will respect your family's decision not to press charges and make no effort to dissuade you—although the actions of these men were reprehensible. However, Officer Middleton must file a report and I will forward it to my superiors. Any decision to prosecute will be made at a higher level than police captain—by the Cook County State's Attorney. That being said, I would be surprised if the prosecutors do not decide to respect your expressed wishes."

Sam almost chuckled when O'Malley said he would not try to talk Luis and Rosaline into filing charges. Of course, he wouldn't. There was no desire on the part of a Chicago police captain to take on the mob or the CIA.

*****

An inoculation is the controlled release of a limited amount of a disease into a body to initiate that body's immune reaction—a reaction that protects the body from the full power of the disease.

In this instance, the Mafia and CIA's plan—the metaphoric disease—might embarrass Castro by claiming that Fidelia Garcia was really Castro's illegitimate, abandoned and unloved daughter. But Fidelia's life and the lives of Luis and Rosaline would have been ruined by those public claims.

However, an inoculation—the release of a limited amount of information in a controlled manner—could change the environment. If successful, Fidelia, Rosaline, Luis, Sam and Isabelle would not be at risk.

*****

A few minutes after the meeting with O'Malley, Rosaline, Luis and Fidelia were standing in front of the precinct station with Sam. Luis invited Sam to join them for lunch. Sam said, "No, I need to get home. Isabelle is probably sitting on pins and needles. However, Luis—I do have one question for you. This is a pretty dumb thing for me to ask at this point, but it's been nagging at me. I really am curious. Did you ever pitch to Fidel Castro?"

Luis laughed, looked down and shook his head while saying, "Yes, yes I did."

"How did it go?"

"Well—it went like this. I pitched to him four times. I think it was either 1946 or 1947. Anyway, Castro was a good ballplayer. The son of a bitch got three hits off of me in four at bats."

*****

On the flight home, Sam couldn't stop thinking about how nice it would be to see Isabelle when she met him at the Airport. He thought about how good he felt about things in his life—how his life—his own personal poem so to speak—was turning out so differently than it had for the character Le Roux in Kees' poem *The Crime Club*.

For Sam, the clues had led somewhere. And he was able to see beyond the walls. In fact, he was feeling as if any case could be solved.

Life was good.

*****

It was about seven when Sam walked out of the Minneapolis/St. Paul International Airport terminal. He saw the 1959 Rocket Oldsmobile waiting about fifty feet away. As he walked to the car, he was thinking how sweet those taillights looked.

Sam was famished. Isabelle stopped at a White Castle on the way home. Sam downed a few of those delicious small burgers, a bag of fries and a coffee-flavored milk shake. The buns on White Castle burgers were always so fresh.

*****

The next morning, after lingering over an excellent cup of coffee and a large hot cinnamon roll, Sam continued to implement the inoculation. He called and left a message for the Minneapolis Police Officers to whom he had made his report on Agent Wozniak—aka Howard Hunt. An hour later, they returned his call and agreed to come to Sam's home that afternoon.

Sam gave them the same report that he had given to Captain O'Malley in Chicago. were expressionless. As they listened to Sam's report, the two Minneapolis Police officers occasionally exchanged glances with one another.

After Sam told them they weren't pressing charges, one of the officers said, "You might not be pressing charges, but I think the FBI is not going to be too happy with this character, Howard Hunt. I doubt you'll hear back from the FBI. But I can guarantee you they will do their follow up with the CIA—behind closed doors. This guy Hunt sounds like a real asshole. He may not end up in jail, but my god, the idiot should not be working for the government. He ought to be doing something that doesn't put him in a position of power—something without access to power—like a ditch digger—or even a plumber."

*****

The following Sunday, Sam bought a copy of the San Francisco Chronicle. On the first page of the second section, he found what he was looking for.

ABE GREENE

Our Cuban Flower Child… The daughter of Castro?

June 26, 1966

I was sitting at home, minding my own business the other day, and I get a call from a private dick from the Midwest. This PI tells me he wants to meet me at the Top of the Mark. He said he'd bring along a young Cuban flower child. The PI tells me that this girl's dad, a friend of Castro, died in the revolution. The catch you ask? The CIA and the Mob want to pretend the girl is really Fidel Castro's daughter. They figured if they can control the girl, they can embarrass Castro. They are so sly!

So, I figure—this, I cannot miss. I show up and meet the dick and one of our hippies…a beautiful young flower child. The girl ran away from her Midwest home five months ago because her grandfather's buddy was asking her to go live with him. The buddy, alias the mobster, loves the girl like a daughter—no really! He and the buddy's buddy (who is in the CIA) visited this girl and got her to skip a class and talk to them. They want her to live with the mobster…or the grandfather…oh, I guess they are flexible. But they truly want to help her—really.

Six years ago, the girl's mother and her daughter moved away from Miami because the grandfather wanted the daughter to marry the mobster. This was all becoming a bit confusing.

So, I called the grandfather. He lives in Miami now, but spent most of his life in Cuba…back in the good old days when our good friend Batista ran the show. I asked the old man if he likes Castro. "No. I hate Castro." Then I ask if his granddaughter's father is Fidel Castro. He says, "Well maybe." I say, what does "well maybe" mean? No answer. So, I ask him if he wanted his daughter to marry the Mafia guy. He says "I wanted her to marry him but she wouldn't."

Finally, I ask about the mobster's buddy, the CIA guy. Grandpa says he hardly knew him. Didn't the CIA guy visit Grandpa with a couple of mobsters in January? Grandpa says he probably shouldn't answer any more questions. That seems like the smartest thing he said during the entire conversation!

This is getting complicated. I'm asking myself "Who's on first?" To clear things up, I call the mobster. I asked him if he wanted to know where the girl was. He said, "Sure. Can you help me?" He would make it worth my while. Worth my while? What is he talking about? I tell him I am a reporter…I can't take a bribe unless it's a really, really big bribe! Evidently our conversation is no longer worth his while…he hangs up on me!

So, wanting to be a responsible reporter, I call the police department in the girl's home town. Yes…the girl went missing and yes…the players are as advertised above!

The news for our mobster and his CIA buddies…the Bay of Pigs is over…you didn't win! The news for San Francisco residents…. you think we're nuts here? Try the east coast. They're really crazy there!

•• ••

*****

The next day, Sam received an air mail special delivery package from Mexico City. He was confused at first, thinking that he must have left something in his hotel room or at the airport with his name and identification on it.

When he opened the package, he realized it actually had been forwarded from Cuba. Sam laughed as he tore off the paper packaging and saw the wooden box. He knew what it was. It was a box of cigars, but not just any cigars. It was a box of Cohiba Corona Especials. There was a brief hand written note on the box. The note said, *Well done and thank you. —F.*

Isabelle watched Sam open the package. Then she went into the kitchen and came back with two glasses of scotch on the rocks. "Inspired by what you told me about your dinner with Fidel Castro, one of the first things I did when I got back from Cuba was buy a bottle of Chivas Regal. Why don't you light a couple of those cigars? I've never had a Cohiba. It will be something new for me."

They sat there, in the living room, sipping slowly from their glasses of Chivas, smoking their Cohibas.

Then Isabelle looked Sam in the eye and said, "I think that you should save the rest of those Cohibas."

Sam asked, "Why is that?"

She waited for a moment, took his hand and put it on her stomach and smiled. Then she said, "You will want to share them with our Cuban friends in January—you know, after our baby is born."

9 781956 920048